UNKNOWN REASONS

Joan Hall

PrimaCasa Press, Lower Burrell, PA15068
PrimaCasa Press is an imprint of AIW Press, LLC.
https://aiwpress.com

The characters and events in this book are fictitious. Any
similarity to real persons, living or dead, is entirely
coincidental and not intended by the author.

ISBN-13: 978-1-944938-22-2

To my brother, Walter, with much love. My interest in music began with me listening to your 45s before I could even read record labels. Later, as young adults, we made countless trips to the mall and record stores to add to our vast music collection. Though our tastes sometimes differ, you helped develop my love of music and encouraged me to live my dream of becoming a writer. I am forever grateful.

Prologue

Driscoll Lake, Texas
October 2011

He stepped out of the shadows, leaving the cloak of darkness, and crept toward the abandoned factory. His pulse quickened with excitement as he neared the building. On the other hand, it could be nerves. A solitary streetlight illuminated his path for several feet between the fence and an abandoned boxcar.

But there was little to worry about. It was Friday night, and many of Driscoll Lake's residents would be at the football game.

It was hard to remember a time when fire didn't captivate him. He learned how to start a flame without the benefit of matches or a lighter and delighted in holding a magnifying glass in a position where the sun reflected on dry leaves, causing them to smolder.

Fire was essential. People used it for cooking. It gave off warmth and provided a source of light.

One small spark could quickly develop into a roaring flame. And a roaring flame was powerful. It could destroy. Even kill.

His first arson occurred at a vacant house on the outskirts of Driscoll Lake. It was a favorite place for teenagers to hang out and smoke or drink beer.

The blaze had been an accident. He was sitting on the rickety back porch of the old structure puffing on a Marlboro when he heard a car. His mother would have been furious to know about his newly acquired habits, although he often thought she suspected something. She seemed to have a sixth sense about certain things. It was possible she had followed him, so he tossed the cigarette and ran for cover in the nearby woods.

When the car passed by without stopping, he waited a few minutes before walking back toward the house. Half way across the yard, he came to an abrupt halt and stood, mesmerized, as the discarded cigarette ignited the dry grass next to the porch.

A smile spread across his face when he saw the flames reach the dry wood. The thought occurred that he should find a place where he could call for help. But he remained motionless, his heartrate increasing as the fire began to spread. It soon engulfed the entire house.

The distant sound of fire trucks jolted him from his reverie and he rushed back to the safety of the woods. He could hardly contain his laughter as he watched the firemen in their futile attempt to save the structure.

He had done this! It no longer mattered that he was an outcast. Fire gave him control and a place of power over others. And the best part was they wouldn't even know he was the one in charge.

Investigators questioned several teenagers known for hanging around the old house, but everyone denied being there. Without any eyewitnesses, it was hard to prove arson. After several months, they ruled the fire an accident. But that didn't stop rumors and speculation from sweeping the town.

The following summer, he started a grass fire on the road to Brewster. Investigators also ruled it an accident.

There were a few other blazes, spread out over a period of a few years. All of them appeared to be accidental, and no one tied them together.

After high school, he managed to control his desires. Almost fifteen years had passed since his last arson. But this year the entire state of Texas was suffering from a severe drought. Wildfires were rampant. In Bastrop County alone, over thirty-thousand acres and sixteen hundred homes and buildings had burned. The massive fire began in early September and was still not officially contained.

Firefighters, already stretched thin, were weary. What better time to start an "accidental" fire? The old building that once housed Cameron Manufacturing was the ideal spot.

No one would have a reason to be at the deserted place, but he couldn't afford for anyone to see him. With a waxing moon in the sky, it was best to avoid being out in the open. He would use a cigarette again, and no one would be wiser. The dead weeds would ignite in seconds. By starting the fire at the back of the building, it was less likely anyone would see him.

While he waited for high thin clouds to cover the moon, a man squeezed through an opening in the fence and started walking toward the loading dock.

Why was Curtis Lawrence here?

He squatted behind the boxcar. The judge stopped for a moment and looked around, but then he continued walking toward the dock, unaware of being watched.

Crouching, he edged closer, paused, and listened as Curtis Lawrence entered the adjacent office building and closed the connecting door behind him.

A smile spread across his face. This was perfect. The fire would eliminate two of his problems—the run-down building and the judge. Soon everyone in Driscoll Lake would be pointing fingers.

He reached into his pocket for a Marlboro and a lighter and took a few puffs before dropping the cigarette on the ground.

Chapter 1

Driscoll Lake, Texas
July 2012
Rachel Jackson sat at a picnic table outside the pavilion in Driscoll Lake City Park. She scanned the crowd gathered for the annual Independence Day celebration. Brian Nichols was supposed to meet her a half hour ago. He was late. Again.

She tapped her foot. Why couldn't people be on time? Taking a deep breath, she tried to calm herself. Brian wasn't usually late. At least, she hadn't noticed his tardiness until recently.

A young couple with four children stood nearby. The parents' hands were full with food and drinks from one of the vendor booths. One of the children tugged at the man's arm.

"Daddy, I'm hungry. Can we eat now?"

"As soon as we find a table," the man replied.

"Please, sit here." Rachel smiled.

The young mother started to protest. "We don't want to take your seat. I'm sure we'll find something soon."

Rachel got up from the table. "It's okay. I'm supposed to meet someone, but he isn't here yet." She took a few steps when she heard someone call her name and turned to see Alan Davis.

"How are you?" the young attorney asked.

She pursed her lips. "I'm fine."

"Seems I can't ever reach you by phone. Want to grab something to eat and then watch the fireworks?"

Rachel looked away. Many women would be flattered by his invitation, but she wasn't one of them. She had been out with Alan once and vowed it was the last time. He was too arrogant and self-centered. "No, thanks. I'm waiting for someone."

"Oh? Who?"

"Not that it should matter to you, but I'm meeting Brian. He's running a little late but should be here any minute."

"Brian Nichols? I heard you've been seen around town with him several times."

"We're friends."

"If friendship is the only thing between you two, what would it take to convince you to go out with me?"

"For starters, I don't mix business and pleasure."

"What makes you think we would talk business? You're not even one of my clients." His cell phone rang. He pulled it from his pocket and looked at the caller ID. "Excuse me. I need to take this call."

Rachel rolled her eyes. During their only so-called date, Alan had been on the phone almost constantly. Not only that, he spoke loud enough so others nearby would hear him, leaving Rachel with the impression he wanted to portray an air of importance.

Why had she been reluctant to reveal Brian's name to Alan? She wasn't even sure how she would classify her association with him. Friends? Former high school classmates? Two people who once conducted a business transaction? Acquaintances who sometimes got together for dinner or a movie?

She started to leave when Alan ended the call.

"Sorry about that. It was important."

"My point exactly. Business and pleasure." Rachel turned to retreat and stopped in her tracks. Brian was coming toward her. If only she could ignore the quick acceleration of her pulse each time she saw him. But it was becoming increasingly hard to deny her feelings.

Maybe it was his enigmatic personality. Most of the time, he acted like a responsible business owner. But sometimes the unruly teenager he had been shone through—the one responsible for juvenile pranks, the one who defied authority. The rebel who frequently gave his mother grief. The would-be rock star.

Today was one of those times. Brian wore jeans and a *Dark Side of the Moon* t-shirt. His hair was a little long, and he had a hint of five o'clock shadow on his face. It only served to enhance his rugged good looks. While she respected the man he had become, she had to admit Brian's one-time rebellious side fascinated her.

Having grown up in a wealthy family, where everyone expected her to maintain a certain social status, Rachel had often longed to be more impulsive. Even after her mother's death, when she went to live with her father in Austin, she remained the dutiful daughter.

Now as a respected physician in the community, she needed to act accordingly. She wouldn't do anything to jeopardize her career. But Brian's carefree lifestyle intrigued her, and she admired him for his relaxed attitude.

He smiled as he approached. "Sorry I'm late. Had to stop at the nursing home. I hadn't seen Mom in a few days and thought I'd better check in."

"How is she?"

Brian shrugged. "Good days and bad days. Today was one of the bad ones."

"Hate to hear that."

"Guess it's to be expected, but not easy to accept. Was that Alan Davis I saw talking to you?"

Rachel rolled her eyes. "Yes. He wanted me to go out with him. That's not the first time he's asked me."

"Oh? And what did you say?"

Rachel lifted her eyebrows. Was Brian jealous? "I told him no. He's too pretentious. Thinks highly of himself, that's for sure. And he can't seem to stay off his phone."

"A lot of people are like that these days."

"I know, but with him it's different. I keep my phone turned on in case someone from the hospital needs me. But Alan acts as if the phone calls make him important. He makes certain someone overhears, but none of the conversations I've heard are anything that couldn't wait until another time."

Brian reached into his pocket, pulled out his iPhone, and powered it down. "No interruptions for us tonight."

Rachel smiled.

"Have you eaten anything?"

"Not yet. I was waiting for you. We'd better find a place to view the fireworks soon."

"Why don't you find somewhere to sit and I'll grab the food. Do you have a preference?"

"A burger sounds good. We can do picnic style. Maybe near the pond."

"Okay. I won't be long."

Rachel walked until she found a smooth patch of grass. It would be a perfect place to view the fireworks. Sirens wailed in the distance as she sat down.

It didn't take long for Brian to find her. "This is from Mary's booth. Mayo, Pepper Jack cheese, avocado, and no lettuce. Hope I got it right."

"Perfect." She couldn't believe he remembered her preference. Mary ran a popular cafe in town. Rachel had run into Brian there one night, and they had decided to sit together.

They ate in silence, enjoying the cool, gentle breeze. A pair of ducks wandered up from the nearby pond, and Rachel tossed them a couple of bites of her hamburger bun. The ducks gobbled up the bread and trotted closer, hoping for more.

"Guess I shouldn't have encouraged them. They may not leave us alone." But her concern soon faded when someone else tossed a handful of food on the ground, and the ducks waddled off in that direction. She smiled when she recognized the couple that purchased her family's home last year. As much as Rachel hated to sell it, she knew she had made the right decision. The new owners had four children—two preteens, a six-year-old, and a toddler. The mother spread a blanket on the ground, and they all sat down together.

A wave of longing washed over Rachel as she watched the family interact with one another. Seeing them together was a reminder of the emptiness within her.

"Do you know those people?"

She had been self-absorbed in her thoughts and almost forgot Brian was sitting beside her. "What did you say?"

"The family sitting over there. Thought you might know them."

Rachel nodded. "They're the ones who bought my home. The older kids are into horseback riding. The father trains horses and the mother gives riding lessons. Nice family."

"Ever wanted children of your own?"

His question took her by surprise. It seemed so personal. A subject only two people who shared a close relationship would discuss. Yet she felt comfortable confiding in him. "I always pictured myself as a mother. It doesn't look like it's going to happen. My biological clock is ticking."

"A lot of women wait these days. You're still young."

"Yeah, well, I'm not even married and that—" Rachel turned away, embarrassed she was about to reveal such personal information with him.

Brian smiled. "If you were married, we wouldn't be here together having this conversation."

His words put her at ease. "Probably not."

He lay back on the grass and clasped his hands behind his head.

"Tired?" Rachel asked.

"A little. I gave my workers a day off, but I spent most of it in the office going over blueprints and balancing the books."

"Thought you were going to hire an office assistant."

"The fire at the old factory put my plans on hold. But let's not go there. I wouldn't want you to accuse me of mixing business and pleasure." He winked.

"Can't imagine you doing that." Rachel looked across the pond. "Looks like they're getting ready to start the fireworks." Her cell phone rang, she reached into her purse. "Sorry. Guess I shouldn't have been so quick to judge Alan." She frowned when she looked at the caller ID. "It's Matt."

Brian sat up as Rachel answered the call.

"Hey, Matt. What's up? ... Brian? Yeah, he's with me now... What? Where? Sure, I'll tell him... Okay, thanks."

She ended the call and turned to Brian. "Matt's been trying to call you. There's a fire in the Woodland Hills subdivision. It's one of your new houses."

***

Brian arrived at the house as the firefighters sprayed water on the last of the smoldering embers. This morning, a house stood on the site—almost sixty percent complete. Now there wasn't much left but the concrete foundation.

He got out of his truck as Police Chief Matt Bradford approached him.

Matt shook his head. "Hate this happened. Tried to call you several times."

"I was with Rachel. I turned off my phone so we wouldn't be disturbed."

Matt raised his eyebrows.

Brian frowned. "Nothing like that. We met at the park and had planned to watch the fireworks. Rachel kept her phone turned on because she was on call. I shouldn't have turned mine off. Maybe if I had got here sooner—"

"Wouldn't have made any difference. By the time the firefighters arrived, it was too late to save the structure. At least they were able to prevent it from spreading to other houses."

"That's a good thing. Does anyone know how it happened?"

"Not yet. The fire marshal is here. I'm sure he'll want to talk with you."

"Richard Abbott? That ought to be special. You know how he feels about me. He practically accused me of setting fire to the old factory last year."

"Don't let him get to you. I'm sure he'll put aside his personal feelings and not allow them to interfere with his job."

"I wouldn't count on it. He's still convinced I was the person responsible for sending his son to prison."

"That wasn't your fault."

"Tell that to Abbott. He also thinks I was responsible for Clay's drug habit. Abbott believes since I did other stuff, doing drugs would have come naturally. It's people like him who won't let me forget the past."

Stan Gardner, the Fire Chief, walked over to them. "Hey, Brian." Stan looked back at the blackened embers. "Tough luck."

"If you believe in such a thing."

Stan frowned. "Luck. Coincidence. Whatever you want to call it. Were you building this house for someone?"

Brian shook his head. "No, it was a spec."

"I assume you had insurance."

"Can't get financing without a builder's risk policy."

"Abbott said he's bringing his team in tomorrow. And I assume the insurance company will want to investigate."

"Probably. I'll call my agent first thing in the morning."

"If they have any questions for me, I'm available."

"Thanks, Stan. I appreciate it. Need anything else tonight?"

"No. Abbott said to tell you he'd contact you."

"I'm sure he will." Brian turned and walked away. Inside his pickup, he powered on his phone and called Rachel's number.

"Hey, there," he said when she answered.

"What happened?"

"Don't know yet, but the house is a total loss."

"I'm sorry."

"Yeah, well. Stuff happens. At least no one was hurt. Are you still at the park?"

"Stephanie's with me, but we're leaving now. The show is over."

"Sorry this ruined our evening."

"Not your fault. I'm going home. Want to come over for a while?"

"Maybe another time. I wouldn't be good company right now. Besides, it's getting late, and I have a lot of things to take care of tomorrow."

"I understand. Call me."

"I will." Brian pressed the button, ending the call. He drove in silence, arriving at home around eleven o'clock. The house was dark. It looked lonely and had an emptiness about it that furnishings couldn't fill. He walked inside and threw his keys on the kitchen counter. Without bothering to turn on any lights, he walked into what he called his music room and sat down on the sofa.

Nine months, two building projects, two fires. What were the odds? Maybe it was a run of bad luck like Stan said. But Brian didn't believe in luck. Things happened. Period. But whatever the reason, he knew one thing. The first fire had hurt him financially. This second one was sure to put an even greater financial strain on his business.

If only he hadn't invested so heavily into renovations on the old factory. As far as the house, even with insurance, he wasn't sure he could secure financing for another one at this point. The downturn in the housing market didn't help matters.

Brian shook his head. Time to think about all that tomorrow. He turned on the stereo. Music always had a calming effect on him. He leaned back on the sofa, stretched out his legs, clasped his hands behind his head, and thought of Rachel.

Maybe he should have taken her up on her offer. At least he would have some company. She always acted as if she understood. Never judged or criticized him. At times, he could talk to her easier than he could to Matt. And Matt was his best friend.

Why did he always seem to turn to her only when something was troubling him? Yes, they occasionally had dinner together, but only if they happened to run into one another somewhere. Rachel's invitation to the Independence Day celebration had taken him by surprise. It wasn't a real date, but it was a step in that direction. Maybe he would ask her out sometime.

But most likely, he wouldn't. Rachel came from a different world—a wealthy family. He carried enough baggage from his background to sink a ship. She wouldn't want a relationship with someone like him. They wouldn't even have a friendship had it not been for her selling him the old factory.

Soon, lulled by the music, he closed his eyes and fell asleep.

***

He was careful not to let anyone see him as he watched the flames shoot into the night sky. The rush of adrenaline when he heard the fire trucks was familiar. Welcomed. Desired. He had felt it when he started his first fire as a teenager, and it never grew old.

He chose tonight's target carefully. A new subdivision with only a few occupied homes lessened the chances of anyone seeing him. Woodland Hills was the perfect place. But even then, it couldn't be just any house. It had to be in a cul-de-sac, and it had to belong to a particular builder.

He scanned the area first and found one with a Nichols Construction sign in the yard.

Other houses on the street were in various stages of construction, and none of them occupied. The Nichols house had a wooded area behind it that led to an equally isolated adjacent street, providing the perfect escape route.

Not only that, he found a spot where he could watch, and no one would be able to see him.

He drove by the area that morning and almost made a mistake. A middle-aged woman was walking her German Shepherd when he neared the house. She had eyed him warily, probably wondering if he intended on doing her any harm. From the looks of that dog, she had little to worry about. It would probably tear apart anyone who attempted to harm its owner.

She called out to him as he slowed to turn around.

"You must be lost," she had said. "No one lives on this street yet."

"Yeah, I took a wrong turn. Looking for Chestnut Lane."

"It's the fourth street on the left. You're on Hickory. Visiting someone?"

"No. Looking at the possibility of buying a house here."

"There aren't any for sale on Chestnut."

"Guess someone gave me wrong information. Thanks for telling me." He drove away as fast as he could without arousing suspicion. He hoped she hadn't made a note of his license plate number. But even if she had, there wouldn't be any reason to tie him to the fire. He waited until almost ten hours after his encounter with her to start the blaze.

Still, he would need to be more careful next time. And there would be another fire. It was only a matter of deciding when and where.

Chapter 2

Brian spent the first part of the following morning dealing with his insurance company. It wasn't how he had envisioned his day. First, he spoke with his agent, who promised to do everything he could to expedite the claims process, then an adjuster called.

"I assume there will be an investigation," the adjuster said.

"Yes. The county fire marshal's office is taking care of that."

"We'll stay in contact with them. I'll go out to the property and have a look around, but we can't pay off until investigators have determined the cause."

"I understand." Brian hung up the phone. Just great. That's all I need.

He also had to deal with his workers and inform them of the fire.

The painting sub-contractor called to remind Brian he still needed to pay them for work they had already done. "I realize the claim can take a while to process, but I pay my workers weekly. I had someone out there yesterday since we've been behind schedule."

"I'll send your money as soon as I can. But I need to know who you sent over there. The fire marshal may have some questions for him."

"Just have them call me. I'll deal with it." The contractor hung up the phone before Brian could respond.

Who had put a burr under his saddle? Phil Jennings had done several jobs for Brian. He never failed to pay him.

The day worsened when Richard Abbott showed up at ten o'clock.

"We've already been out to the site. The preliminary investigation indicates the cause was due to human involvement."

Brian took a deep breath and exhaled slowly. "Meaning arson?"

"I didn't say arson. What makes you think that?"

"You said there was human involvement. I assumed—"

"Not clear yet. It could have been accidental or intentional. We do know the fire originated in a trash pile behind the house. Were you there anytime yesterday?"

"I gave my crew a day off."

"That doesn't answer my question. Were *you* at the construction site yesterday?"

"No. I had no reason to be there. Nor did any of my workers. However, the painter said he had someone over there."

"What's his name?"

"I don't know the worker, but the sub-contractor is Phil Jennings. He said to call him if you have any questions." Brian took a piece of paper, scribbled the name and phone number, and gave it to Abbott.

"Thanks. I'll call him."

"So where were you all day? Stan Gardner told me they had trouble reaching you by phone."

"Why the interrogation?"

"Just covering all my bases."

And you're enjoying every second of it. "Okay, I spent most of the day at home."

Abbott raised his eyebrows.

"Alone. I came here to the office around three o'clock to catch up on some paperwork and then went to the nursing home to visit my mother. It was probably around six-thirty. I stayed there for a couple of hours."

"Can your mother verify this?"

"Does she need to?"

"Maybe. I assume you can count on her to vouch for you."

Only if she remembered. Dorothy Nichols still recognized her son but often forgot his visits. Brian first noticed the short-term memory lapses almost a year ago, and they had increased the past several months.

So far, she still had her long-term memory, but just a few weeks ago, she spoke of her husband as if he was still alive. Thomas Nichols had been dead for more than fifteen years. Whether she would remember Brian's visit was anyone's guess.

"My mother has memory lapses and doesn't always recall when I'm there. However, several nurses saw me."

"Where did you go after you left the nursing home?"

"To the city park. I met a friend."

"Who was this friend?"

"Rachel Jackson."

"Ah, yes. The good doctor. I recall she came to your defense last year when questioned about the factory fire. Nice to have friends like her."

Brian's face grew warm, and a vein pulsated in his neck. Was Richard Abbott insinuating Rachel hadn't told the truth? How dare he question her integrity? "What's that supposed to mean?"

"Getting defensive, aren't you? Sometimes the people closest to us can't or won't see the truth. It's obvious you and Rachel are, shall we say, friendly."

"My relationship with Rachel is none of your business. But you're right about the people we are close to not being objective. You're still blaming me for your son going to prison. I didn't put him there. If he had been innocent, he wouldn't have had to do time."

It was Richard Abbott's turn to look angry. "Don't you dare mention my son. He has nothing to do with this. However, you did cost him five years of his life."

"No, he did that to himself. But you know that. You just don't want to face the truth."

"If you hadn't—"

"If I hadn't what? I gave him ample chances to redeem himself. More than most people would." Brian stood up from his desk. "Now, if you have any more questions for me, let's get on with it. Otherwise, get out of my office. I have a business to run, and you have an investigation to complete."

Abbott rose from the chair and walked to the door. He opened it to leave but turned back. "You haven't heard the last from me. In fact, if I find something—anything— suspicious, I'll reopen the case on the fire at the factory." He slammed the door as he left.

***

"Rachel, I can't think of anyone I'd rather have take over my practice than you."

Dr. Henry Jacobs was a long-time family physician in Driscoll Lake. Some of his patients were third generation, Dr. Jacobs having served as the family doctor for their parents and grandparents. His retirement would leave a gap, much like Miles Parker's retirement from his law practice earlier this year. Both instances made Rachel realize how much Driscoll Lake had changed and continued to change.

"Thank you." Rachel looked around the room. She recalled several visits here as a child when Dr. Jacobs had been her family physician.

"You do realize you can make more money in your present situation."

"Yes, but money isn't all that's important."

"Tell me, then." He leaned back in his chair and linked his fingers together. "Why do you want to leave the hospital and go into private practice?"

"For one thing, it's the hours. I have an on-call rotation at the hospital, subject to being called all hours of the night and having to work two weekends out of each month. Sometimes it's hard to have a social life with a schedule like that."

"I see. An attractive young woman like you must have several men knocking at your door. Any young man would be lucky to marry someone like you. You have your mother's gentle nature and unassuming personality. She was a wonderful woman. Her death was so tragic. So untimely."

Rachel's eyes misted, and she blinked back tears.

"I'm sorry," Dr. Jacobs said. "I didn't mean to bring up old memories."

"It's okay. I had to relive it all over again last year, but I'm glad I—that Stephanie Harris and I—finally know the truth."

"I'm sure you are."

"Back to your question about taking over your practice, the main reason is you've worked hard throughout the years to build it. People trust you, and your retirement will leave a void. I can't ever be the person you are, but I want to help these patients. Not everyone is fond of seeing physicians who are part of big health care conglomerates. Some of them still like the hometown feel of a private practice. I believe, having grown up here, I can continue to provide the kind of personal touch with their care."

"That's the answer I was looking for. I've had several offers and interviewed each prospective buyer, but I don't believe any of them has what it takes to continue this practice. You do, and you've convinced me. Your offer is fair. I'll contact my attorney to begin drawing up the necessary paperwork."

Rachel's eyes sparkled with excitement. "I'll do my best not to let you down."

"I'm not worried about that. How much notice to you need to give the hospital?"

"At least a month. Wish it could be sooner."

"That won't be a problem. It will take a while to get all the paperwork in order. If you would like, I'll stay on for a while to help with a smooth transition."

"I think that's an excellent idea."

"There's one other thing. I have a few patients at Woodbine Nursing Home and make visits there. Would you have a problem with continuing that?"

"None at all."

"Good. Several of the patients you probably know, but I can go with you the first time."

Rachel stood up to leave and extended her hand. "Thank you, Dr. Jacobs."

"On the contrary. I should be the one thanking you. I made my wife a promise that I would retire before I reached seventy. I only had four months left. She was about to give up on me. Until you made an offer, I was ready to reconsider."

***

Rachel walked out of Dr. Jacob's office and stopped to soak in the late afternoon sunshine. The heat was typical for July, but the evening promised to be pleasant.

She found it hard to contain her excitement and wanted to share her good news with someone. It was Friday, and she felt like celebrating. After getting into her car, she took her phone from her purse, and called Brian's number. They hadn't spoken in a few days.

He answered on the second ring.

"How are you doing? Any news about the fire?"

"Richard Abbott came to see me yesterday. He had plenty of questions. Said there was evidence of human involvement."

"Meaning arson?"

"Not necessarily. It could have been accidental. To tell you the truth, I think Abbott would like nothing better than to tag it as arson and pin the blame on me."

"Why?"

"Long story. But that's enough about me. I want to put the fire out of my mind—at least for a while. What's up with you?"

"Remember when I said I might not have to worry about being on call at the hospital for long? I have some good news and want to celebrate. Got plans for tonight?"

"No. I'm on my way home now. Figured I'd order pizza or something."

"Don't. Let's go out to dinner."

"Okay, where and when do you want to meet?"

"I'll pick you up. Say around six-thirty? Dress casually."

"Can't refuse an offer like that. I'll be ready."

***

Rachel pulled her shiny new red Corvette convertible into Brian's driveway at exactly six-thirty. He must have been looking out the window because the front door opened and he walked outside the instant she arrived. Why was it her heart rate accelerated each time she saw him? The black t-shirt accentuated his muscles. Although his work involved physical labor, he apparently worked out in a gym. Rachel suddenly realized how little she knew about him and what he did in his spare time.

Brian climbed into the passenger seat. "Didn't know you had a 'Vette. What happened to your SUV?"

"Traded it a few weeks ago. I know it's silly, but every time I drove it, I was reminded of Phillip, and the night he demanded I drive to the factory. I was sure he planned to kill me. I didn't know he had lured Kyle and Stephanie there. Curtis Lawrence may be a weasel, but if it hadn't been for him, Kyle wouldn't have been the only one to die."

"Witnessing his death couldn't have been easy for you."

Rachel shook her head. "I watch patients die all the time. When I did ER rotations, I treated victims of gunshot wounds, traffic accidents, stabbings, and such. But watching Kyle bleed out, knowing there was nothing I could do... It's different when the victim is someone you know."

"It still bothers you, huh?"

"Yeah."

"If you ever need to talk to someone, I'm available."

"Thanks. I've spoken to a colleague on several occasions. She's a psychologist. And Stephanie and I talk about it sometimes."

"The two of you have become close over the past year."

"We have. I'm excited about being her maid of honor. It's been fun helping plan the wedding. Things are easier now that she's living here full time."

"Matt is happier than I've seen him in a long time. I think he had feelings for her back in high school."

Rachel put the car in reverse. "Thought I would leave the top down. It's a beautiful evening."

"Good idea. Where are we going?"

"To a new cantina outside Brewster. Hope you like Mexican."

Brian smiled. "I'm from Texas, aren't I?"

They drove to the restaurant in silence, any conversation being difficult over the noise of the highway. Rachel glanced at Brian a few times. She was happy for Stephanie and Matt, but the thought of seeing another one of her friends getting married served as a reminder of her own unwed state. Several of her med-school friends had married. Some already had several children.

Even her younger half-sister tied the knot last year. She had told Henry Jacobs one of her reasons for wanting to get away from the hospital was the inability to have a social life. Funny, but being able to set her hours would do little to change things.

She had no social life except for an occasional dinner with Brian. She couldn't call them dates. They were two friends who occasionally got together. And he seemed to like things just as they were. He hadn't so much as hinted he was interested in being anything else. They wouldn't even have a friendship if she hadn't sold him the old factory buildings last year.

"Popular place," Brian said as Rachel drove into the crowded parking lot.

"It's always like this, but I made reservations. Thought we could dine outside."

Once they sat down, it didn't take long for a waiter to take their drink order.

"Margarita on the rocks," Rachel said.

The waiter turned to Brian. "And for you sir?"

"Just iced tea. Unsweetened."

After the waiter left the table, Rachel said, "I'm sorry. I forgot you don't drink. Should I have ordered something else?"

"It's okay. It's not as if I'm an alcoholic who is tempted every time I'm around booze. I just don't want to become one. Now, tell me your news."

***

Rachel decided to put the top up for the drive home. During dinner, she and Brian had engaged in a lengthy conversation, discussing plans for her new private practice as well as his work on the renovation of the old Cameron office building. He told her about his idea for what was once the factory. He had to alter his original plans due to the fire last fall.

"It means a lot to me to see how much you care about restoring the place," she had said. "The property was in my family for a long time."

But Brian was silent after they got in the car, and Rachel reached for the button to turn on the radio. They neared the outskirts of Driscoll Lake when a popular classic rock song played from the car's speakers. Rachel glanced over to see Brian softly singing the words.

"Good song," she said.

"Yeah. With a subliminal message."

"Oh, yeah?"

"Maybe not so subliminal, but if you pay attention to the background vocals, you'll know what I mean."

"I know the words. The guy is afraid of having his heart broken."

Brian was silent.

"Who broke your heart? Your ex-wife or someone else?"

"Who said I'd had my heart broken?"

"No one. It just seems— I'm sorry, I shouldn't be asking you such personal questions."

"It's okay. Angie and I parted by mutual consent, although I blame myself for our marriage failing. I was too busy building up my business than to concentrate on making things work."

"Did she know you were trying to establish yourself when she married you?"

"Yes."

"Then she should have been more understanding."

"We weren't suited for one another, anyway." He paused for a moment before looking at Rachel and continuing. "And nobody else has broken my heart."

"How did you know what I was thinking?"

"Most women would want to know. Not that I think of you like I do other women."

Did he just say that? Rachel slowed the car to turn into Brian's driveway, parked, and turned off the engine. "Thanks for celebrating with me tonight."

"I'm glad you asked. I'm sure there were others you could have invited."

"I wanted to celebrate with you."

Brian turned to look at her, and their eyes met. "Really?" He looked away but made no effort to get out of the car.

What was he waiting for? Rachel fidgeted with her key ring. Brian's reference to the song may not have meant about having one's heart broken. He may have been referring to the part about not wanting to fall in love. But both had been dancing around this friendship thing for almost a year. Brian wasn't going to make the first move. If he wouldn't, she would. The close quarters of the car made it easy. She reached for his hand.

"Brian, I enjoyed being with you tonight."

He turned, a look of surprise on his face. She leaned toward him and touched her lips to his. The kiss was light, but he moved closer, deepening and lengthening the kiss. When Rachel responded, he suddenly pulled away and reached for the door handle.

Brian cleared his throat. "I'd better go inside. Busy day tomorrow."

She rubbed her forehead, took a deep breath, and exhaled slowly. "Guess I'll see you around sometime."

"Uh, sure. Okay." Brian got out of the car and closed the door. Then he hurried up the sidewalk, unlocked his door, and stepped inside. He didn't even turn around to look back.

Rachel lowered her head and rested it on the steering wheel. Somehow, she had missed the signals he'd been sending her. How could she face him again knowing he wanted nothing more than friendship? Without feeling the humiliation of rejection?

Straightening, she started the car, put it in reverse, and backed out of the driveway.

Chapter 3

Mid-morning sunlight streamed through Brian's bedroom window. He opened his eyes slowly and rolled over to look at the clock. He rarely slept this late. Then again, he usually slept through the night. Last night he tossed and turned until almost three in the morning, thinking about his evening with Rachel.

What had happened? She was a beautiful, desirable woman who had made it clear she wanted more than friendship. But what had he done? Turned her away. Why?

He knew the reason. It was the same excuse he had used for months. He couldn't get past their different backgrounds. Last night she drove up in a brand-new sixty-thousand-dollar sports car. She could have easily afforded one four times that amount.

Rachel spent money as if it was nothing. How could he compete with that? Sure, he could provide her a comfortable home and necessities. The average middle-class lifestyle. But he would never be able to give her what she was accustomed to.

Brian got out of bed, walked into the bathroom, turned on the shower, and adjusted the temperature to a comfortable warmth. He lingered beneath the warm spray until he relaxed.

Back in the bedroom, he pulled on a pair of jeans, not bothering with a shirt, then walked into the kitchen. He hit the brew switch on the coffee maker before peering into the refrigerator. At least he had done a decent job of stocking it this week. He had all the makings for breakfast tacos.

After months of having bare cupboards, he decided to start cooking more meals at home. He would never be the type of cook his mother once was, but he could manage. It wasn't as if he had any prospects for a wife in the near future.

Wife. He couldn't picture Rachel being the kind of wife who would have dinner for him each evening. She was a professional who had a successful career. Certainly not the stay-at-home-mother type.

But he recalled their conversation at the park from a few nights ago. Rachel had said she wanted children. Apparently, unlike some modern women, she wanted to do things the old-fashioned way. Marriage first, then children.

Rachel again. She seemed to occupy his every thought. He had enough on his mind with business issues and the fire. The last thing he needed right now was the entanglement of a woman in his life.

***

Rachel hurried to answer the doorbell, surprised to see Stephanie.

"Hope this isn't a bad time. I was driving by and took a chance on you being here."

"Glad you're here. I was just about to have coffee on the deck. Would you like a cup?"

"Thanks. Sounds good."

Rachel nodded toward the French doors that led outside. "Go ahead. I'll grab the coffee and be there in a couple of minutes." In the kitchen, she poured two steaming mugs of her favorite morning blend and then went outside.

Stephanie took the mug from her and inhaled the rich aroma before taking a sip. "Thanks. This is good."

Rachel sat down. "I always begin my day with coffee."

"I never used to drink it, but thanks to Matt, I recently started."

"Getting excited about the wedding?"

"That's an understatement. I know September will be here before I know it, but it seems like an eternity. Did you know I had a crush on Matt in high school?"

"Brian said Matt had feelings for you back then."

Stephanie smiled. "Brian said that? When?"

"Last night."

"If I'm not wrong, that's the second time the two of you have been out this week."

"Can't really call either occasion a date. And I had to ask him both times. Sometimes I wonder why I keep pushing him."

"He's never asked you out?"

Rachel shook her head. "Not really. We went to a new Mexican restaurant in Brewster. But let's not talk about Brian and me. Have you spoken to Christine lately?"

"Some. She's still grieving for Kyle. And no matter how many times I've told her I don't blame him for keeping silent all those years, I'm not sure she believes me. In fact, she sometimes acts as if it's her fault."

"I haven't talked to her much. She took a leave of absence from her job after Kyle died. Maybe asking her to be in the wedding will help her realize it's time to start living again."

"I hope so. Christine has been hurt enough. Speaking of living, what about you? Seeing anyone besides Brian?"

"No. Who has time? I've been too busy."

"Sounds like an excuse."

Rachel shrugged. "I assume you and Matt will live in his house."

"You're changing the subject, but yes. Matt is already converting the loft for my writing nook. And it makes sense since the house is larger."

"I would venture a guess that you don't want to live next door to your in-laws. At least not during the first years of your marriage."

"You're right. I love Nell and Dan, and they aren't intrusive, but I don't want to be in their back door."

"I can understand."

"I've decided it's time to sell Helen's cottage. It's small but would be a good home for a retired couple or a starter home for someone."

"Probably wasn't an easy decision. I know how hard it was for me to sell our family home."

"Lots of memories there, but it's time to put aside the past."

Stephanie took a sip of coffee. "So, tell me more about you and Brian."

"You're not going to give up, are you?"

"No."

"We're friends. That's it." Rachel lowered her head. "I would like it to be more, but he seems content for things to remain as they are."

"Have you told him?"

"Not in so many words."

"How do you think he feels about you?"

"I'm not sure. Sometimes he acts as if he wants to deepen the relationship, but for some reason, he seems to be holding back. I can't imagine why. I guess he has a lot on his mind."

"How so?"

"The fire last fall at the factory and now the one in Woodland Hills. He hasn't said anything, but I'm sure they've caused him a bit of a setback in his business. The last thing I want to do is push a relationship on him at this point."

"Maybe you should talk to him. Sometimes it's hard for men to show their emotions, but I've seen the way he acts around you. When we were inside that burning building last year, he was so protective of you. It's obvious he cares. You may be the one who has to make the first move."

Rachel sighed. "I did last night. Didn't seem to work."

"You mean asking him to dinner?"

"No. I kissed him."

Stephanie raised her eyebrows. "What did he do?"

"He responded at first. Even took the initiative to deepen the kiss. Then he made some excuse and got out of the car."

"Maybe you took him by surprise. I still think he cares about you. Just give him time."

Time. That's what she'd been giving him. How much longer would she be willing to wait?

***

The thrill had vanished in the three days since the fire and already the old longings stirred within him. It was time to start thinking about his next move.

If only he could ignore his feelings, but they had been there too many years. And the need was escalating. As a teenager and young adult, he set fires at random. But this time, each one would be carefully planned and timed. Investigators were leaning toward the last blaze being accidental, just as they had the others.

Starting another fire so soon was so tempting, but it would arouse suspicion. That was something he couldn't afford to have happen. This time, he had a mission. A purpose for each fire. A target. And he wasn't going to allow anyone or anything to stop him.

Chapter 4

Matt Bradford leaned back in his chair and looked at the two men sitting at his desk. Carlos Gonzales was a trusted colleague and friend. He was thorough in his work and kept an open mind during investigations. Too bad he couldn't say the same about Richard Abbott.

To be fair, most of the time Abbott did a good job as county fire marshal. He wasn't a dishonest person. But he seemed to have a grudge against Brian, and it clouded his judgment on the investigation of the Woodland Hills fire.

Damn shame, too. Brian didn't deserve the animosity. What began years earlier escalated when Brian provided eye witness testimony against Abbott's son and helped send him to prison.

It would be hard for a father to see his child turn to a life of crime. Matt liked to think he would be reasonable if he had a child of his own. Richard Abbott certainly wasn't doing his son any favors by ignoring his problems.

Almost two months had passed since the Woodland Hills fire. Abbott was dragging his feet on the investigation, and Matt wanted answers. "So, what do we have?"

"The fire started in the trash pile behind the house. There is clear indication of human involvement, but not enough evidence to rule arson. At least not yet." Abbott added with a smirk.

"The same as what the preliminary investigation revealed." Matt had hoped Abbott would have something more.

"Yes. As you already know, a painter was at the house earlier in the day and said he threw some old rags into the pile that had paint thinner on them. Someone probably tossed a cigarette, although the painter said he isn't a smoker. Could have been teenagers sneaking around. It didn't take much for the cedar siding to ignite."

"Then you believe it was an accident?"

"I'm still not convinced, but I can't prove otherwise. Same thing at the factory. We think a tossed cigarette caused that fire. However, I believe it's possible the same person is responsible for both incidents and made them appear to be accidents."

"Any suspects?"

"I've heard Brian Nichols is having financial troubles. He owns both places. Could have done it for the insurance money."

Matt's nostrils flared. "That's ludicrous. You can't base an investigation on rumors and assumptions."

Carlos, who had watched the interchange between the two men, spoke up. "Do you have any evidence to tie him to either instance?"

"No. But don't tell me you've never solved a case by going on your gut instinct."

"Not without sufficient evidence to back it up," Carlos said.

Matt nodded at him. It was Carlos's intuition that something was amiss in the original investigation into Stephanie's father that led to the real killer. Turning back to Abbott, he said, "Do you have any evidence that ties to Brian? Other than your opinion?"

Abbott lowered his head. "No."

"Then there shouldn't be any reason for you not to release your findings to Brian's insurance company," Carlos said.

Matt drummed his fingers on his desk. "This could have been settled a long time ago if you hadn't dragged your feet."

"I wanted to make sure I had conducted a complete investigation."

"No one can accuse you of not being thorough," Matt said.

"Look, I came here as a courtesy because the fire occurred within the city limits. I didn't have to tell you anything."

Matt nodded. "No, you didn't. And I appreciate you coming."

"You'll have a copy of my complete report first thing tomorrow morning, as will the insurance company." Abbott stood to leave the room but turned around as he got to the door. "I know Nichols is your friend. But I don't believe you're seeing him for what he is. Everyone knows the sort of things he did as a teenager."

Matt watched him leave before turning to Carlos. "He's the one who can't see the truth."

"I agree. But at least we can put this behind us. Let's hope we don't have any more suspicious fires."

***

Brian glanced at the caller ID, recognizing the number for the claims department of his insurance company. He took a deep breath before answering. "Hello."

"Mr. Nichols? This is Jake Osborn calling regarding your claim on the Woodland Hills property. I'm happy to say we finally received the fire marshal's investigation report. He ruled it accidental. We'll be sending a check to your bank within the next couple of days."

Brian closed his eyes and let out a long breath. "That's good to know."

"I apologize for the process taking so long, but the initial report didn't rule out arson. We had to make certain before proceeding, in case investigators considered you a suspect."

"Me?"

"I'm sorry. Didn't mean to imply you would do anything like that. I meant no offense. But we've seen a lot of instances where the property owner was responsible."

"I understand. You're doing your job."

"I spoke with the fire marshal on several occasions in an attempt to expedite the claim, but he was adamant."

"Wouldn't expect any different from him. I appreciate your call." Brian hung up the phone and rubbed his forehead. He had felt a headache coming on all morning, so he pulled a bottle of acetaminophen from his desk and swallowed a couple of pills.

Even though it was a relief to hear from the insurance company, the fact that Richard Abbott was responsible for the delay was enough to send his blood pressure skyrocketing. But no sense dwelling on the situation. It was time to move forward.

The report cleared him of any wrongdoing. Now it was time to start cleanup and rebuilding—something he was sure the neighbors and other builders would appreciate. A burned-out shell of a house in a new subdivision didn't look good for homeowners or prospective buyers.

Brian spent the rest of the morning arranging for someone to start the clean-up process. It was noon when he looked at his watch. Time to grab a bite of lunch. Rosa's Taqueria was his usual lunch hangout, but he had already eaten there twice this week.

He looked outside. The weather was unseasonably cool for late August. Temperatures in the mid-eighties with low humidity. The thought of staying cooped up in the office all afternoon didn't appeal to him. He needed to get outdoors. Soak up some sunshine. Breathe.

Rachel took Thursday afternoons off. He picked up his cell phone and pressed the speed dial for her number. He hadn't seen her much in the past few weeks except in casual passing. Nor had they talked on the phone. She had been busy establishing her new practice, so he figured that was the reason for her lack of communication.

Or maybe it was because of how he turned away from her the night she kissed him. What else was he supposed to do? Invite her into his house? Their relationship was nowhere near that stage. The way things were going in the car, it would have been too easy to take things to the next level.

"Hello, Brian. What's up?"

Brian closed his eyes at the sound of her voice. He had missed her. More than he cared to admit. "I got word the fire was ruled accidental, and my insurance company is issuing a check. Thought if you didn't have any plans for this afternoon we could grab a burger or hot dog and go to the park. It's a beautiful day, and I didn't want to spend it in the office."

"Wish I could, but I have other plans."

"I see."

"I'm having lunch with Stephanie and Christine."

"Oh, okay." Had he just sighed? He didn't want her to realize his disappointment, but she must have picked up on it.

"Hey, I'll see you tomorrow, remember? I suppose Stephanie will seat us together at the rehearsal dinner."

"That is tomorrow. I almost forgot. If you haven't already made plans, I could pick you up."

"I'd like that."

"Then it's a date." Poor choice of words. It occurred to him he had never asked her out for a real date.

"I'll be ready." Rachel paused for a moment. "Sorry about today. A picnic in the park would have been fun."

"We'll do it another time. Guess I should check with Matt to see if he needs anything. After all, I am the best man."

"I'll see you tomorrow night. And hey, good news about the fire."

"Yeah, it is." Brian hung up the phone. It *was* good news. But he couldn't ignore a nagging sensation that his troubles had just begun.

***

"When does your mother arrive?" Rachel asked Stephanie as they drove toward Riverbend Ranch.

"She and my stepfather are due to arrive in Dallas at three. They'll probably get here sometime around seven. They want to take me, Matt, and his parents out for a late dinner."

"How does your mother feel about you moving back to Driscoll Lake?"

"She didn't have much to say. I don't expect her to visit often. Now that we learned the truth about Dad and since I told her how nice everyone had treated me here, she seems to be okay with it. Although I confess, I never thought she'd come back."

"You and I eventually did."

"Yeah, and I'm glad. Before my father died, he and Mom were good friends with Matt's parents. Mom and David enjoy traveling, much like the Bradfords do, so I think they will get along. I'm just glad Mom waited until today to arrive."

"Why is that?"

"She was disappointed when I didn't want a formal wedding. If I had done things her way, I would have married in church wearing a long white dress with a ten-foot train and a half-dozen bridesmaids dressed in pink or some other pastel color. A short ivory-colored wedding dress, two attendants, and midnight blue bridesmaid dresses aren't her style."

"She wouldn't try to interfere, would she?"

Stephanie slowed the car as she turned into the entrance of Riverbend. "Let's put it this way. She strongly suggests things. I did consent to one request."

"What's that?"

"For my stepfather to walk me down the aisle. I hadn't planned that until recently. I walked alone at my first wedding, but David and Mom had only been married a short time. David told me he realized he could never take my father's place, nor would he want to. However, he said it would be an honor for him to give me away."

"That's nice."

"Yeah. Too bad it isn't my father."

"I know. Sometimes when I think of Mother and all the things we missed..." Rachel looked out the window.

"I'm sorry. I feel bad about what I said. I'm trying to keep my mother from planning my wedding, and you give most anything to have your mom around."

"Don't feel guilty. I understand. Phillip robbed both of us. Somehow I think your father is smiling down upon you and is happy about your marriage." She saw Stephanie wipe tears from her eyes. "Now I've made you cry. Look out!"

Stephanie slammed the brakes but not in time to keep from bumping the pickup that crossed in front of them.

Rachel jumped out of the car first and ran to the other driver. "Are you crazy? What do you think you're doing? Look what you've done!"

The man stepped back. "I… I was—"

Stephanie hurried to his side. "Are you okay?"

"I'm fine. You barely bumped me."

"I'm so sorry. I should have been paying closer attention."

Seeing the Riverbend Ranch sign on the side of the vehicle, Rachel said, "I gather you work here?"

An older man pulled up in an all-terrain vehicle. "What's going on?"

"Had a little accident, boss. But this lady—"

"I'll handle things from here. Haven't I told you about driving too fast? What's it going to take to make you pay attention?"

"Please, sir," Stephanie said. "It wasn't his fault. I wasn't paying attention and drove through the yield sign. Your employee had the right of way."

"He still could have been more observant. If there's any damage to your car, Ms.—

"Harris. Stephanie Harris."

"Ross Hunter."

Rachel walked to Stephanie's car to look. "I don't see any damage."

"What about the pickup?"

"Looks like a scratch or two. Nothing to be concerned about. Not the first scratch, and it won't be the last."

"Then, if it's all right with you, let's forget about this and move on."

Hunter looked at the Colorado license plate on Stephanie's car. "If you're sure... I see you're from out of state."

"I recently moved to Driscoll Lake. And I'm positive everything is okay." Stephanie shook the man's hand before she and Rachel got back in the car.

"Are you okay?"

"Yeah. Didn't need anything like this to happen two days before my wedding. But it could have been worse."

"I guess so. That guy should have used more caution."

"Rachel, it was my fault. Everything is fine. Christine is probably waiting. Let's have lunch."

Chapter 5

Brian looked in the mirror and tugged at his collar. He wasn't accustomed to wearing a tie, and he felt constrained. According to Rachel, the near last-minute decision for the men to wear vests and ties was Stephanie's attempt to appease her mother. Kathryn Armstrong felt long-sleeved shirts and jeans were a bit too informal.

By the time Rachel and Brian arrived for the rehearsal, the tension was thick enough to cut with a knife. Matt was trying to console Stephanie, who had threatened to call off the entire affair in favor of the two of them having a simple ceremony before a judge.

When Rachel noticed Stephanie's tears, Brian saw a spark of anger in her eyes. She pulled Stephanie's mother aside, and the two of them left the room. When they returned a few minutes later, Kathryn talked to Stephanie, who seemed to relax. Afterward, everything went as scheduled.

Later, at the rehearsal dinner, Brian had a chance to ask Rachel about her encounter with Kathryn. "What did you say to her?"

Rachel raised an eyebrow. "Not nearly as much as I wanted to. I told her to back off because Stephanie had planned and paid for the type of wedding she wanted. I said if she didn't go along with plans, she could march herself back to Georgia."

"You didn't?"

"I did."

"That's my girl." Brian blushed as he realized he'd spoken the words aloud.

"What?"

"I said, 'atta girl.'"

Brian smiled as he remembered the conversation. He hadn't fooled Rachel, but she didn't seem to mind. Her talk with Kathryn had worked, Stephanie's only concession was the ties and vests.

At least the temperatures were cooler than usual for early September. It could be worse. They could be having a formal wedding in the middle of July where he had to dress in a tuxedo complete with a cummerbund and bow tie.

But it didn't matter. If wearing formal attire had been required, Brian would have done so to support his best friend.

"Me too, buddy." Matt appeared beside him in the mirror, also adjusting his tie. "Kathryn can be a bit controlling. I went along for Stephanie's sake and not hers."

"Figured your future mother-in-law to be the take-charge type."

Matt rolled his eyes. "Yeah. Steph was already nervous. She didn't need the added stress of her mother's interference."

"At least we're still allowed to wear our jeans." Brian chuckled. "Did you see Kathryn's eyes last night when the recessional began to play?

Matt nodded. "I don't think 'You Make My Dreams' is her idea of a proper song for such an occasion."

"She'll get over it."

"Yeah. Funny thing. Kathryn's husband seemed to enjoy the choice of music. David is okay. I like him." Matt paused for a moment. "To be honest, I think Kathryn's behavior is due in part to her being back in Driscoll Lake."

"A place she thought she'd never set foot in again. I can understand, in a way. A lot of people mistreated her and Stephanie years ago."

"Yeah."

"I will say she was cordial to me last night. Asked about my mother and said she had hoped Mom would be able to attend the wedding. I think she meant it."

Matt's other groomsman, Jason Elliott, stuck his head in the door. "It's time."

Brian looked at Matt. "Are you ready for this?"

Matt grinned. "What do you think?"

They walked together and took their places beneath the archway. After ushers seated the parents, Pachelbel's Canon began to play. Brian thought of the three women about to walk down the aisle. All of them went through a difficult time last year. Rachel and Stephanie having to relive the tragic death of a parent—themselves facing an almost certain death at the hand of a ruthless killer. Christine losing her husband and learning he withheld knowledge that could have cleared Stephanie's father of wrongdoing years earlier.

Now, a year later, they came together to celebrate the beginning of two people joining their lives. Most people waited in anticipation of the bride, but when Rachel began walking down the aisle, Brian's eyes were only on her. The late afternoon sunshine highlighted her dark auburn hair, and he couldn't help notice how the midnight blue dress swirled around her long, shapely legs. Her eyes met his, and she smiled as she stood across from him.

When Stephanie took her place at the altar, and the minister began the ceremony, Brian found it difficult to concentrate on the words. He couldn't help but imagine what it would be like if it were Rachel and him in place of Matt and Stephanie. But even as the thought crossed his mind, he knew it was impossible.

***

Rachel sat at a table with Christine and looked around the room at the wedding guests. "Lots of people here tonight."

"Yeah. Not surprising. Even Stephanie's mother seems to be having a good time."

"Even with the 'unconventional' wedding?"

Christine laughed. "Unconventional in Kathryn's eyes. I overheard her say the choice of music was Stephanie's idea."

"She once told me how she and her father shared a similar taste in music. Her mother prefers classical."

"Stephanie's father is the reason for a lot of sixties and seventies music?"

"Yeah, but it sounds pretty good to me." Rachel paused for a moment. "How are you doing these days?"

"I'm hanging in there. Starting to get out more."

"You haven't mingled much tonight. Outside the bridal party dance, you've kept to yourself."

"Jason was kind. He's the first man I've danced with since Kyle's death." She nodded to the man sitting with his wife a few tables over.

Rachel squeezed Christine's hand. "Sorry. I'm sure that was hard."

"What's your excuse?"

"What are you talking about?"

"I seem to recall you've danced only once."

"I've been too busy." Rachel looked around the room. "Say, isn't that the FBI agent who helped Carlos with the investigation last year?"

Christine turned her head. "Vince Green? Where?"

Rachel nodded. "Standing next to Carlos."

"This is the first time I've seen him dressed in something other than a business suit."

"Do you know him well?"

"Not really. We spoke several times last year when they thought Curtis was involved with Phillip in the embezzlement case. Vince seems nice enough. Why do you ask?"

"He keeps looking this way. Go talk to him."

Christine shook her head. "No. I couldn't do that."

"Why not?"

"Come on, Rachel. Give me a break."

"Okay. I'm not trying to push you into anything. Just want to see you have a good time tonight. You deserve that much"

"It's not like you've been a social butterfly tonight, either."

"Yeah, well." Rachel laughed. "I guess we're sitting here like two wallflowers without a date for the prom."

"Hello, Rachel."

She turned to see Alan Davis standing beside the table. She'd seen him among the guests and had tried to avoid him. Why was he even at this wedding? It wasn't as if he was a close friend of the bride or groom. "Care to dance?"

Rachel hesitated. Alan would persist, and Rachel had no desire to cause a scene by refusing. It wasn't as if Brian was spending any time with her. He'd made himself scarce, hanging around the band and conversing with members when they took a break. She didn't have him to come to the rescue, although the prospect of that happening sent a shiver of excitement through her.

She turned to Alan. "Are you sure you can put your phone away long enough? I'm surprised you didn't have to take an important call during the wedding ceremony."

"I know proper etiquette. Give me that much credit."

"All right. One dance."

Alan was a smooth dancer. He led well and kept a reasonable distance between them. But he wasn't Brian. She glanced across the room and saw him talking to Matt's father.

When the song ended, Rachel nodded and smiled. "Thanks."

"Turning away from me so soon?"

"I said one dance. Anyway, I should get back to Christine. She's having a bit of a hard time tonight." But when she turned, she saw Christine dancing with Vince Green.

"She looks fine to me. Can't use her as an excuse."

"I don't need excuses." She walked back to the table and Alan followed. "Why are you following me? Is there something you need?"

"Pity a beautiful woman like you is here alone. Unless of course, your 'friend' is your date tonight. He seems to have been busy all evening."

"I assume you're talking about Brian. Yes, he's my friend. No, we didn't come together. And yes, I'm perfectly fine being alone. You don't have to hang around. I danced with you, so be satisfied with that."

"I thought maybe after this is over we could —"

"No."

"You don't even know what I'm about to say."

"Whatever it is, the answer is no."

"But—"

"Hey, Rachel. Mind if I join you?"

Rachel looked to see Brian standing nearby. "Please do."

Brian sat down next to her. "Hope I'm not interrupting anything."

"You're not." She glared at Alan.

"Guess I know where I stand. Too bad. We could have had a good time." Alan turned and walked away.

Rachel shook her head. "Jerk."

"I have a few other choice words for him, but I'll refrain from using them."

Rachel laughed. Alan was his own worst enemy. He was too arrogant. It wasn't as if he was unattractive—quite the contrary. His icy blue eyes, neatly trimmed light brown hair, and impeccable taste in clothes was enough to make most women swoon. But he wasn't Brian.

The man sitting beside her was the antithesis of Alan. He wore his dark brown hair slightly long. His brown eyes were warm and inviting, and he was more comfortable wearing blue jeans and a t-shirt than business clothes. Alan represented stability and security. Brian was the rebel. Dark. Dangerous. And Rachel was far more attracted to him.

"Sorry I haven't been around much tonight."

"I'm fine. It's not as if you have to keep me entertained."

"You looked like needed rescuing."

"Thanks. Alan is an arrogant jerk. I've been trying to keep Christine company, but she's dancing with Vince Green."

"Good for her. So how about it? Want to dance with me?"

I'd like nothing better."

***

Brian took Rachel's hand and led her to the dance floor. The tune was upbeat, and Rachel was surprised at the ease in which Brian twirled her around. Despite his carefree attitude, he wasn't one to socialize a lot.

Maybe it was because of his past, especially his teenage years and the fact his father had been an alcoholic. He had hinted as much on a few occasions, but Brian was never one to open up to her completely. She guessed if he confided in anyone, it would be Matt.

Rachel had been surprised at their friendship. Before she moved away from Driscoll Lake as a teenager, Matt and Brian ran in different circles. Matt was the golden boy of the high school football team. Not only was he a star athlete, but he also excelled in his studies. She was surprised to learn Matt decided to enter law enforcement. If anything, she would have guessed he would have become an accountant like his father.

Brian, on the other hand, often ran with the wrong crowd—the ones who defied authority. The students who would sneak away from school to smoke or have beer parties outside of town. And even though he never spoke of his father in favorable terms, like Thomas Nichols, Brian chose to become a carpenter.

Somehow, Brian and Matt had become close friends. Although Brian had never said, Rachel got the feeling their friendship went back a long way.

The song ended, and she smiled. "Thanks. This was fun. I didn't know you danced so well, although it shouldn't surprise me, knowing how much you love music."

"You have a few surprises of your own."

"Oh yeah?"

"Like the hummingbird on your shoulder. Never imagined you having a tattoo."

"Maybe I have a few more surprises."

His eyes narrowed. "You mean you have others?"

"Just the one. What about you? I figured you the type to have body art, yet I've never seen any."

Brian cocked an eyebrow and lowered his voice. "Not that I wouldn't care to show you, but this isn't the time or place."

Rachel's face reddened.

He laughed. "I don't think it would be appropriate to take my shirt off."

"Oh, okay." She shivered under his gaze.

"Cold?"

"No. I'm fine." She stepped back, thinking Brian was ready to sit down.

"Not so fast. We haven't slow danced yet." He pulled her close as the lights dimmed and "Waiting For a Girl Like You" began to play.

If Alan had tried to get this close to her, she would have slapped him right there on the dance floor. But being in Brian's arms felt like the most natural thing in the world. She laid her head against his chest, and he pulled her even closer, resting his chin on top of her head. Their bodies molded together, and she became oblivious to her surroundings.

But after a few minutes, she remembered they were in a public place. Driscoll Lake had plenty of gossips, and some of them were present. No reason to give anyone cause for idle chitchat. At any rate, they were at the wedding of their closest friends. Rachel would not disgrace the event because she was having a hard time keeping her hands off the best man.

She pulled back and put a little distance between them.

Brian whispered in her ear. "Not a bad idea. Although I prefer you much closer."

"You do?"

"Oh, yeah."

She smiled but allowed herself to get lost in the moment—and the words of the song.

***

The interaction between Brian Nichols and Rachel Jackson made for some interesting speculation. They tried to pass their relationship off as being good friends, but he could see it was more than that. He'd heard rumors to the fact. If that dance was any indication, those rumors were true.

He made certain to keep an eye on them the remainder of the evening. They were never far apart from one another. Even danced a few more times, although nothing like that intimate moment they shared earlier.

If he were a betting man, they would leave together. Her house or his? Maybe it was time for a change of plans.

No. It was too soon. He had other work to do first. A little while longer, and then he would destroy his nemesis forever.

Chapter 6

The next two weeks were both busy and productive for Brian. Crews had cleaned up the building site, and all that remained now was the concrete foundation. On Monday, his workers would start framing the new house. Things were starting to look up.

He spent most of Friday afternoon in his office. It was almost five-thirty when the phone rang. He hoped it would be Rachel. They hadn't seen one another since the wedding, and he missed her. It would have been great if they had been able to leave together that night, but Rachel had driven Christine to the wedding.

Probably just as well. After that one dance, he wouldn't have wanted to be responsible for what might have happened had he taken her home.

But Rachel always called him on his cell phone. When he looked at the caller ID, he was surprised to see the number of a real estate office.

"Nichols Construction."

"Mr. Nichols? My name is Kimberly Eves, and I'm with Caldwell Realtors in Brewster. I wondered if I might have a word with you. Is this a good time?"

"Sure. What can I do for you?"

"It's regarding a piece of property—the old Cameron Manufacturing site. An out of town investment firm contacted me asking if you might be interested in selling."

"No, selling isn't a consideration. We've almost finished the first stage of renovations. The first tenant will occupy a space in early December."

"I see. What are your plans for the factory section?"

"I'm not sure how much you know about the place, but last year's fire necessitated some changes to my original plans. I had to delay the second phase but hope to begin work next spring or early summer at the latest."

"Sounds like selling is out of the question."

"It is. Did this company indicate why they are interested in the property?"

"No, but they're willing to offer a generous price."

Kimberly Eves named off a figure well above the current market value. Even with all renovations completed, the property wouldn't be worth that much money. Whoever was behind this had inside knowledge of Driscoll Lake's economy. They must anticipate additional growth which in turn would bring increased business opportunities and revenue.

If it were only a matter of money, Brian would be foolish not to accept. But restoring the place meant much more than financial gain. "Tell them I'm not interested."

"Not interested? You're sure about this. After all, you wouldn't be able to get that price from anyone else."

"You heard right. The property isn't for sale."

She sighed. "Okay, but if you reconsider, don't hesitate to give me a call."

Brian hung up the phone. An offer like that would enable him to pay off his existing debts and replenish the money he'd taken from savings to purchase the Cameron property. He shook his head. No matter how tempting the offer, he didn't want to give up his dream.

His stomach growled, reminding him he didn't eat lunch. Without giving the matter another thought, he called Rachel's number.

"Hi, Brian."

"Got any plans for tonight? Thought we could go to dinner together."

"I wish I could, but I promised Christine I would have dinner with her. She's starting to socialize more, and I feel she needs someone. Sorry."

"I understand. Glad she is starting to come around. What about tomorrow night?"

"Now I really feel bad. I'm driving to Austin first thing in the morning to spend the weekend with my father and step-mother. I won't be home until Sunday night."

"Okay. Hope you enjoy the time with your family."

"I'll call you when I get back. We'll do something together next week."

"Sounds like a plan."

Brian hung up the phone. Another night alone. Looks as if it would be an evening of eating pizza and watching whatever he could find on Netflix.

***

Several months had passed since Rachel last visited her family in Austin. The five-hour drive took almost six thanks to bumper-to-bumper traffic when she reached Georgetown. She sometimes missed the Austin nightlife, especially the music scene. But she didn't miss the congested freeways and crowds of people. Rachel shook her head. She had indeed settled into small-town life.

She noted the familiar sites of the LBJ Presidential Library and Darrell K. Royal-Texas Memorial Stadium on the University of Texas campus. She had done her undergraduate studies at UT and remained a loyal fan. She jokingly told others she bled burnt orange.

The tall skyscrapers made it increasingly difficult to see the State Capital Building, but when she finally caught a glimpse of it, she knew she wasn't far from the Colorado River and the turnoff to her father's house.

Rachel looked forward to spending the weekend with her family. She thought she would be the only one present, but when she arrived, both her siblings were there. Her brother Cade, in his third year of residency, managed to have a free weekend.

The big surprise came when her sister Nicole announced she and her husband were expecting their first child the following May. Although she was excited about Nicole, the news was another reminder that she was unmarried and childless.

Nicole was the youngest, ten years Rachel's junior, and would be the one to have the first grandchild. Rachel tried to reason because Nicole hadn't chosen to go to medical school like herself and Cade, it made sense that she was the first to marry and have children. But she was only kidding herself. Somehow Rachel was allowing life to pass her by.

Even Cade confided to Rachel that he was getting ready to pop the question to his longtime girlfriend. The news left her even more melancholy. It was hard to be excited for her siblings when she was unmarried and childless—and would be for the foreseeable future, if not longer. She didn't sleep well Saturday night. When she did manage to drift off, she dreamed of Brian. When she was awake, she kept thinking about the dance they shared at the wedding.

She awoke early on Sunday morning, dressed, and tiptoed downstairs to the kitchen. Pouring a cup of coffee, she took it outside to the patio. The September morning was crisp and cool, even for Austin. However, it would be warm enough for a swim later, and she was glad she brought her swimsuit.

Rachel took a sip of the hot liquid. She needed the caffeine. Was there ever a time when Brian didn't occupy her thoughts? He had sounded disappointed on Friday when she said she couldn't have dinner with him.

It then occurred to her she could have invited him to come to Austin. The house had plenty of room, and her father and Cecelia wouldn't have minded an additional guest. Would he have accepted her invitation? She reached for her phone to dial Brian's number but realized it was too early. He might not be awake at six-thirty on a Sunday morning.

When she heard the patio door open, she turned to see her father. He kissed the top of her head before sitting next to her. "I see you're still an early riser like me."

"It's in my blood, I guess."

"Your mother always liked to sleep late. I often told her she wasted the best part of the day."

"Yeah, that was Mom, all right." Rachel looked at her father. Ron Jackson was still a handsome man, even though his auburn hair had begun to show traces of gray. Rachel got her hair and eye coloring from him. Her mother was the opposite with a fair complexion, blond hair, and blue eyes.

"So, how is my little girl?"

"Dad, I haven't been your little girl in a long time. In case you haven't noticed, I'm about to be on the back side of thirty."

"That's still young. You're just beginning to live. So, what's troubling you?"

"Am I that transparent?"

"It wouldn't have anything to do with your sister being pregnant and your brother getting engaged, would it?"

Rachel's father had always been perceptive. "I'm happy for both of them. And anyway, I've been busy with my new practice and other stuff."

"Is there a man in your life?"

Rachel jerked her head in surprise. "No. Yes. Sort of. We're friends, that's it." Rachel wondered how many times she had used that terminology to explain her relationship with Brian.

"Who is he? What's he like?"

"His name is Brian Nichols. He's lived in Driscoll Lake all his life. Owns a construction company. I sold him the old factory buildings last year, and he's making them into a place for restaurants and specialty shops."

"Sounds like he has a level head. What about his family?"

"An only child. His mother has rheumatoid arthritis and is in the early stages of dementia. She lives in a nursing home now. She once worked at Cameron. His father is deceased."

"And how does Brian feel about you?"

"I wish I knew. We sometimes meet for dinner or a movie. He called Friday night and asked me out, but I had already promised a friend I would have dinner with her. I told him I would give him a call next week."

"Sounds like something could be developing there."

"I don't know. When I ki—" Rachel stopped before she said too much. There were some things one didn't tell their father, like oh yeah, Dad, I practically threw myself at him, and he turned away.

"Maybe you'd feel more comfortable talking to Cecelia. She's a good listener."

Rachel shook her head. "No, it's okay." There was a long pause before she asked, "Dad. What happened between you and Mom? Why did your marriage fail?"

"It was my fault. Your mother wanted me to stay and for us to work things out, but I couldn't get over our backgrounds being so different. I wasn't accustomed to having money, and I resented the fact that she could afford the nicer things in life. I wanted to be able to buy them for her."

"Did you tell her that?"

"Yes. I told her my situation before we married. She knew I grew up poor and worked to put myself through medical school. It didn't matter to her. She just wanted us to be together. I think she would have given it all up if I said the word."

"What happened?"

"I wanted to be able to provide your mother with the lifestyle she was accustomed to. Although I received scholarships, I still had a ton of student loans. She wanted to pay off my debts, but I wouldn't hear of it. Pride, I guess. I knew it would take me a while to establish my reputation as a surgeon and build up my practice, but I also knew I'd eventually get there. I didn't want her to support me in the interim.

"Anyway, you know how tough it can be those first few years after medical school. Residency, then a surgical internship. We began to argue a lot. I moved out and filed for divorce. Madelyn only wanted a chance at happiness, and I blew it."

"And then she married Phillip. Did you ever regret leaving her?"

Ron paused for a moment before answering. "Yes. Many times. Don't get me wrong. I love Cecelia. She has been good for me. Because of her, I have two other children. But I can't help but believe if I hadn't divorced your mother, she would still be alive today."

***

Although Rachel intended to leave Austin shortly after lunch, she didn't get away until almost five. Which mean she wouldn't arrive home until nearly ten. And that was barring any accidents, road construction or heavy traffic. She was nearing Waco when she reached for her phone and pressed the speed dial for Brian's number.

"Rachel, where are you?" His voice came through the car speakers.

"Just outside Waco. Didn't leave Dad's house until late. My brother and sister were also in town."

"A little family reunion, huh?"

"Yeah. And everyone had news to share. Cade is getting married, and Nicole is pregnant." And the older sister is still single and childless. She didn't dare say that aloud.

"So, you're gaining a sister-in-law and becoming an aunt."

"Yeah. It looks that way. I had hoped to get away earlier so we could have dinner together tonight. Looks like I won't be home until late."

"That's too bad. I was looking forward to seeing you."

"How was your weekend?"

"Believe it or not, I took it easy. Went to see Mom a couple of times. Other than that, I stayed home. Not much else to do."

"I look forward to returning home and a more laid-back atmosphere. Austin is— I'll just say Austin is Austin and leave it at that."

"A big city."

"Yeah. And growing bigger every day. Even Dad said something about moving away after he retires."

"Can't blame him. Guess I've lived in a small town too long. Having some downtime wasn't so bad. I had a lot of thinking to do."

"Oh yeah? Want to talk about it?"

"Got a call on Friday from a real estate agent asking if I would be interested in selling the factory site."

Rachel's heart sank. She couldn't imagine someone else owning what was once her family property. "What did you say?"

"I told the agent I wasn't interested, but the offer is very generous. It's from an investment company that is interested in acquiring properties in Driscoll Lake."

"But you're so close to finishing the first stage of renovation. Don't make any hasty decisions."

"I won't rush into anything. Thought I'd give it a week or two. If these people want the property bad enough, they'll wait."

Rachel slowed the car. "I'd better get off the phone. I'm on the outskirts of Waco and traffic is getting thicker. I'll call you in a couple of days." She pressed the button to end the call.

Brian was thinking of selling the property? No way. Not if there was anything she could do to prevent it from happening.

Chapter 7

Two days had passed since Brian admitted to Rachel he was tempted to sell the old factory site. She didn't like the idea of someone other than Brian owning it. The property had been in her family too long, and she hated the thought of some outside company destroying a part of the town's history. If she could do anything to stop the potential sale, the property was not going to fall into the wrong hands.

She would repurchase it from Brian to prevent that from happening, even though she had no use for the buildings. Last night she thought of a solution. She was eager to tell him her proposal.

Several times during the day, she picked up the phone to call him but changed her mind. This was something they needed to discuss in person. She left her clinic immediately after seeing her last patient of the day, leaving her staff to lock up for the night.

Rachel drove to Brian's office, hoping to find him there. Disappointed, she decided to see if he was home. He was in the front yard when she arrived.

"What brings you here?" He smiled as she got out of her car.

"Wanted to talk to you about something."

"Sure. Come inside."

Rachel liked the looks of the house. The outside was a combination of brick and fieldstone—a popular style these days. "You have a nice house. I take it you built it yourself."

"My crew did most of the work, but I had a hand in the design. Planned it as a spec, but we finished it around the time of my divorce, so I decided to move in. Look around if you'd like. Want something to drink?"

"Sure." Rachel strolled down the hall. She liked the contemporary look of the place. It was masculine. The decor, or lack thereof, could use a feminine touch. But the place was clean and neat. He probably had someone to clean for him. She had to admit the minimalist look appealed to her.

She walked down the hall and saw the master bedroom door was open. She couldn't resist looking inside. Like the rest of the house, the decorations were minimal, and the room had a masculine feel.

An earth-toned comforter covered the king-sized bed. A glass brick wall separated the master bathroom, giving the entire master suite a feeling of openness. Inside the bathroom was a whirlpool tub and separate double shower.

Rachel felt her face grow warm and she hurried from the room. She didn't want Brian to catch her in his bedroom. She suddenly felt as if she had invaded his private space.

"I only have bottled water," Brian called from the kitchen. "My refrigerator is often bare."

"Water's fine."

In another room, she found drums and stereo equipment. Framed photos of album covers adorned the wall. An electric guitar and amplifier stood in one corner next to a chair. A futon sat against one wall.

Rachel remembered when Brian played drums for the high school band. He was good.

"I see you found my music room."

She turned at the sound of his voice. "Yeah. Nice. I knew you played drums back in high school. Didn't know you also play guitar."

"Some. Music is my outlet."

"I might have guessed. Wasn't your biggest desire to be the next Ringo Starr?"

"Don Henley."

"What?"

"Don Henley. I was an Eagles fan. Beatles too, of course. Their music influenced a lot of people."

Rachel walked to the drums and tapped lightly on one cymbal. "I gather you still play."

"Yeah. I recently joined the band that played at Stephanie and Matt's wedding."

"Good for you. Somehow the band's name fits you."

"Radical? You think I'm a troublemaker?" His words were teasing.

"No, but you've always been a free spirit. Tell me more about the band."

"I'm the youngest in the group, so we do a lot of classic rock. We play at private events and on occasion at local clubs."

"That's why you kept talking to the band members the night of the wedding?"

"Yes. The drummer was leaving, and I had already spoken to the group's founder earlier. A couple of days later, I sat in on a session, and the other members accepted me unanimously."

"That's great. How did you become an Eagles fan?"

"My mom liked them, so I grew up listening to their music. When they got back together for the *Hell Freezes Over* tour in '94, I saw them in concert at Texas Stadium."

"Funny how many of our generation are drawn to the music our parents listened to."

"A lot of the stuff out these days is junk. And I'm not really into the country music scene. Sometimes I think I should have been born during the baby boom."

Rachel smiled. "You know what they say about that generation."

"Yeah. Mom is still young at heart, but it grieves me to see her like she is. She's too damn young to have dementia. And then there's arthritis."

"Unfortunately, neither disease isn't always a respecter of age." Rachel turned and looked out the window. "Of course, my mom will always be young in my mind. She was only five years older than I am now when she died."

"You still miss her, don't you?"

"I miss what we could have had. A mother should see her daughter grow up, go to college, get married, have children. Phillip Denton robbed her of all that. All because of his greed. She was an innocent victim who didn't deserve to die. Neither did Stephanie's father."

"No, they didn't."

"At least I have the consolation of knowing Phillip is rotting in hell. He's getting what he deserves."

"I guess I don't have to ask how you feel about him."

"Phillip's actions cost so many people—including your mother. I hate him for what he did. If Mother had never married him, she'd be alive today."

"And you would have never left Driscoll Lake."

"Yeah, well Mother was always unlucky in love. She and my father couldn't make a go of their marriage. Their backgrounds were too different. I always believed she married Phillip on the rebound."

"Is that why you've never married? Afraid you'll repeat the mistakes your mother made?"

Rachel jerked her head and looked at Brian.

"I'm sorry," he said. "I have no right to ask you that."

"It's a fair question. I guess I'm just waiting for the right man to come along."

"I gather he hasn't."

Rachel turned to look into Brian's eyes. "Maybe he has and doesn't know it."

Brian lowered his head. "Whoever he is, he'll be one lucky guy." He stood up and walked to the set of drums.

Rachel cleared her throat. "Tell me more about the band. I'd like to hear you play sometime."

"I hope I can keep playing with them. The two fires have caused a bit of a setback for me, so I'll probably be doing more of the work myself. That way I don't have to pay a full crew. Unless I decided to sell the factory."

"Let's talk about that. It's the reason I stopped by. I have a business proposition for you."

"A business proposition?"

"Yes. I think you already know when I sold the place to you, someone else made an offer for the property. It was much higher than what you offered, but they wanted mineral rights which I refused to sell."

"I recall you mentioning something about it. Go on."

"The property was in my family for generations. It wasn't easy to let go, although it made sense. I liked your ideas and plans for the place. The fire was a setback, but I'd like to see you continue with your original plans."

"I'd like nothing better, but financially I'm not sure it's possible."

"That's where I'd like to offer you a partnership. I'll provide the financing and include enough for you to pay off any existing loans. You'll do the restorations and retain ownership of the property. I'll be a silent partner."

"I'd still have to make payments to you."

"Not until you've completed the work and begin leasing space to tenants."

"That's very generous, but what's in it for you?"

"The satisfaction of knowing the owner is someone who cares. Someone who wants to restore the place and not destroy it. Someone who looks to the future while still caring about the past."

"This project was a longtime dream of mine. Selling the property wouldn't be an easy decision. I don't know what to say."

"Say yes."

***

Friday morning, Rachel's phone rang as she drove to her office, and she pressed the button to listen to the call.

"Hey, it's Brian. I wanted to catch you before your first patient arrives."

"I'm on my way to the office right now."

"Have dinner with me tonight. Unless you have other plans."

"I don't."

"Good. I'll make reservations at Riverbend."

"Riverbend? That sounds great."

"I'll pick you up at seven."

"I'll be ready." Rachel ended the call. Her day had just gotten brighter. She had something to look forward to. Not the usual dreary Friday night.

It was mid-morning before she realized he had asked her out on a real date. At least, that's how she looked at it.

Their times together, other than when she asked him out a few weeks earlier, had been instances of running into one another and deciding to eat together or catch a movie. This was different. Riverbend wasn't a run of the mill "let's grab a bite to eat" place.

Maybe tonight would be a turning point in their relationship.

***

Rachel spent most of the afternoon trying to decide what she would wear for her evening with Brian. In the end, she chose a simple sleeveless black dress and black wedge sandals.

When the doorbell rang, she hurried to answer. Brian leaned against the door jamb, his arms folded and legs crossed at the ankles. He wore a long-sleeved button-down shirt, jeans, and a jacket. He straightened as she opened the door.

"Wow," she said.

He raised his eyebrows. "I would have dressed like this a long time ago if I'd known you'd react like that."

"Guess I've grown accustomed to seeing you wear t-shirts most of the time."

"Yeah, well, I thought I'd do something different tonight. Still wearing my jeans, of course."

Rachel smiled. "Come inside for a minute. I'll get my purse."

Brian followed her and stood in the living room. He looked around. "I like what you've done with this place. Looks nice."

"You were the builder? I didn't know."

"One of my earlier projects."

"I love the house. You're very talented."

"One of the things my father did right. He was a good carpenter before he became an alcoholic. Taught me a lot when I was young."

"I don't think I've ever heard you say anything positive about your father."

"Not much to say." Brian shrugged and looked away. "Our reservation is for seven-thirty."

"I'll only be a minute." Rachel hurried upstairs. The September evening could be a bit chilly, especially if they dined outdoors, so she grabbed a lightweight chiffon shawl. When she walked back down the staircase, Brian was waiting at the bottom.

"You look beautiful tonight." He took the shawl from her and wrapped it around her, his hands lingering on her shoulders.

Rachel shivered, remembering the feel of being in his arms. "Thanks," she whispered.

Brian's voice was husky. "Yeah, uh, guess we should be going."

***

Brian showed Rachel a side of him she had never seen before. He acted like a perfect gentleman, opening the car door for her, holding the door of the restaurant, and making sure she was seated before he took his place beside her. While she appreciated his thoughtfulness, she found equally attractive, if not more so, the rebellious side of him. The once would-be rock star with the devil-may-care attitude.

When the waiter appeared at their table, Brian asked, "Would you care for a glass of wine?"

"Not tonight. I think I'll have unsweet tea."

Brian nodded to the waiter. "Same for me."

Rachel studied the menu. "Do you come here often?"

He shook his head. "Figured this was a special occasion."

"Then I'm flattered."

After they placed their orders, Brian said, "I've thought about your offer the past few days."

"Have you reached a decision?"

"I accept."

Rachel smiled. "You don't know how happy I am to hear you say that. This will be a first for me."

"I think you're the right partner."

"A silent one. You're the expert. I'm not."

"Bet you could learn."

"If I had the right teacher."

"Oh, I could handle that."

Rachel's face grew warm, suddenly aware of the hidden implication. She cleared her throat. "As much as I would like to handle this on a handshake, my lawyer has advised that we draw up papers."

"Wouldn't have it any other way. Always best to do things right—even if it's among friends. But let's leave the business talk for another time. I want to enjoy tonight."

The dinner conversation was pleasant. They talked about her new practice and Brian's new venture with the band.

Once they finished their meal, the waiter appeared. "Would either of you care for coffee and dessert?"

"Just coffee for me." Rachel looked at Brian. "They have a decadent strawberry pie, but there is no way I could eat an entire slice. The portions are large."

"Why don't we share?"

Rachel felt a little flutter in her stomach. Although innocent, there seem to be an implied intimacy with sharing food. "Sure."

"A slice of strawberry pie. Two forks, please." Brian said to the waiter.

"Well, that's interesting," Rachel said as she looked on the opposite side of the room.

"What?"

"Alan Davis is here with Heather Stevens."

"Alan and Heather? I thought she didn't work for him any longer."

"She doesn't. Miles Parker made sure of that before he retired. Maybe they have more than a working relationship."

Brian glanced in toward Alan's table. "He's welcome to her."

"I seem to recall you taking her out one night."

"Big mistake on my part. I remember that occasion. We ended up at Mary's with Matt, Stephanie, Christine, and Kyle. You were there with Alan."

"You saw us? Going out with him was one of the biggest mistakes I ever made. I kept glancing in your direction, hoping you would rescue me. But you all seemed to be having a good time."

"Guess so. I would have, had it not been for Heather."

"As far as I'm concerned, she and Alan deserve one another."

***

Controlling his anger was difficult. Seeing Brian Nichols and Rachel Jackson together in what appeared to be an intimate dinner meant he would have to change his plans. If they were together all night, Brian would have an alibi.

He had intended to start another fire tonight. Had the details already worked out. The target carefully chosen. It was time to raise the stakes. This time there wouldn't be any doubt the fire was arson.

What was one more day? He had waited this long. It would take patience and persistence to finish this job, but he vowed to see it through to the end.

Chapter 8

Matt Bradford turned to look at the bedside clock. Who would be calling at four o'clock on a Sunday morning? When he saw it was the fire chief's number, he got out of bed and stepped into the bathroom to take the call. No reason to disturb Stephanie.

"Sorry to bother you," Stan Gardner said. "There's been another fire."

Matt rubbed his forehead. "Where?"

"A residence on Meadow View Lane. Homeowners weren't home. Thanks to an observant neighbor, we were able to extinguish the blaze before it destroyed the house. Most of the damage was to the garage and kitchen area."

"I'm sure it's too early for any clues as to the cause."

"Nothing yet, but I've already notified the fire marshal's office. The neighbor who reported the fire also said he saw a suspicious person earlier."

"I'd better get over there and question him." Matt ended the call and walked back into the bedroom to get dressed.

Stephanie stirred in the bed and opened her eyes. "What's wrong?"

"A house fire. No one was injured, but a neighbor reported seeing a suspicious person in the area. With Carlos on vacation, I need to talk with the man. Sorry."

"It's okay. I understand."

Matt sat down on the bed and kissed Stephanie on the forehead. "Go back to sleep. I'll be home as soon as I can."

***

Matt first met Vic Stewart two years ago when he reported a break-in at his next-door neighbor's house. Because of Vic's swift actions, police were able to apprehend the suspect before he made off with valuable electronics equipment and jewelry.

He was the type of person most people would appreciate having as a friend. The seventy-five-year-old retired engineer was a keen observer. He looked after his neighbors and watched their homes when anyone was away. Vic was instrumental in starting the first residential crime watch program in Driscoll Lake.

The October morning was chilly, so Vic invited Matt and Fire Marshal Richard Abbott into his home to talk

"Care for a cup of coffee?" Vic said before motioning them to sit down at the kitchen table.

"None for me," Matt said.

Abbott was quick to assume the lead. "No, thanks. You say you saw a suspicious person not long before the fire?"

"It was a couple of hours earlier. I was up late watching TV—can't sleep much these days—it was well after midnight when I decided to go to bed. When I checked the front door, I saw a man walking along the sidewalk in front of Tippet's house."

"What time was this?"

"Around one-thirty. I turned on the outside lights. Those floodlights are bright, you know. The man kept walking in the same direction, but it seemed to me he picked up his pace somewhat. I did notice he was smoking a cigarette.

Since he didn't try to run or hide, I figured it could be someone visiting one of the homes at the end of the street."

"Did you get a good look at him?" Matt asked.

"Couldn't see his face, but he was tall, brown hair, probably mid-thirties. About the same age as you, chief. Not that I would ever think it was you."

Matt smiled. "I understand."

"Anything else you remember?"

Vic shook his head. "Nothing. No, wait a minute. There is something. Earlier last night, I saw a small white car drive by. It may have been a Honda or a Kia, but I'm not certain. Now that I think about it, the driver could have been the same man I saw later."

"Did this happen close to the same time?"

"No, I saw the car much earlier. Around seven in the evening."

"Thanks for giving us the information. We'll check with other neighbors to see if anyone saw something. Appreciate your time." Matt stood up from the table, a signal to Abbott it was time to end the discussion.

They walked outside together.

"What do you think?" Abbott asked.

"Vic's always been reliable. He isn't one to call the police unless he has a good reason."

"If the fire turns out to be suspicious in origin, we may have a lead."

"It's a long shot, but if that's the case, this would be worth looking into."

Stan Gardner approached them as they crossed the street. "We're wrapping up here. No chance of the flame reigniting. We've assisted in securing the scene. Thought you'd want to know we found footprints beneath a back window and a cigarette butt."

Matt looked at Abbott, the unspoken word between them clear. This evidence could be the first sign that someone intended to set the fire.

***

Rachel spent most of Sunday morning lounging around the house. If there was one thing she missed most about her family home, aside from the memories, it was the pool. Maybe she would look into having one built before next summer. An early morning swim was her favorite exercise. Not that she would have gotten in the water today. The October day was chilly. She couldn't even get excited about climbing into the hot tub.

Brian hadn't called since Friday night. Although he had taken her to a nice restaurant, she couldn't help but believe it was to show gratitude. A way to "seal the deal" of their partnership. The chemistry they shared at the wedding wasn't present. Sure, he walked her to the door and even kissed her goodnight, but there was no deep-seated passion. It was more of a perfunctory kiss. Even his remark indicated such. "I'm not in the habit of kissing my business partners."

So that's what he thought of her? Had their friendship even been replaced? Maybe she'd made a mistake in offering to finance the renovations. Many women in her place would feel used.

But if that were the case, he would have likely taken the relationship deeper and then approached her about financing the project. But that didn't happen. She hadn't attempted to hide her feelings about him. In fact, if Christine hadn't ridden with her to the wedding…

Rachel shook her thoughts aside. If anything, someone might think she was using a business partnership to get closer to Brian. That wasn't the case. The first time he made an offer to buy the buildings, she had thought he was the right person. Before then, she didn't know much about him even though they attended two years of high school together. But that was a long time ago. Brian had changed since then.

Sighing, she sat down on the sofa and turned on the television, hoping to find something interesting to watch.

She thought about calling Stephanie to see if she would like to go to a movie but quickly nixed that idea. Stephanie was newly married now. And it was Matt's day off. Enough said.

Christine was starting to socialize a little more but had mentioned something about spending the day with her daughter, Emily. No way would Rachel interfere with their time together. A year after her father's death, Emily still showed signs of withdrawal.

Any other time she would call Brian. But not today. They would need to talk once her attorney drew up the paperwork for the business agreement. Until then, she would give him a little space.

Rachel decided to order pizza and spent the afternoon watching movies. So much for an active social life. She would have had more excitement if she had been on weekend rotation at the hospital.

***

Sunlight streamed through Brian's bedroom window, awakening him. He looked at the clock. It was almost noon. He hadn't slept this late since his teenage years. The band had played at a private party the night before. It lasted until well after midnight. By the time they packed up their instruments, he didn't arrive home until almost three in the morning.

Stretching, he got out of bed and went into the bathroom to take a shower. A few minutes later, he pulled on a pair of jeans, went into the kitchen, and peered into his refrigerator. He was falling back into his old habits of not going to the grocery store. The few items in the fridge were several days old. The last thing he needed was food poisoning. Nothing else to do but go out. He went back into the bedroom, finished getting dressed, and hurried out the door.

He decided to eat at Rosa's Taqueria. Not only was it one of his favorite places, but it was less likely to be crowded there. When he walked inside Rosa's, he was surprised to see Matt there—and wearing his uniform.

"Hey man," he said. "What's up? Figured you'd be at home today."

"Carlos is out of town, so I had to help with a house fire investigation."

"A house fire? Where?"

"Charles Tippet's place on Meadow View. Do you know him?"

"I built the place. Hardest person I've ever worked for. We had more than a few disputes. He still doesn't like me. What happened?"

"Tippet and his wife were out of town. Thanks to a watchful neighbor, the fire was contained to a small portion of the house."

"Any idea as to the cause?"

Matt shook his head. "Not yet. But we have evidence the fire may not have been an accident."

***

Last night he made a narrow escape. Who would have thought anyone living in a retirement community would be awake at almost two in the morning? When a neighbor turned on his floodlights, it was hard to stay calm. He would have to be more careful next time.

The ideal way would have been to climb over the back fence of the Tippet home. However, that would have required crossing through someone's backyard. It would have been easier to choose another house, but he had selected this one for a reason. He knew the history between Brian Nichols and Charles Tippet.

The only regret he had last night was the fact he hadn't been able to watch the blaze. After seeing the neighbor, it was too risky. Not to worry, however. He was already planning the next fire, and he would make sure he could be in a position to watch.

Chapter 9

Brian was surprised when he looked at his watch and saw that it was almost seven-thirty. He needed to work in the office, having spent the last three days at his various construction sites. Now that things were looking up financially, it was time to hire an office assistant. He made a mental note to phone the newspaper office in the morning and inquire about placing an ad.

Two weeks had passed since his "date" with Rachel. She hadn't called or stopped by since then. He'd spent a good deal of time trying to figure out what had gone wrong. The evening had progressed nicely, and Rachel acted as if she enjoyed herself. Until he took her home. When he kissed her, she didn't respond. Very different from the passionate woman who had come on to him in her car only a few weeks earlier.

The only time he had seen her was when they signed their business agreement in her lawyer's office. She had acted professionally. Almost distant. Rachel didn't even call him with the appointment date—instead, she left it up to the attorney. If a business relationship was what she wanted, then that's what he would give her.

He would be lying to himself if he said he didn't want more. And he felt sure she wanted him. But he didn't deserve someone like Rachel. And she needed someone who could give her the lifestyle she was accustomed to.

Brian got up from his desk and began to turn off the office lights when he heard the sound of an automobile outside. He glanced out the window to see Matt getting out of his pickup truck.

"Hey, man," Matt said as he walked inside. "Just driving by. Didn't expect to see you here so late."

"Lost track of time."

"Glad you are here. I know this is short notice, but Stephanie and I would like for you to come to dinner on Friday. Stephanie is inviting Rachel. It's our first time to entertain since our marriage and who better than our best friends?"

"Rachel coming?"

"Don't know yet. Stephanie was supposed to talk to her today."

"She may not come if she knows I'll be there."

"Thought you two were friends. After seeing the two of you together at the wedding, it wouldn't surprise me to know there was something more."

Brian shrugged. "Yeah, I thought so too, but for some reason, she's been avoiding me the past couple of weeks."

"Oh, yeah?"

"Yeah. Since the night I took her to dinner at Riverbend. I keep trying to think what I might have said or done to set her off."

"You took her to Riverbend? That's where I took Stephanie for our first real date. Must have been a special occasion."

"That's sort of what I had in mind, although we did have some business to discuss. I thought Rachel would like it, but..." Brian shook his head. "I don't understand what happened."

"Just when you think you've got a woman figured out, they do something totally unexpected."

"Tell me about it."

"If it's any consolation, I gave up on trying to understand women a long time ago."

"Even your wife?"

"Especially my wife. But I love her just the same. I hope you'll come on Friday—no matter what is going on with Rachel. It would mean a lot to Stephanie and me."

"I'll be there."

"Good. See you around seven."

***

Rachel was hesitant about accepting Stephanie's invitation when she learned Brian would be there. The last thing she wanted was for any tension between the two of them to spoil the evening. But in the end, she accepted, not wanting to disappoint her friend.

Matt greeted her at the door.

"Come in. Glad you came tonight. Brian should be here soon. Stephanie is in the kitchen."

"Hey there," Stephanie called out.

Rachel inhaled a mouth-watering aroma as she walked in the kitchen. "Need any help?"

"Thanks, but I have it under control. Hope you don't mind Tex-Mex tonight. Enchiladas, charro beans, rice, and guacamole."

"Can't think of anything I'd like better."

"Funny. All the years I lived away from Texas, I never lost the craving for good Tex-Mex. By the way, Matt picked up stuff for margaritas. Want one?"

Rachel frowned. "I, uh. Sure."

"Don't worry. I have plenty of non-alcoholic drinks for Brian. Matt told me he doesn't drink."

Was her concern for him that transparent? She glanced around the house. Although she had only been here one other time with Stephanie before the wedding, already she could see a bit of feminine touch. Stephanie had placed candles on the dining table. A basket of fruit sat on the kitchen counter. Framed photographs adorned one wall near the front entrance, including some candid shots taken of Matt and Stephanie at the wedding and on their honeymoon.

Rachel thought of Brian's house. She had ideas of how to make it appear more like a home. With just a few— Whoa, girl. She was treading where she didn't belong.

Something warm and furry at her feet caught her attention. Stephanie's cat rubbed against her legs. "Hey, Whiskers. How are you doing, little guy?" She reached down and scratched him behind the ears.

"Sorry about that. Whiskers doesn't meet a stranger. Matt, would you mind taking him into the bedroom?"

"Sure." Matt was just walking into the kitchen. He reached down, picked up the cat, and left the room again.

Rachel smiled and glanced at her watch. It was already 7:20. "Wonder what's keeping Brian?"

"It's okay. We didn't plan to eat right away. I'm sure he'll be along shortly. In fact, I heard a car door. It's probably him."

The doorbell rang, confirming Stephanie's assumption.

"Sorry I'm late," Brian said when Matt opened the door. "Went by to see Mom after work and got tied up. I spent the day at the factory site and had to stop by the house to shower."

"It's okay, man."

"Hi, Brian," Stephanie said. "How is your mother?"

"Not too bad today. She was in a talkative mood, and I lost track of time."

"Perfectly understandable. Enjoy those moments while you have them."

Brian looked at Rachel. "How are you?"

"I'm fine. And you?"

"Okay. Busy. But that's a good thing."

***

Brian was cordial during dinner, answering Stephanie's questions about the old factory project, but he had little to say to Rachel. When the meal ended, she quietly exhaled. It was bad enough that she felt the tension in the room, but she sensed Matt and Stephanie were also aware. That wasn't good. Not on their first time to entertain as a couple. Especially since their best friends were responsible for the friction.

Stephanie's words jarred her from her thoughts. "Matt and I thought it would be a good time for our first outdoor fire of the season."

"Sounds good," Brian said.

Rachel cleared her throat. "I probably should go before it gets too late."

Stephanie looked surprised. "It's still early. Wish you would stay. It's not like you're on call at the hospital or have patients to see in your clinic tomorrow."

"No, but—"

"Then there's no excuse. You and Brian go outside. Matt and I will clean up here and join you in a few minutes."

"I'll help." Rachel started to rise from the table.

"No. Matt can do it."

He raised his eyebrows and nodded in acknowledgment.

Rachel didn't miss the exchange between them. Okay, she would play along with their game. For now.

Matt stood up from the table, took a box of matches from the kitchen counter, and handed them to Brian. "I already have wood in the fire pit. Do you mind lighting it?"

"Sure." Brian took the box and walked out the door.

Rachel had little choice but to follow him. She walked along to the cobblestone patio, waited while he put a match to the dry wood, and watched it begin to flame. The air was a little a little chilly, so she walked closer to the fire and sat down. "Nice night."

"Yeah." Brian took a chair beside her.

"I like what Matt has done here. Makes me want something similar in my backyard."

"Sure."

What was with him? "Maybe it's better if I do leave. At least you might have a good time if I'm gone."

"Rachel, stop with the small talk. What's bothering you?"

"What's bothering me? I should ask you the same thing. All evening you've acted like you have a thorn in your flesh."

"Maybe I do."

"And I suppose I'm the one who put it there."

"You might say that."

"Me? What did I do?"

"It's what you haven't done. Since the night I took you to Riverbend, you've made yourself scarce. You haven't called or come around—even had your attorney contact me about the partnership paperwork."

"I thought that's how you wanted it."

"Why would you think that?"

Rachel got up from her chair and walked to the edge of the yard. "What else was I supposed to think? You take me out for a roman—uh, a nice dinner, but when we got back to my house, you acted as if kissing me was a chore. Then you said something about not being in the habit of kissing your business partners. I figured if a business partnership was all you wanted, then that's what you would get."

Brian walked to her and put his hands on her upper arms. "And I thought that's what you wanted. I'll admit I didn't handle the situation the best way but did it ever occur to you there was another reason I held back?"

"Another reason?"

"Believe me, Rachel, you mean a lot more to me than just a business partner."

Rachel moved closer to him and put her arms around his waist. "I feel the same way about you."

"I don't think either one of us can deny—"

Brian's words were cut short by the sound of a door opening. Stephanie and Matt walked outside.

"I think we need to continue this conversation," Brian whispered.

Rachel looked into his eyes and smiled. "I think you're right."

***

After the brief conversation with Brian, Rachel relaxed and was able to enjoy the rest of the evening. The tension that had hung in the air earlier was gone. Brian pulled his chair close to her. It was hard for her not to reach out for his hand, but she held back. They were still trying to figure things out. No reason to go public yet—even to Stephanie and Matt.

She sensed Brian was anxious to continue their earlier conversation. It was hard to sit still when she and Brian had unfinished business. But it was an enjoyable evening. It wasn't that long ago when Rachel would never have dreamed the four of them would be sitting together as friends.

Stephanie lived in Denver and had vowed never to return to Driscoll Lake. Matt once lived in Dallas. After years of living in Austin, college, and medical school, Rachel hadn't given much thought to returning. Only Brian had stayed in the area. But it seemed as if fate had brought them all together.

The last of the flames had died down, and only smoldering embers remained when Matt's cell phone rang. He removed it from his pocket and looked at the caller ID. "It's Carlos." He turned away to take the call. When he walked back to the fire, he had a somber look on his face.

"There's been another arson. This time it was at Manny's Pizza. The building was a total loss."

Brian looked surprised. "Manny's? I remodeled the place for him a few months ago. He was just getting his business built back up. Damn shame."

***

Two nights later, another fire occurred at an unoccupied house on the outskirts of town—the house where Brian once lived with his parents. Despite the heat of Abbott's suspicions falling on him, a chill skittered up Brian's spine.

Someone was targeting him.

Chapter 10

Matt had come to respect Andrew Reeves in the few months he had served as mayor of Driscoll Lake. He showed a genuine interest in the city's residents and supported continued economic growth.

The fact that three suspicious fires had occurred within the past few weeks had many citizens concerned. So it didn't come as a surprise to Matt when Mayor Reeves called a meeting that included him along with Fire Chief Stan Gardner, Detective Carlos Gonzales, and Fire Marshal Richard Abbott.

The mayor was quick to get to the point. "I think we'll all agree this rash of fires has us all troubled. The sooner someone catches the person responsible, the better for everyone. Tell me what you have."

Richard Abbott spoke first. "While all of the fires are of suspicious nature, the last three are most certainly arson."

"All fires? What other ones are you talking about?"

"The one at the Woodland Hills subdivision in July and the fire last year at the old Cameron buildings."

"What do you base your suspicions on?" Andrew Reeves asked.

"Each fire has a common thread. Brian Nichols."

Matt was quick to speak. "Oh, come on man. You're not going to start that again. You have no proof."

Stan Gardner shook his head. "I can't see how Brian could be involved in any of this."

"Nevertheless, I'd like to hear what you have to say." The mayor nodded for Abbott to continue.

"Nichols owns both the factory and the house in Woodland Hills. He was the building contractor for the Tippet residence, did a remodel job for Manny, and the house that burned last night was his childhood home."

Matt snorted. "Interesting theory but it doesn't prove anything. You'll need more evidence than that. It could just be a coincidence."

"Five separate fires a coincidence? I don't think so."

Carlos spoke up. "Maybe they aren't a coincidence."

Matt looked at him in surprise. Was Carlos going to turn against Brian as well?

"Hear me out. Richard is correct in that Brian has either a direct or indirect connection to each location. It's possible both of the earlier fires weren't accidental, and the arsonist is targeting him. Someone out for revenge."

"Makes more sense than anything I've heard." Matt glared at Abbott.

"That's ludicrous. I'm telling you, Nichols is the one responsible for all this. You can't see the truth because he's your friend."

Matt sat forward in his chair. "And you can't be objective because you blame him for what happened to your son."

"That's not true. I—"

The mayor held up his hand. "Gentlemen, please. We're here to discuss how to solve a crime. Not create more problems."

"I apologize, Mayor Reeves." Matt took a deep breath. "However, I do think it would be a good idea to bring in outside investigators. Someone with more resources and who can look at the situation without bias."

Abbott was quick to speak up. "Mayor, I already have a team working on this. I believe by pulling together we can solve this without outside assistance. Carlos, you're a detective. What do you make of it?"

"Wait a minute. I was a homicide detective in San Diego. I don't have any experience in arson investigation. I'm with Matt. We need additional resources."

"Absolutely," Stan Gardner said.

"I agree. As mayor, I'm concerned about the safety of our citizens. We should consider ourselves fortunate no lives have been lost. Richard, it's not that we're saying you're unable to do your job. Just allow someone to help. Put a task force together. The sooner we get this behind us, the better."

Abbott sighed. "Okay. I'll call the feds."

***

When Matt learned an agent from the Department of Alcohol, Tobacco, and Firearms would be arriving in Driscoll Lake, he offered to have the investigation's headquarters at the police station. "We have a couple of vacant offices and an interrogation room. If the need to expand happens, I'm sure we can use the community center or another public building."

Mayor Reeves agreed.

It wasn't a surprise that Richard Abbott had protested. "But Mayor, my office already has a lot of pertinent information in our case files. We have plenty of space and the resources to help."

The mayor stood his ground. "All the fires have occurred in Driscoll Lake. With your office being in Brewster, it's best to let the ATF set up here."

Abbott frowned but had little choice in the matter. Matt guessed he felt as if he was losing control. Why did it matter? Everyone needed to leave their egos at the door. It wasn't a competition. Everyone's job was to find the person responsible and put an end to the wave of crime. Some citizens and business owners were already getting nervous wondering if there would be another fire, and if so, where.

Agent Greg Sikes arrived in town on Tuesday afternoon. Matt guessed him to be around forty years old—a bit younger than expected—but with years of experience. According to Abbott, he had worked a series of high-profile arson cases on the east coast before transferring to the Dallas Field Division.

Matt stood and shook his hand when the investigator walked into the office. "Agent Sikes. Glad you're here. I understand you're the lead investigator, and I won't interfere, but you'll have my department's full support and cooperation if needed."

"Thank you, Chief Bradford. My goal is to bring about a swift conclusion to the investigation. I often work alongside local law enforcement agencies."

"The fire marshal will fill you in on his investigation so far."

"He tells me he has a suspect. What's your take on it?"

"I'd rather not say until you look into the case files. However, if you have any questions for me, I'm available."

If Sikes was surprised by Matt's statement, he didn't show it. "Fair enough."

***

Brian worked in his office Tuesday afternoon. He had a couple of responses to his ad for an office assistant. One wanted full-time work only, the other lacked experience.

After having spent more time at the factory site, he realized how much he missed that aspect of his business. If he had the right person to run things at the office, he could devote more time to doing what he loved best—building things.

Too bad he couldn't find someone like his mother. She had been a dedicated assistant to Stephanie's father until his death. Later, she worked in Dan Bradford's accounting office. In fact, if she was able now, Brian had no doubt she would be willing to run things here.

He shook his head. The memory lapses were becoming almost a daily occurrence as evidenced by his regular visits. He had visited her the past three days. How much longer would she even remember her son?

Because of spending so much time with his mother, he had neglected someone else important to him. Rachel. They still had unfinished business. He looked at his watch. It was almost four. He picked up the phone and pressed the speed dial button, hoping to catch her between patients.

Rachel answered right away. "I was wondering when you would call."

"I'm sorry. I've been spending a lot of time with Mom. She's had a rough few days."

"Yeah, I know. I was at the nursing home yesterday and looked in on her. She talked about your father as if he was still alive."

"That's been happening a lot lately. Something she never did before."

"I don't think I have to tell you things will get worse."

Brian rubbed his forehead. "No. You don't. But that's not the reason I called. We need to finish our conversation from the other night."

"Good. Do you have plans for this evening?"

"I've neglected things here in the office. Planned to work late. Tomorrow is payday, and I'm still not finished writing the checks."

"You still need to eat dinner. I have one more patient to see. Why don't I grab Chinese takeout and stop by around six?"

"Best idea I've heard all day. See you soon." Brian hung up the phone and returned to his paperwork, hoping to finish before Rachel arrived.

About an hour later, he heard the sound of a car door outside. Hoping it was Rachel, he looked out the window to see Heather Stevens. What business did she have with him? Too bad the door wasn't locked. She walked into the office wearing a short skirt, stiletto heels, and a low-cut blouse.

Whatever game she was up to, Brian wasn't interested. "What can I do for you?"

Heather walked to his desk, sat on the corner, and crossed her legs. When she spoke, her voice was low and sultry. "You could do lots of things for me."

"Let me rephrase. What business do you have here today?"

"I hear you're looking for someone to run your office. I came to apply for the job." Heather ran her fingers along the edge of the desk, and they came to rest on a stack of paperwork.

"You're here for what?"

"From the looks of things, you could use some help."

"What makes you think you're qualified for the position?"

"I worked as a receptionist for Parker and Davis. Answered the phones, took messages and greeted clients as they arrived."

"You had time for all that? Thought all you did was spread gossip."

Heather lowered her head. "That was a mistake. I learned my lesson."

"Any experience with accounting software or word processors. Balancing accounts?"

She leaned closer to him. "No, but I'm sure you could teach me."

"If I had time to do that, I wouldn't need an assistant. You've wasted both your time and mine by coming here. I can't and won't hire anyone who doesn't have the skills and qualifications for the job."

"But I—"

Brian stood up and walked toward the door when he saw Rachel's car. "But nothing. If you're looking for a job, you've come to the wrong place. And now, if you'll excuse me, a friend is here. And I'm busy."

Heather looked out the window. "Friend, huh? I saw the two of you together at Riverbend. Looked like more than friendship to me."

"It's none of your business. Time for you to leave."

"I can see where I'm not wanted." Heather turned and stalked out the door.

She was right. He didn't want her around. The woman had a lot of nerve. He'd give her that much. Brian turned and smiled as Rachel got out of her car. "About time you got here." They walked into the office together, and he locked the door behind him. "Don't want any more unexpected visitors."

"What was Heather doing here?"

"Can you believe she had the nerve to ask for the office assistant's job?"

"You're kidding? Someone needs to teach her how to dress for a job interview."

"For real."

"Oh, so you noticed?" Rachel teased.

Brian looked at her. She was wearing jeans and a cream-colored sweater and still looked far more attractive than Heather in her provocative attire. "Didn't do a thing for me."

"Hungry?" Rachel held up the bag containing the Chinese takeout.

His eyes narrowed. "Yeah."

She laughed. "For food."

"Rachel, I—" His words were cut short by the ringing of his cell phone. Brian took it from his pocket and looked at the caller ID. "It's the nursing home."

"Better answer it."

"Brian Nichols... Yes... She did? When... Okay, I'm on the way." He ended the call and turned to Rachel. "Mom slipped on the floor of her room and fell. They're taking her by ambulance to the hospital in Brewster. She may have broken a hip."

"Oh, no. I can drive you there."

"It's not necessary."

"No arguments. I'm going with you."

***

Heather waited until she was a few blocks from Brian's office before she pulled the car to the side of the road. She reached for her cell phone to call the all too familiar number.

"Well?" Alan asked.

"No."

"What do you mean no?"

"I mean no. He told me I wasn't qualified for the job."

"I knew that, but that wasn't your real purpose in going. What did you do? Go in there dressed in proper attire for an admin assistant? Or worse, like someone's grandmother?"

"Certainly not! I tried playing the part of seductress, but it didn't work."

"And why not?"

"He isn't interested. It's Rachel he wants, not me. By the way, she showed up before I left."

"Why was she there?"

"Do you have to ask that? Especially after seeing them together at Riverbend?"

"Tell me something I don't already know. I swear, Heather, sometimes you are so—"

"Don't you dare call me stupid. Otherwise, I won't tell you what I learned."

Alan sighed. "Okay, sorry. What is it you know?"

"My little visit wasn't all in vain. Brian has a new business partner. I saw some paperwork on his desk."

"Oh, yeah? Who is it?"

"None other than Rachel Jackson."

Chapter 11

Matt's first impression of Greg Sikes was positive. The agent was a no-nonsense individual who was dedicated to his job. He was also an early riser, having arrived at the station early Wednesday morning. When Matt walked through the door at seven, the dispatcher told him Sikes had been there since five.

After grabbing a cup of coffee, Matt went into his office and closed the door. Like everyone else in Driscoll Lake, he wanted the arsonist caught before another fire occurred. Heaven forbid if any lives were lost. He had taken his second sip of coffee when he heard a knock on his door and looked up to see Sikes through the window. Matt motioned him inside.

"Sorry to bother you first thing, but I'd like a word."

"Of course," Matt said. "Have a seat."

"I reviewed Abbott's notes, including ones on the earlier fires that were ruled accidental. I'm inclined to agree with his assessment that all five fires are related."

"How do you figure that?'

"I believe the first two were set intentionally and made to look like accidents. With the drought last year, it didn't take much with the dry brush and weeds to cause that place to go up in flames. All fires started at the back of the buildings, and all have a common link."

"What would that be?"

"According to Abbott, Brian Nichols."

"Then you suspect him?"

Sikes nodded.

"I don't agree."

"I hear the two of you are friends."

"He's my best friend. But that doesn't matter. I would still find it hard to believe he was involved."

"Is it true he had a juvenile record?"

Matt shrugged. "Criminal mischief. Lots of teens have done much worse. Happened a long time ago. People grow up. They change. Abbott doesn't like Brian. Don't allow him to influence you."

"Who says that's what I'm doing? The report indicates both you and Nichols were at the factory last fall when the first fire occurred."

"That's correct."

"Mind telling me what happened?"

"I went there because a friend—she's now my wife— was in danger from a ruthless killer. He lured her to that place along with two other people, Rachel Jackson and Kyle Lawrence, with the intent to kill them. When I arrived, Brian was already at the factory."

"What was he doing?"

"Not sure. He was near the front gate. Getting ready to leave."

"Did Nichols say why he was there?"

"He didn't need to explain. He owns the place. I did ask what he was doing and whether he had seen anyone or anything."

"So you were curious. What happened next?"

"I explained what was happening. We heard a gunshot and ran toward the building. When we got near the front entrance, we saw flames behind the factory. We heard a second shot, and I ran into the building."

"He didn't go inside with you?"

"No. Stephanie, Rachel, and Curtis Lawrence—that's Kyle's father—managed to escape through a broken window. Brian heard the glass break and went to help them. He was about to come inside for me when I stumbled outside. Had smoke inhalation."

"Think any of the others would be willing to talk to me?"

"I'm sure both Stephanie and Rachel would. Kyle was killed, along with the murderer, Phillip Denton. Curtis Lawrence is in prison."

"Would Nichols talk?"

"I'm sure he will. If you consider him a suspect, he'll be anxious to clear his name. I'll call him."

"Let me know what he says." Sikes stood up and left the room.

An hour later, when Matt phoned Brian, he learned that Dorothy Nichols suffered a fall and would be undergoing surgery. Sikes would have to wait another day.

***

Dorothy Nichols' surgery was successful and there were no complications. The surgeon told Brian he expected her to make a full recovery. After a few days in the hospital, she would need rehab. Knowing she exhibited signs of early Alzheimer's disease, the doctor recommended a facility in Brewster that also provided physical therapy.

When the neurologist came by the next day, he was honest with Brian. "Your mother won't be able to stay in assisted living any longer. It's no longer safe, and she needs dedicated nursing care. It's something for you to consider while she's in rehab. You may want to consider making the change now. Woodbine has an excellent Alzheimer's unit.

Brian knew the day would come, but he was not ready for it now. Still, he wanted to do the right thing for his mother. Maybe he would discuss the situation with Rachel. Ask her for advice.

Rachel. They still needed to talk about their relationship. Maybe tonight. Things seemed to keep getting in the way.

When his phone rang, he was surprised to see the number for the Driscoll Lake Police Department. He answered right away. "Hello?"

"Brian, this is Matt. How is your mother?"

"Doing okay. Surgery went well. She'll need a few weeks to recover. What's going on?"

"An ATF agent is here to help investigate the recent arsons. Sikes would like to talk with you."

"Why me? I don't know anything."

"He seems to think the fires are connected to you."

"You're joking?"

"Afraid not. I told Sikes it was ludicrous to think you're involved, but—"

"Abbott got to him."

"Yeah. Anyway, the ATF agent has set up investigation quarters here at the station. Would you be able to stop by and talk to him this afternoon?"

"It's not convenient, but if it means clearing my name, then yes, I'll do it."

"I told him you'd want to. Word of warning. He's questioning the fire at the factory and the one at your house in Woodland Hills."

"Even though they were accidents? Why?"

"Sikes seems to think someone set the fires deliberately."

Brian sighed. "Okay. I need to go to Brewster to check on Mom after lunch. I'll come by around four."

"I'll tell him. Sorry about this."

"Not your fault."

***

Brian arrived at the station shortly before four.

Matt met him in the lobby. "This guy doesn't pull any punches. He's a straight shooter."

"Good. Then we can get this over and done soon."

"Want me to sit in with you?"

Brian hesitated before answering. If this investigator was anything like Abbot, he would need Matt's support. On the other hand, to go into the room with your best friend, who happened to be the chief of police, could be interpreted as a sign of weakness. "Why? Afraid I'll lose my temper?"

Matt shrugged.

"Unless Abbott got to him, there shouldn't be any reason for me to get angry. I have nothing to hide."

"I know that."

"Thanks for the offer, but I'll be fine."

Famous last words.

Greg Sikes stood up and extended his hand when Brian entered the office. As Matt indicated, Sikes got right to the point. "Thanks for coming in. As you know, we're investigating the rash of arsons in recent weeks. Need to ask you a few questions."

"Okay."

"So far there has been a direct or indirect link to you with each of the fire locations."

"What do you mean?"

"You built the Tippet house, did a remodel job at the pizza place, and the last fire was located at the home where you lived as a teenager."

"You'll find I've done work on a lot of houses and businesses. Doesn't mean anything. As far as the last fire, my mother moved from that house five years ago."

"And your father?"

Thomas Nichols was the last person he wanted to discuss. "Dead."

"Any siblings?"

"None." Where was Sikes going with this?

"Does your mother still own the home?"

Brian shook his head. "Sold it when she moved to assisted living."

"Any other connection to the house?"

"I grew up there, but I'm certainly not emotionally attached to the place."

"Doesn't sound like you have good memories of living there."

"Not particularly. If you want my opinion, someone did the world a favor." Great. That was the wrong thing to say. Brian shifted in the chair, wishing he could recall the words."

Sikes raised his eyebrows. "Oh yeah? What makes you say that?"

Swallowing hard, he said, "The structure wasn't in good shape. That's all."

"I see. So you weren't anywhere near the place the night of the fire?"

"No, I was not.

"Then let's talk about the fire in Woodland Hills and the one at the factory last year."

"They were ruled accidental."

Sikes ignored Brian's words. "The house under construction in Woodland Hills, were you at the building site anytime that day?"

"I already went over this with Abbott. I wasn't there."

"Tell me what you know about the factory."

"I'll tell you what I can."

"Chief Bradford says when he arrived that night, you were already on the premises."

"That's correct."

"Exactly why were you there?"

"No reason in particular. I had recently bought the property. Had a lot on my mind. Just needed to go someplace quiet to think."

"Did you go into the building?"

"No."

"Not even when you knew people were inside?"

"Shortly after Matt arrived, we heard a gunshot and ran toward the building. I started to go in, but Matt told me to wait. We didn't know who fired the shot or how many people were involved. He asked me to call 9-1-1 and went in himself."

"Did you make the call?

"Yes. The flames had already started to spread. I looked around, hoping to find some water where I could wet my shirt and put over my mouth to protect against smoke inhalation. I heard glass breaking and went to help Rachel and some others get out the window. I was about to go in to look for Matt, but he came outside."

"You're telling me you never entered the building?"

"That's right."

"At any time, did you go to the back side of the property?"

"No. In fact, except to open the front gate, I never got out of my pickup until Matt arrived."

"Then you didn't see anyone else around? Anything out of the ordinary?"

"Nothing."

"Some people would think it suspicious that you were even there."

"Coincidence."

"Think so? Even Chief Bradford said he had doubts."

"Matt said that?"

"Surprised?"

Brian's face grew red. "Yes. I am."

"That angers you?"

"If your best friend questioned you, wouldn't you be angry?"

"I suppose I would. That's all I have today. Thanks for coming in." Sikes stood up.

"Is this the part where you're going to tell me not to leave town?"

"This isn't a joking matter."

"I'm not joking. And for the record, I have no intention of going anywhere. Not now. Not ever."

"That's good because I may have some more questions for you later on."

"Fine." Brian rose from the chair, turned and stalked out of the room.

***

Brian took a few deep breaths, trying to calm himself before confronting Matt. His face was warm and a vein pulsed in his neck. Even his best friend was suspicious of him? This was the second time Matt had questioned his actions. Brian was inclined to overlook last year's incident with Stephanie. This time there was no excuse. How dare Matt question his reasons for being at the factory?

Enough was enough. No sense in waiting to calm down—that may never happen. He stormed into Matt's office without knocking.

"What the hell did you tell Sikes about me?"

Matt looked surprised. "What do you mean?"

"Cut the crap. You sold me out, and you know it. Bad enough to have Abbott questioning my actions, but you? I thought we were friends."

"We are."

Brian raised his voice. He was sure others could hear him, but he didn't care. "Yeah, well, friends don't stab friends in the back."

"I didn't do that. Look, Sikes wanted you in here yesterday. I was the one who told him he would have to wait until today because of the situation with your mother."

"And I'm supposed to be grateful?"

"I thought you would be. What exactly did Sikes say?"

"That you wondered why I was at the factory the night of the fire."

"I think there's been a misunderstanding."

"I'd say so. It's bad enough that Sikes is on Abbott's side, but now I guess you are, too."

"I'm on the side of the truth and—"

"Well, look for the truth somewhere else. I didn't set those fires. And while you're at it, stay out of my life." Brian stormed from the room, slamming the door behind him.

Chapter 12

After he left the police station, Brian got into his pickup truck and drove around for a couple of hours. Why was this happening again? First Abbott, now Sikes. After wandering for a while, he ended up at the old factory site. Déjà vu. He'd done the same thing a year ago. Where, according to Abbott and Sikes, the string of arsons began.

He parked his truck near what was once the old office building and turned off the engine. A lot of things had happened the past year. The structure had gone from being abandoned to almost being destroyed by fire to being a renovated building in which the first tenant would soon occupy. His longtime dream was about to become real. But what good would it do now? Abbott, the ATF agent, even his best friend believed he was responsible for starting the fire.

Brian closed his eyes and remembered the night of the fire. When he learned Rachel was inside, he—

He shook his head, unwilling to consider what life might have been like if he had lost her.

Lost her? Rachel had never been his. Friends, yes. Business partners, yes. But she meant much more to him. No doubt, there was a chemistry between the two of them. He felt it. Rachel did, too. The night at Matt's house they had started a conversation they never got to finish. Too many things had interfered. And with the mood he was in tonight, this wasn't the time.

But he needed her. Rachel never judged him. She would never believe he was responsible for the fires.

***

Stephanie laid the book she was reading on the end table and curled her legs beneath her. Whiskers hopped onto the sofa and lay down in her lap. It was almost eight o'clock, and Matt still wasn't home. He'd called earlier to say something had come up and he would be late, but she hadn't expected things to take this long.

Matt had left the house before seven that morning. He would be tired after the long day. When she saw headlights in the driveway, she sighed in relief. Depositing Whiskers on the floor, she got up from the sofa and walked into the kitchen to meet him.

He smiled as he walked through the door. "Hi, honey."

Stephanie put her arms around him, and they kissed. "You look exhausted."

"Yeah. It was a rough day."

"Are you hungry? I can make you something to eat."

"No, thanks. Carlos ordered pizza for everyone earlier. But I could use a beer."

"Go sit down and make yourself comfortable. I'll get it for you."

"I won't argue with that idea."

Stephanie walked to the refrigerator, pulled out a Budweiser and opened it before joining Matt in the living room. He had removed his boots, propped his feet on the coffee table, and rested his head on the back of the sofa.

She sat beside him, kissed him on the cheek, then handed him the beer.

He took a couple of sips before sitting the bottle down.

"Want to talk about your day?" Stephanie asked.

"It was one of those where everything that could go wrong did."

"Oh?"

"Yeah. Everything from the fire marshal being mad at me to angering my best friend."

"Brian? What happened?"

"First of all, Richard Abbott confronted me. He thinks I went over his head and convinced the mayor to get outside help with the arson investigations."

"But you didn't do that."

"No. The mayor called the meeting and suggested that himself. I did agree, as did Carlos and Stan. Abbott's not objective. He doesn't have the resources the ATF has to conduct a proper investigation. We have a serial arsonist running around. Abbott keeps wanting to blame Brian."

"Brian? Why?"

"Three of the fires were on property belonging to him."

"Three?"

"His Mom's old house, the one in Woodland Hills, and the factory site.

"I thought the first two fires were ruled an accident."

"They were, but Abbott admitted to having doubts. Guess he's convinced Sikes."

"Even if they were arson, it doesn't mean Brian was involved. And how do they figure the others were related?"

"The third fire was at a house Brian built. There was a dispute between him and the owner."

"So what if the properties all have a direct or indirect connection to Brian? That doesn't make him an arsonist."

"I know that, but Abbott believes he has motives. He claims Brian has had financial problems and set the factory and the house on fire to collect insurance money. The fire at the Tippet house was for revenge."

"That's ridiculous."

"I told him that, but it's hard for Richard Abbott to look at Brian with an open mind. It's a long story involving his son. He and Brian hung out together as teenagers. The kid later made a lot of wrong choices in life and Abbott blames Brian. Hard for him to be objective."

"What's your take on the agent?"

Matt took another sip of the beer. "Sikes is a no-nonsense guy. I thought he would be unbiased. Guess I was wrong."

"What do you mean?"

"Sikes questioned me about the fire at the factory."

"What did you tell him?"

"I told the truth. I said something to the fact that I wondered why Brian was there that night. When Sikes called him in for questioning, he apparently twisted my words to make Brian believe I doubted his innocence. Brian, being Brian, got angry and stormed out of my office before I could explain."

"Sikes considers him a suspect?"

"I told him he was wrong. He wouldn't listen, but I'm not going to stand by and allow him to destroy an innocent person."

"What will you do?"

"Sikes is in charge of the investigation, but if he doesn't back off Brian, I'll talk to the mayor. Carlos seems to think, and I agree, that someone is targeting Brian. Wish we could figure out who it might be."

"I can't imagine Brian being angry with you."

"It's not the first time. Last year, when Curtis Lawrence ran your car off the road, Brian was involved in an accident around the same time. When you said the vehicle was a dark extended cab Ford, and I saw Brian's dented truck, I wondered if he was to blame."

"What reason would he have had to kill me?"

"None. And I realized that. Trouble was I allowed my emotions to cloud my judgment. Someone didn't want you here, and I was so afraid of losing you that I didn't think clearly."

"But the two of you obviously patched things up."

"Yeah, we did. Until now, that is. I shouldn't have said anything to Sikes. I didn't know he would take it the wrong way. Now Brian doesn't even have his best friend to talk to."

"Maybe he'll talk to Rachel. I mean, they are friends."

"I'm beginning to think there may be more there. I remember something Brian said last year when I apologized for overreacting about your accident. He told me that he might have acted the same way if Rachel was involved." Matt took another sip of beer.

"He said that? I wish the two of them would stop being so stubborn and tell one another how they feel. Then talk to Brian again. Explain. Your friendship goes too deep. He'll understand." Stephanie put her hand on Matt's neck. His muscles were tight and tense. "Turn around," she said. "Let me work some of the stiffness out."

"You're good for me, you know." He sat the bottle of beer down and stretched his legs on the couch with his back toward her. She began massaging his neck and shoulders. After a few minutes, she felt him start to relax.

"That's better," she said. "But probably what you need is a hot shower and to go to bed early."

Matt swung his feet off the couch, turned to her, and grinned. "I think, Mrs. Bradford," he said between kisses, "that's an excellent idea."

***

Rachel spent the afternoon running some much-needed errands—one of which required a quick trip to Dallas. She arrived home around eight-thirty, tired but glad to have put a significant dent in her to do list. Although it was still early, she couldn't think of anything that sounded more appealing than climbing into bed and reading a book.

She rarely had time to read these days. When she did, it was usually a medical journal. None of that tonight. A copy of Stephanie's latest novel had lain on her nightstand for weeks and now was the perfect time to begin reading it.

She went upstairs, changed into her favorite sleep shirt and turned back the covers of the bed. At nine o'clock, the doorbell rang. She got out of bed and looked out the window, surprised to see Brian's pickup in her driveway, and hurried downstairs to open the door. He stood on the porch, hands in his pocket, shoulders hunched, and his head lowered.

"Brian. What's wrong?"

He looked up slowly. "Can we talk?"

"Sure." A thought crossed her mind. "Oh, no. It's not your mother, is it?"

"No, Mom is okay. In fact, she's doing better than expected."

Rachel put her hand to her throat and exhaled. "That's a relief. You had me worried for a minute. Come inside."

Brian walked into the den and sat down on the sofa.

"Looks like you were about to go to bed."

When she saw him standing at her front door, she hadn't bothered to put on a robe. Although the sleep shirt came to mid-thigh, she was suddenly conscious of how she was dressed.

"It's okay. Just planned to read a while. Can I get you something to drink?"

"No, thanks."

Rachel sat on the opposite end of the sofa and curled her legs beneath her. "You want to tell me what's going on?"

"This afternoon an ATF agent questioned me about the fires."

"Why?

"Abbott convinced him the factory fire and the one in Woodland Hills were arson and that I was his prime suspect."

"I thought he ruled those as accidents."

"Abbott now says he has doubts. And then Matt told Agent Sikes that I was at the factory the night of the fire before he arrived."

"You were already there? I didn't know."

"Yeah. I spent most of that evening driving around town and ended up there. I had no idea what was going on inside until Matt arrived. I told Abbott about it when he investigated last year. Matt made certain Sikes knew I was there."

"You wouldn't expect him to lie, would you?"

"Matt lie? Not him. He's too perfect."

"This doesn't sound like you. If you don't have anything to hide, then Matt telling his side of the story shouldn't make a difference."

Brian jerked his head toward her. "You think I'm hiding something? So now you also doubt me?"

"No, of course not. All I'm saying is because you're innocent, it shouldn't matter what Matt says. Anyway, he's not the type to sell you out. He wouldn't do that to his best friend."

"That's what I thought. But he told the ATF agent he had questions about why I was there."

"Are you sure he said that?"

"Yeah." Brian got up from the sofa, walked to the French doors, and looked outside. "I did something today I'm not proud of. After I spoke to the agent, I went to Matt's office. We had words."

"What sort of words?"

"I told him to stay out of my life."

"You didn't."

"I know it wasn't right, but I'm so tired of fighting my past. Why can't people forget?"

"The things you did as a teenager were nothing more than juvenile pranks. Lots of kids did things worse than painting the town water tower or papering the math teacher's house."

Brian turned around to face her. "Then you don't know. It happened after you left Driscoll Lake."

"What?"

"About the time I stabbed my father."

Rachel gasped. "I didn't know that."

He sat down next to Rachel. "I stayed out too late one night. Hanging out with the guys. I had given up drinking by then—did that just before your mother died. Didn't change anything else about my behavior, though. I was seventeen and rebellious.

"I never paid attention to rules. Mom wanted me home by eleven, but I think it was sometime around two in the morning when I finally walked through the door. Dad was waiting for me. As usual, he was drunk. We started to argue."

"Did your father hit you?"

"Yeah. In all honesty, it was the first and only time he was physically abusive. I hit back. All this time Mom was begging us to stop. Things got pretty loud. I think the next-door neighbors heard and called the police. Dad lunged at me again. We were in the kitchen, and I grabbed a butcher knife and stabbed him."

"Was it self-defense?"

"I've always said so. But if I'm honest, I don't really know. He was drunk, and that made him unpredictable. He'd already been violent that night and was coming at me again. But again, he was drunk. That also made him unstable on his feet. I could have overpowered him pretty easily, probably even without the knife. So, was it a knee-jerk self-defense reaction, or was it a bad decision? I don't really know. Anyhow, by the time the police arrived, Mom had already called for an ambulance."

Rachel took his hand. "I had no idea. Did you go to jail?"

"Yeah. They locked me up My father went to the hospital. Mom, of course, was torn between wanting to help me and making sure Dad was okay."

"That must have been tough on her."

"Tell me about it. She got Dan Bradford involved, and he got me out the next day. Dad's injuries weren't life-threatening. He got out of the hospital in a couple of days. Didn't press charges."

"I had no idea. That must have been hard for you."

"Even more so on Mom. Between losing her job at Cameron and dealing with my father, she didn't need the added headache of having a rebellious son."

"What happened after that?"

"Mom recognized I needed help. After she talked to Matt's dad, he began to help me. Became my mentor. Made a big difference in my life."

"Dan is a good person."

"Yeah. He helped me to see my father in a different light. I realized alcoholism is an illness. Matt was also there for me. That's when we became friends."

"I wondered about that. When I lived here before, the two of you didn't run in the same crowd. I'm curious. If your father didn't press charges, then it's not on your juvenile record. Why the problem with people remembering your past?"

"Come on Rachel. You know how it is here. Word spreads. People knew what happened. The gossips had a field day, saying what I did was only a matter of time."

"Yeah, that's one thing about living in small towns. Everyone knows everyone else's business. Still, all that happened years ago. People know you for the person you've become, not who you were."

"You would think my best friend would realize that."

"In spite of what happened between you and Matt today, he's still your friend. Why not apologize?"

"I don't think I'm ready."

"At least think about it.

Brian glanced at his watch. "It's getting late. I should go." He stood up and walked to the door.

Rachel followed him. "I'm glad you stopped by."

"Sorry to have unloaded on you. Sometimes I think you're the only one who trusts me. This is the second time Matt has had questioned my actions. Last year, it was the deal with Stephanie."

"And I told you then his feelings for her clouded his judgment."

"What's his excuse now?"

"Brian, he's just doing his job. There's an arsonist on the loose, and they need to cover all bases. It sounds to me like you're as much a victim as anyone. Whoever this person is, it seems they have targeted you—or those you care about."

"Then why can't anyone else see that? I guess the things I did as a teenager will follow me the rest of my life. Why can't people believe I've changed?"

Rachel walked toward him and put her arms around his waist. "I believe you. And I believe in you." She looked into his eyes.

Brian's eyes met hers. "I'm glad someone does." He lowered his head and kissed her, lightly at first, but when Rachel put her arms around his neck, months of pent-up passion released itself. He pulled her close to him and deepened the kiss.

When he broke the kiss, his voice was husky. "I'd better go."

"Why?"

"You know the reason."

"Brian, it's okay. We're both adults."

"Rachel, I… I want to be with you, but I'm not ready… I mean, I'm not prepared. I don't have—"

Rachel pulled out of his embrace, turned toward the door, and fastened the deadbolt. "I don't care," she whispered.

Brian pulled her into his arms for another passionate kiss before she took him by the hand and led him upstairs.

Chapter 13

The pale light of dawn had started to appear when Rachel woke the following morning. In the western sky, a full moon dipped near the horizon and cast its light through the bedroom window. She stirred and looked at the man sleeping beside her. Brian lay on his side, facing her.

How she longed to run her fingers through his tousled hair, to trace the words of the tattoo on his upper left arm. Reaching toward him, she paused. Bit her lip. Pulled her hand back when she read the words indelibly inked on his body.

A simple statement. "Let it be..." Had he chosen it because of the song or some other reason? Was it the often-misunderstood person crying out, "I am who I am. Let me be me."

He had a tattoo of a panther on his other arm. He'd played in the high school marching band, one of almost two-hundred Driscoll Lake Panthers to take the field. And although he loved the music, Rachel couldn't imagine that being the reason for the tattoo. A panther was wild and untamed. Although Brian wasn't the same person she'd known years ago, she often sensed his untamed spirit.

Now that it was almost morning, she had time to think about what they had done. She was a medical professional and knew what consequences could result from their actions.

Rachel did a quick mental calculation and breathed a sigh of relief. Cyclically-speaking, she was in the "safe zone." Everything should be all right.

She quietly slipped out of bed, put on her robe, then walked from the room, smiling as she stepped around the pieces of clothing strewn on the floor.

Downstairs, she placed a pod of hazelnut in the Keurig and hit the brew switch. When it was done, she took the cup outside to the deck then sat in her favorite lounge chair. A cool breeze blew, and the early morning sun cast long shadows across the yard.

Sipping her coffee, she pondered her relationship with Brian. They had crossed a line last night. But that's what she wanted—a romantic relationship. Why did she always have to make the first move?

Brian had wanted to wait. What would happen this morning? Would he pull away again? If he did, there was no one to blame but her for destroying what they had. They could hardly go back to being "just friends."

It was almost a half-hour later when she heard a sound and turned to see Brian standing in the doorway. He was fully dressed but made no effort to walk closer to her.

She stood and walked toward him. Her voice wasn't much above a whisper. "Hi."

"You were up early."

Rachel chewed on her lower lip. She had always prided herself on being a person in control. But things were different with Brian. She could never tell what he was thinking. Remembering the time she'd initiated a kiss, and he'd backed away, she was certain he had second thoughts about last night. "Yeah, I… I'm usually an early riser."

Then he smiled. "I guessed that."

Relief washed over her. "And I gather you're not."

"Only when I have to. Come here." He pulled her into his arms and pressed his lips to hers.

This was real. This was right. When he ended the kiss, Rachel drew him back to her for an equally passionate one. But when she let out a soft moan, Brian pulled away.

"Is something wrong?"

"Didn't want things to get out of hand again."

Again? What did he mean by that? He was having regrets. "No, of course not. After all, we wouldn't want to give the neighbors a show." She turned and stormed into the house, fighting the tears that threatened. But she would be damned if she let him see her cry.

The door closed with a soft click. Brian had followed her inside.

"There's coffee in the kitchen if you want some before you leave."

"That sounds like a dismissal," Brian said.

"Patients to see this morning. Still need to shower and dress."

"Will I see you tonight?"

"I, uh, I don't know. There's a seminar at the hospital in Brewster this evening. I need to attend."

"Look, Rachel, about last night—"

"Let's not talk about it now."

"We have to talk sometime. We can't just pretend it didn't happen."

"I know. But not now. I need time." Time to prepare myself for your rejection.

Brian sighed. "Then maybe it's best I leave."

"I'll, uh, call you in a few of days."

Brian sighed and walked toward the foyer.

As he opened the door, Rachel said, "Brian. Maybe the timing wasn't right, but I don't regret what happened."

Brian stopped but kept his back toward her. "Rachel, I—. Never mind." He walked out the door and closed it behind him, leaving her alone.

***

Brian started his pickup and backed slowly out of Rachel's driveway. He didn't see anyone stirring about on the street, but he knew behind the windows of houses people had eyes. Anyone could have seen him arrive last night and know that he hadn't left. And Rachel's comment about the neighbors left him a bit unsettled.

Why should they care what people thought? He and Rachel were both consenting adults. But he did care. Most people thought of Rachel as strong and independent, but beneath the surface, he saw a vulnerable woman. One who longed to be protected. One he wanted to protect.

There were plenty of gossips who would love to spread the news that a member of one of Driscoll Lake's most prominent families was involved with someone like him. Someone from a middle-class family. Someone with a shaded past and an alcoholic father.

Rachel had never acted as if the difference in their backgrounds bothered her. She never seemed like a spoiled little rich girl—and she had every reason to act like one.

Maybe he was reading more into Rachel's comment about neighbors than was necessary, but something she had said a few weeks ago bothered him.

"Mother was always unlucky in love. She and my father couldn't make a go of their marriage. It wasn't either one's fault, but their backgrounds were too different."

Rachel's father had come from a middle-class family. He'd worked hard to put himself through college and medical school. He was now a well-known surgeon in Austin—his life very different from his growing-up years.

But even with all he'd accomplished, he couldn't make his marriage to Madelyn Cameron work. Madelyn had come from a wealthy family. Their pasts were wildly different.

What had Rachel been saying? That any relationship between the two of them would turn out like her parents' had? He was getting ahead of himself. Neither of them had mentioned the word marriage. Until last night, they'd only been good friends.

He'd heard her wake this morning. When she turned toward him in the bed, it took every ounce of his control not to reach for her again. Funny how the light of day put a new perspective on things. He should have insisted on leaving last night before things got out of hand.

It wasn't that he didn't want it to happen. He had wanted Rachel for a long time. But they should have waited. What if Rachel became pregnant?

What had he done? He'd just made his life more complicated. As if he needed more complications right now.

When he pulled into his driveway, he killed the engine and sat quietly for a while. Brian wasn't one to kiss and tell, but he needed to talk to someone. Someone who could look at things objectively and wouldn't spread gossip around. Matt would understand.

But yesterday Brian had alienated his best friend. And there wasn't anyone else he felt comfortable discussing the situation with. The only other person he ever confided in was Rachel. This time the issue was with her, and she said she needed time. He would have to suffer the consequences of his actions alone.

***

The weekend had been the longest one of Brian's life. Rachel hadn't called or even sent a text. When she said she needed time, he expected to hear from her within a day or so. But three days had passed with no word from her. Had their actions closed the door on their friendship, too? He didn't want to consider the possibility.

How could they continue to call themselves friends? The relationship had taken a step beyond that, and it would be nearly impossible to turn back. And since he had words with Matt, he had no one to talk with. If Kyle was still alive—

No, he'd never been close friends with Kyle. At least, not close enough to confide anything to him.

Brian had spent most of the weekend brooding. He visited his mother a couple of times. Surprisingly, she'd been coherent during both visits. Enough to know something was bothering him.

He tried to shrug it off. "A lot is happening now. The first tenant will soon occupy the factory, and there are still a few things to complete."

"Tell me, where is your friend?"

"Matt? Busy, I imagine. You know he recently got married. I'm sure he'd rather spend time with Stephanie."

"I'm not talking about Matt. I mean Rachel. She was with you the night they brought me to the hospital. Thought she might come with you to visit me."

"Rachel is also busy. And as for her reasons for being here that night, she had stopped by my office when I got the call about you. She could see I was upset and offered to drive me."

"She cares about you. I could see it the other night. Rachel's a sweet girl. I think the two of you are perfect for one another."

"Mom, she's hardly a girl. She's a grown woman with a promising career. And as for us, we're friends. That's all."

"Not what I saw the other night. She sees you as much more than a friend. And if I'm not wrong, you feel the same way about her."

Brian stared pointedly at his mother.

"All right. I won't say anything else."

On Monday morning, Brian decided he couldn't continue to mope around. No matter what happened with the fire investigation and with Rachel, he had a business to run. When he peered in his refrigerator, he found it nearly empty and decided to go to Mary's for breakfast.

He sat at a table near a window. A waitress asked if he wanted coffee.

"Yes, please." He opened the menu. An omelet sounded good, and Mary had a variety of choices—even a "build your own" cheese omelet with a variety of extras to add.

The waitress returned with the coffee. "Ready to order, sir?"

"I'll have the cheese omelet with bacon, onion, mushrooms, and jalapeños with a side of hash browns. Biscuits, but no gravy."

"That's a bacon and cheese omelet?"

"Yes. With onions, mushrooms, and jalapeños."

"Okay, bacon and cheese omelet with onions and mushrooms."

"And jalapeños."

"Hash browns or home fries?"

Hadn't he already told her that? "Hash browns."

"Toast or biscuit and gravy?"

Brian tried to hide his annoyance. Was she even listening to him? "Biscuits."

"Would you like gravy?"

"Fine." He didn't, but she'd probably bring it no matter what he said.

"I'll have it right out to you."

If this were any indication, the day would only get worse. His suspicion was confirmed when Matt came through the door and walked to his table.

"What do you want?" Brian didn't attempt to hide his displeasure.

"We need to talk."

"I think we did enough of that the other day."

"No, we didn't. You talked. But I have something to say now. There's been a misunderstanding, and I need you to hear me out. I'm going to sit down, so unless you want to cause a scene, you'll listen to what I have to say."

Brian shrugged. "Suit yourself."

Matt took a chair opposite of him.

The waitress returned. "Would you like a menu sir?"

Brian rolled his eyes. Here we go again.

Matt shook his head. "Just coffee. Black."

"Coming right up."

Was this the same confused person who took his order a few minutes ago? Was there something different in the way he and Matt communicated? Maybe people just paid more attention to Matt.

After the waitress left, Matt said, "Look, I don't know what Sikes said to you, but I told him it was ridiculous to think you were involved. I did say something about wondering why you were at the factory that night, but I also said you didn't need a reason to be there since you owned the place."

"Go on."

"It's no excuse, but having to relive that night when I knew Stephanie was in danger wasn't easy."

Brian knew the feeling. When it came to Rachel, he didn't always think with a level head. "I know."

"Our friendship goes back way too far. I'm sorry for any misunderstanding. I don't believe you're responsible for any of the fires, and I'll fight Sikes and Abbott with everything I have to prove your innocence."

"Thanks, man. Appreciate it. I guess I'm still too sensitive about certain things. Too quick to jump to conclusions. I would have thought I'd gotten over all that by now."

"I've never been in your situation, so it's hard for me to imagine what it must have been like for you."

"Consider yourself lucky."

"You know if you don't want to talk to me, Dad is always available. He'd be happy to lend an ear."

"I know that. Anyway, I can't keep using the past to make excuses for my behavior. I should have waited until I cooled down before confronting you the other day."

"If I'd been in your situation, I probably would've acted the same way. I shouldn't have been thinking about what might have been. Stephanie made it out alive. I don't need to keep re-hashing things."

Brian smiled. "Understandable, but that's twice you've allowed your feelings for Stephanie to cloud your judgment."

"Yeah, well, women will do that to you."

Brian looked out the window. "Don't I know it?"

Matt raised his eyebrows. "I assume you're talking about Rachel. Couldn't help but realize Stephanie and I interrupted something when you guys were at our house. How are things between the two of you?"

"Complicated." And getting more so by the minute. He took a sip of coffee.

"Want to talk about it?"

Brian sighed. "Yeah. It's just that I—"

Matt's cell phone rang. "Hold that thought." He spoke into the phone. "Bradford...Yeah...Okay, I'll be there in a few."

"Something come up?"

"Yeah, sorry. I need to get to the station." He stood and threw some bills on the table. "Breakfast is on me. We'll talk later."

Chapter 14

Greg Sikes had spent the past four days viewing the investigation reports on each of the fires. There was little doubt the earlier incidents at the properties owned by Brian Nichols were arson, carried out by the same person. What he couldn't figure out was why the arsonist waited almost nine months between the first and second fires.

He had grilled Nichols hard the other day, but he had a purpose in doing so. Perpetrators often crack under pressure. Brian didn't waver. But Greg didn't believe in coincidences. Each location had some connection to Nichols. Abbott was adamant that Brian was the arsonist, but there wasn't any concrete evidence to support his theory.

It wasn't hard to see Nichols and Abbott despised one another. Greg wasn't sure of the reason for the animosity. It probably wouldn't be hard to find out in a small town like Driscoll Lake. He could ask Chief Bradford. But unless it related to the investigation, it was none of his business. He had more important things to do. At any rate, he wasn't on Bradford's list of favorite people right now. Wouldn't be wise to ask, especially when the subject had to do with Brian Nichols.

On Monday morning, Sikes entered his office and closed the door. He had enough information on the case to obtain a criminal profile. He picked up the phone.

A familiar voice answered. "Etheridge."

"This is Sikes. I need you to do a profile for me."

"New investigation?"

"Yeah. In a small town called Driscoll Lake."

"How many fires?"

"Five so far. Hope we've seen the last of them, but I doubt it."

"Okay, tell me what you've got."

Sikes gave him the most important points of his findings. "I'll email you more details."

"Any witnesses?"

"Shortly before the third fire at the Tippet residence, a neighbor reported a suspicious person in the neighborhood. Unsure if it's related."

"Does this town have a high crime rate?"

"No. There was a murder here last year. Turned out to be related to a twenty-year-old crime. Ironically it happened at the site of the first fire and on the same night."

"Think there is a link?"

"Not to the murderer."

"I'm sensing there may be another connection."

"I'd rather not say. You'll see my report."

"Any suspects?"

"The fire marshal has one, but again, I want to keep an open mind. I need more than circumstantial evidence to make an arrest, even if I do suspect someone."

"Okay, I'll look over your report and get back to you soon."

***

A week had passed since Brian had seen or talked with Rachel. Several times he had picked up the phone to call her but each time changed his mind. Rachel had said she would call him. But she hadn't.

Did she no longer want to see him? Had their friendship meant nothing to her? Was he just a one-night stand? He couldn't imagine Rachel thinking of him in those terms.

As the week wore on, his frustration increased. He'd even snapped at his mother during one of his visits—something he quickly apologized for. And when Friday afternoon came, with still no word, he decided to swallow his pride. He picked up the phone and called her number. One ring. Two. Three. Thirty seconds seemed like an eternity.

Dammit, Rachel, pick up. They couldn't keep avoiding one another. Finally, an answer. Voicemail.

"Hi, this is Rachel. Please leave a message, and I'll get back to you."

Yeah, right. Brian started to hang up but changed his mind. It was time to put an end to the silence between them. "This is Brian. It's been a while. I've been waiting to hear from you. Call me." He paused. "If you won't talk to me as a friend, then please speak to me as a business partner. There's something we need to discuss." He pressed the end button and placed the phone back into his pocket.

He'd made the first move. Now it was up to her.

**

It was almost five when Rachel saw her last patient of the day. If she had ever looked forward to a weekend, this was one. Several patients had called asking for appointments, and add-ons extended her workday.

After making sure the rest of the staff had left, she went into her office and closed the door. She didn't eat lunch, but a package of peanut butter crackers would have to suffice. She'd think about dinner later.

Rachel pulled her cell phone from her purse to check for calls. Her pulse quickened upon seeing a missed call and voicemail from Brian. She had avoided talking with him, wanting to postpone what she perceived to be the inevitable. But he had called her. Maybe... Whatever the case, it was time to face whatever happened. She held her breath as she listened to the message.

Brian wanted to talk. Okay, that was good. But what did he mean by mentioning their business partnership? That was it. He needed to speak to her about the factory project. Right now, that's probably all that held them together.

She started to press the button to dial his number but changed her mind. Whatever happened, they needed to discuss their relationship in person and not by phone. Hoping he would still be at his office, she gathered her things and left by the back door, locking the building before getting into her car and driving away.

Luck was on her side. Brian's pickup was next to his office building. She pulled into the parking lot and got out of the car. Ignoring the fluttering in her stomach, she opened the door and went inside.

Brian looked surprised. He got up from his desk and walked to greet her, although he acted somewhat reserved. "Hi. Guess you got my message."

"Yeah. I decided to stop by. Thought it was best we spoke in person."

"I agree." He motioned to a chair. "Want to sit down?"

"No, thanks. I can't stay long." Was that a look of disappointment on his face?

"Then let's talk." Brian sat down on the edge of his desk and crossed his arms.

He was waiting for her to make the first move. "About last week, I needed a few days to think. As far as I'm concerned, we're still friends."

"I think we moved beyond the friendship stage."

Rachel cleared her throat. Brian wasn't making this easy. "Yes, I know, but—"

"You said the other day you didn't regret it. Then what's the problem?"

"I don't regret what happened. I do think my sense of timing could have been better."

"Because I showed up at your house upset? You think the only reason I slept with you because I was only looking for comfort?"

"No, but I was the one to come on to you. I don't want anything to jeopardize our friendship. I want us to be able to work together, and I don't want to see the factory project abandoned."

"Friends and business partners. That's all you want? We shared something special that night. Neither of us can deny it."

"I know."

"Rachel, what happened between us was inevitable. Maybe a little sooner than either of us intended, but it happened. The question now is—" His cell phone rang, and he reached into his pocket. Glancing at the caller ID, he said, "It's the rehab facility."

Rachel turned away while Brian took the call. Still, in the small room, she couldn't help but overhear his side of the conversation.

"Are you sure... Did she? Okay, I'll be there as soon as I can. Thanks."

"Something wrong with your mother?"

"She's having a bad day. Been asking for my father. So far, no one has been able to calm her down. They think I might be able to get through to her." Brian rubbed the back of his neck. "I'm sorry. I... We..."

"Brian, don't worry about it. See to your mom. I understand."

"Can I call you?"

"Yes," she said.

Brian was silent for a moment but then smiled as he spoke. "Good. I'll be in touch."

***

Brian was reluctant to leave Rachel, but he needed to check on his mother. He drove straight to the rehab facility from this office.

The charge nurse greeted him as he came through the door. "It hasn't been a good day. She's been asking for your father most of the afternoon. However, when I went into the room to check on her a few minutes ago, she was coherent. Acts as if nothing is wrong. Maybe I shouldn't have called you. It's Friday night, and you probably have plans."

"I don't. And even if I did, it's important for me to know what's going on here."

"She's lucky to have someone who cares. You're a good son."

"I wasn't always this way." Brian turned and walked to his mother's room. He tapped lightly on the door before entering.

As the nurse said, Dorothy Nichols acted as if nothing was wrong. She was sitting in her wheelchair watching her favorite TV show. "Brian! What brings you here?"

He bent down and kissed her cheek. "I came to see you."

"On a Friday night? Can't imagine someone as handsome as you not having a date. At the least, I thought you might be playing with the band."

"No. We didn't have anything scheduled tonight."

"Do I need to remind you how much I'd love to have grandchildren?

Brian winced. It wasn't the first time his mother had told him her desire. But even if he married and had a child within the year, Dorothy Nichols probably wouldn't know her grandchild. Her condition had deteriorated fast over the past few months.

"You'd make a great father."

"I didn't exactly have the perfect role model. Besides, the usual order is to have a wife first."

"I'm sure there are plenty of women willing to fill that role. What about Rachel?"

"Rachel?"

"Of course. She's smart, pretty. Kind and considerate like her mother. Nell Bradford said she'd seen the two of you together several times. Rachel told me the two of you are good friends."

"When did you talk to her?"

"She was here yesterday. Took over for Dr. Jacobs."

"Mom, Rachel doesn't see patients here at the rehab."

Dorothy frowned. "She doesn't? I was certain she was here. Guess I was wrong."

"Mom, you're confusing this place with Woodbine. That's where you talked to Rachel."

"I guess it was at Woodbine." Dorothy grew silent and turned away.

Brian watched his mother as she gazed out the window. She raised an arthritic hand to wipe away a tear that ran down her cheek. He couldn't help but wonder what it was like for her. On several occasions, she had said things that indicated she was aware of her condition. He'd often wondered if knowing her mind was deteriorating was worse for her than the disease itself.

Leaning forward in his chair, he put his elbows on his knees and rested his head in his hands.

"So, what about Rachel?"

Brian looked up in surprise. Her lucidity had returned as if nothing unusual had happened. "What do you mean?"

"We were talking about you settling down and finding a wife."

"Oh, I doubt she would want to marry someone like me."

"What's that supposed to mean?"

"Come on, Mom. Our backgrounds are too different."

"Are you ashamed of your family? It's true that your father was an alcoholic, but before the bottle got the best of him, he was a good man. Had a respectable business."

"I'm not ashamed. It's just—"

"We weren't wealthy like the Cameron family, but it apparently doesn't bother Rachel. If it did, she wouldn't want anyone to see the two of you together."

Brian pondered his mother's words. She had a point. If Rachel cared about their differences, she wouldn't want them to be friends, let alone lovers.

Lovers. They had skirted the issue earlier, but they both knew what they shared was more than a one-night stand.

Chapter 15

Brian visited with his mother almost two hours. Except for the one incident, she was cheerful and talkative and her thoughts coherent. If someone who wasn't aware of her situation were to walk in, they wouldn't be able to guess she had Alzheimer's disease.

He drove slowly during the trip back to Driscoll Lake and pondered the situation. The doctor was right in that the time had come to move her to a place where she had more extensive nursing care. Brian hated to disrupt her life. She had become accustomed to her apartment. But she wasn't able to care for herself any longer.

The fall a few days ago had made that clear. Brian was also concerned that her apartment had a small kitchen. She had always enjoyed cooking, and he feared she might leave a burner on and start a fire. There were too many risks involved. The issue was trying to convince her that moving was for her own safety.

Brian turned off the main highway and drove toward his house. The decision would be difficult, but it was in everyone's best interest. If only he had someone else to talk to.

Rachel would understand. Her house wasn't far. Maybe he would stop by to talk. After their earlier conversation, he knew he could speak to her as a friend. She would look at the situation objectively. Instead of going home, he took a shortcut through another neighborhood toward Rachel's house.

When his phone rang, it took him by surprise. He glanced at the unknown number and debated on whether to answer. But with the Dallas area code, it was less likely to be one of those crank calls that made the rounds.

He pressed the talk button. "Brian Nichols."

"Mr. Nichols, this is Tom Wilson. I spoke to you a few days ago about the possibility of doing a job for me."

"Yes, I remember."

"I realize it's a Friday night, but my wife and I just got in from Dallas. We're only here tonight. On our way to Nashville and plan to leave early tomorrow. Would it be possible for you to stop by and look at our house this evening? We won't be back in the area for a couple of weeks and are anxious to get started on the remodeling."

"Um, sure. Tell me where your house is." Brian pulled to the side of the street. When the man gave him the address, he entered it into the GPS.

"I'm only a few blocks away. I can be there within ten minutes." Brian hung up the phone and pulled away from the curb, unaware he had attracted the attention of a man driving a small white car.

***

The arsonist had picked his target a few days earlier. Now the time had come. Like the other incidents, everything had to be precise. And with the ATF involved, he would have to use more caution. But just a few more fires and his mission would be complete. Too late to back out now.

He decided to drive through the neighborhood and get another look at the house. It had been a long time since he had felt this much excitement about a fire. His only regret was that he wouldn't be able to see the look on Curtis Lawrence's face when he learned his home had burned. At least the judge would know he wouldn't have a house to come back to whenever he got out of prison.

He slowed the car and turned down the street where the Lawrence house was located. Too bad it was vacant. If Curtis wasn't in jail and at home… No, he was getting a far worse punishment. Dying in a fire would be too sudden. Better that he had to sit in prison much like all the people he had sent there. Did Lawrence think about them as he sat in his cell? Wonder how he felt being on the other side?

His face grew red with anger when he saw a pickup truck parked in front of the house. Who was it and why were they there? When he drew closer, he recognized Brian. He drove by slowly and peered inside. Brian was on his cell phone.

Looked as if luck was on his side. Hopefully, someone would see Brian near the scene. If not, he had ways to ensure someone knew he had been in the area. This was perfect. Time to put his plan into action. He drove to his preselected location two blocks over, parked the car, and walked toward the house. Unlike the Tippet home, Curtis Lawrence's house was located in a wooded area with no other homes directly behind it. So much easier to go unnoticed. Best of all, he had a perfect spot to watch the structure go up in flames.

***

When Agent Greg Sikes received the call about another fire, he rushed from his office to the location. Although it was too soon to tell, his instinct said the arsonist had struck again. If that was the case, it was time to bring in a couple of his top fire investigators.

He also wanted to question any potential witnesses before the fire marshal had the opportunity. Abbott had allowed his issues with Brian Nichols to interfere in the investigation, and that wasn't a good thing.

Flames had fully engulfed the house by the time Greg arrived. From the looks of things, there was little chance to save the structure. A crowd of people had gathered to watch. Driscoll Lake police were on hand to control traffic and keep the spectators at bay. Greg was glad Matt was already at the scene.

He parked his car and walked toward the chief. "What do we know?"

"The call came in about an hour ago. Fire started at the back of the house."

"Anyone at home?"

"No. The house belongs to Judge Curtis Lawrence. He went to prison a few months ago, and the house has been unoccupied since then. Someone comes in to check on things on occasion, but that's it."

"Curtis Lawrence? Where have I heard that name before?"

"He was at the factory when it burned last year. You probably saw his name mentioned in the investigation reports."

"Interesting. Does Nichols have any connection to the judge?"

"Not really. Curtis's son Kyle was one of Brian's high school classmates. Kyle was killed last year at the factory."

"I see."

"Still think all the fires are connected?

"Yes."

"It's obvious you think Brian is involved some way."

Sikes nodded his head.

"You're wrong."

"How long have you known him?"

"More than twenty years. Long enough to know he wouldn't do something like this."

"I know he's your friend. Sorry I had to question him the other day, but I'm here to conduct an investigation. I'm not here to be popular."

"I understand."

"I will say he never wavered under pressure. However, I heard I caused a dispute to arise between the two of you. For that, I'm sorry."

"We worked it out. Did you ever consider the possibility someone could be trying to frame Brian?"

Greg shrugged. "It's possible. Do you know of anyone with a grudge against him?"

"Other than Richard Abbott?"

Greg jerked his head in surprise. "Are you saying?"

Matt shook his head. "Abbott isn't an arsonist, but given their history, I'm not sure he's the right person for this investigation."

"I agree. That's why I spoke to the mayor this morning. He wants my department to take over everything. I'm calling in two of my best investigators. They should be here in a couple of hours."

"And Abbott?"

"He doesn't have a say in this anymore. I'll keep him informed as a matter of courtesy and include him in any meetings with the mayor."

"Glad to hear that. Maybe we'll get some answers."

"Have you spoken to any of the neighbors yet?"

"So far no one claims to have seen anything. Hope someone will come forward."

***

The Lawrence house was a total loss. When the firefighters were able to extinguish the blaze, not much remained but a burned-out shell. Curtis's closest relatives were his granddaughter Emily and daughter-in-law Christine. Matt phoned Christine shortly after he got to the scene. She arrived as Matt was about to leave for the night.

"Sorry about the house," Matt said.

Christine shrugged. "Emily and I didn't come here often. Curtis wasn't one to have family gatherings. He considered us family when it suited his image. And you know how he felt about his own son—until it was too late."

"Yeah, I'm sorry. Just thought you'd want to know about the house. Someone will need to tell the judge."

"That won't be me. We're not in contact. And Emily doesn't want any association with him."

"Even though he's her grandfather, I can't say I blame her. How is she doing?"

"Coping. Emily blames Curtis for her father's death. And in a way, I do too."

Matt noticed tears had started to form in Christine's eyes.

"I probably shouldn't have called you."

"It's okay. I...I look at the house and see one more thing that was a part of Kyle's life destroyed. Soon there will be nothing left."

"The house is only material. You and Emily were important parts of his life. You'll always have the memories. Nothing or no one can take them away."

Christine nodded her head. "It's just that Kyle grew up in that house. But you're right. It never was his home. Just another one of Curtis's prized treasures."

"We'll take care of notifying him."

"Thanks. The less I have to deal with Curtis, the better."

Agent Sikes walked up at that moment. "Not much more we can do here tonight. Gardner's men will stay here for a while to help secure the area along with those you've assigned to watch. My team will begin the investigation first thing in the morning."

Matt nodded toward Christine. "Agent Sikes, this is Christine Lawrence. The house belonged to her father-in-law."

Sikes extended his hand toward her. "Ma'am. Sorry to meet in these circumstances."

"It's okay."

"I see. Would you mind answering a couple of quick questions?"

"Sure."

"You probably know Driscoll Lake has had several arsons lately. We won't know about this fire until we begin our investigation, but are you aware if your father-in-law has any enemies?"

"He was a district judge. Sentenced a lot of people to prison. Of course, he has enemies."

"I understand. Anyone in particular stand out?"

"I wouldn't know. We were never close, and I haven't spoken to him since my husband died. Curtis is also ruthless and conniving. I wouldn't be surprised if he's made some enemies outside the courtroom."

"I see. Thank you, Ms. Lawrence. Appreciate you taking time to answer my questions. If you think of something, call me." He handed her a business card.

"Can't imagine anything but okay."

Matt waited until he and Sikes were out of Christine's earshot. "I agree with what she said. Lawrence is a ruthless man. Wouldn't surprise me if he has a lot of adversaries."

"Why is he in prison?"

"Obstruction of justice. Lawrence withheld information about a double murder in which the perpetrator made it appear to be a murder-suicide. He also attempted to kill my wife by running her car off the road."

"A model citizen, huh? Was he charged with anything?"

"He confessed and pleaded guilty to assault with a deadly weapon as well as the obstruction charge. Got a lighter sentence because of it. I figure he'll be out on probation in a few years."

"And Lawrence happened to be at the factory the night of the fire."

"Yes. He figured out Kyle was there and guessed he was in danger."

"You're sure he didn't go there to meet Nichols?"

"That would have never happened, but you'll probably hear the scuttlebutt around town. Lawrence wanted the property. He served on the city council at the time and tried to thwart Brian's plans for the place."

"Interesting. I knew there must be a connection."

The man was arrogant. Matt would give him that much. He seemed as determined as Abbott to place the blame on Brian. At least Abbott had an excuse. Sikes was supposed to be unbiased.

Matt started to walk away when a sudden chill enveloped him. Someone was watching. The arsonist? Matt's eyes scanned the crowd of spectators. Most of the people he knew. One of them could be responsible for starting the fire Arsonists often hang around the scene of the crime, especially when they could blend in with the crowd.

Putting aside his thoughts, he turned and walked away. As he neared his pickup, he couldn't help but remember what Stephanie had told him about the night her father died. How she had known something was wrong long before she learned of his death.

Shaking his head, he climbed into his truck. He was a law enforcement officer. He'd been trained to rely on evidence and facts, not gut instinct. But even so, he couldn't squelch the uneasy feeling.

Chapter 16

Rachel blinked her eyes and tried to determine what sound had awakened her. Her cell phone. Why would someone call so early on a Saturday morning? Looking at the caller ID, she recognized Brian's number. It was already past nine.

"Hello?"

"Hey, there. Were you still asleep?"

Still trying to clear the cobwebs, she said, "Yeah. Stephanie was here until after midnight, and then I couldn't go to sleep. I stayed awake until almost three reading."

"Stephanie was at your house on a Friday night? I'm surprised. Don't tell me there's already trouble in paradise."

"What makes you think that?"

"Just surprised she wouldn't be with Matt, that's all. I mean, it's not like the two of you can't have a girl's night out, or whatever it is you women call it."

She tried to ignore the teasing tone in his voice. "Nothing like that. At least it wasn't planned. Matt and Stephanie were on their way home when he got a call. There was another fire. Since they were nearby, he dropped her at my house."

"You're kidding? Another fire?"

"Wish I was. This time it was at Curtis Lawrence's house. They think it was arson."

"Curtis's house? Guess no one is immune. What time did it happen?"

"Stephanie got here around nine. I think someone reported the fire about an hour earlier."

"Oh, that's just great. Now everyone will think—never mind."

"What's wrong?"

"Um. Nothing. Just thought of something."

"Is it related to the fires? If you know anything, tell the ATF agent."

"He's the last person I want to talk with. Besides, it's not important."

"Are you sure?"

"Yes. Can we change the subject now? I really don't want to talk about ATF agents or fires."

He was keeping something from her. Rachel was sure of it. She couldn't help but believe it was related to last night's fire. Brian wouldn't willingly talk to Sikes, but if he and Matt were on speaking terms, he might open up. Careful on how to approach the subject, she said, "Have you spoken to Matt lately?"

"Yes. Everything is okay between us."

Trying to keep her tone light she said, "So you swallowed your pride?"

"You're saying I'm prideful?"

To Rachel's relief, he didn't sound upset. She laughed. "I didn't want to say it, but—"

"You're right. I am. Actually, Matt found me and apologized. I was wrong about him. Again"

"I'm glad the two of you came to terms. Your friendship goes back too far to let a simple misunderstanding destroy it."

"Yeah, I realize that, now."

"Then you wouldn't hesitate to talk with him if something was on your mind?"

"Rachel, I told you it's nothing."

"Okay. Want to get together tonight?"

Brian was silent for a moment, leaving Rachel to think she'd said something wrong. "Sorry. I'm playing with the band. I would invite you to come, but it's a private party."

"It's okay. I understand."

"No, it's not okay. Seems like every time we try to get together something else interferes."

"Brian. I'm not going anywhere. We'll have other chances."

***

Matt took a deep breath as he entered City Hall and made his way toward the conference room. Mayor Reeves had called a special meeting on Monday morning with Greg Sikes, Carlos, Fire Chief Stan Gardner, and Matt to discuss the arson investigation.

As much as Matt wanted the crime solved, he dreaded seeing Richard Abbott. He wouldn't be happy about being left out of the investigation into the fire at Curtis Lawrence's house. Despite not being present, Matt suspected Abbott would try to find a way to tie Brian to the crime.

His suspicions were correct. Everyone was already seated in the conference room when Abbott stormed through the door.

"I'm surprised anyone invited me to this meeting."

"Why would you think I wouldn't include you?" Mayor Reeves asked. "No matter who conducts the investigation, you should care about bringing a swift resolution to this ordeal. We don't know when or where the arsonist will strike again. I think we all agree he will."

"I am concerned. But no one will listen to me or seems to care about my opinion."

"If you'd looked at this more objectively, you could have played a bigger role. Most of the time the ATF works alongside local investigators. Now, Agent Sikes, what do you have for us?"

Sikes cleared his throat. "Thank you, Mayor. I agree with Mr. Abbott on one thing. I believe Brian Nichols is the link with these fires."

Abbott sat up straighter in his chair and glanced around the room—a smug look on his face.

The mayor looked surprised. "Go on."

"I discussed the possibility with Chief Bradford last night. He and I don't agree on the particulars, but he does have another idea."

Matt nodded. "Carlos was the first one to think someone wanted to frame Brian. I believe the real arsonist is choosing specific targets linked to him. I asked Agent Sikes to consider the possibility."

"That's ridiculous," Abbott said. "You're grasping at straws."

Sikes ignored Abbott's words. "I'm willing to consider Matt's suggestion. Up until the fire last night, we could tie each location directly or indirectly to Nichols. This is different. There is no real connection with Lawrence and Nichols."

Abbott was quick to respond. "Are you kidding me? No connection? Other than the fact it was Lawrence who withheld information that could have led to solving a crime involving Rachel Jackson's mother?"

"That's totally irrelevant," Matt said.

"Oh yeah? It's no secret that Brian and the good doctor are, shall I say, close?"

Sikes sat up straighter. "What are you talking about?"

"Rachel spent twenty years believing the wrong person killed her mother. If she's bitter about Lawrence, she could have confided in Brian. You know, pillow talk? That would be motive enough for him to target Lawrence."

Matt's nostrils flared, and he stood up. "Now you're the one grasping at straws. And your comments about Brian and Rachel's relationship is uncalled for. You need to back off the snide comments."

Carlos put his hand on Matt's arm. Matt looked at him, nodded, and sat back down, but not before sending a warning look to Abbott. He listened as Sikes explained his reasons for reopening the investigations into the first two fires.

Stan Gardner spoke. "I agree with Matt. I've known Brian for a long time and find it hard to believe he is an arsonist."

"What about the fire that happened years ago when Nichols was a teenager? There was a lot of speculation that he was the one responsible," Abbott said.

Matt shook his head. "Those were only rumors."

"I have a question." Stan Gardner cleared his throat. "You mentioned the first two fires were possibly made to look like accidents. With all the other fires, the person doesn't care that we know it's arson. What's your take on that? There is also a gap of almost nine months between those first two fires."

"Not certain. I've sent information to someone I know who is an expert criminal profiler. He should have a report to me in the next few days. We were also able to collect some DNA evidence at both the Tippet and Lawrence homes. We've sent it to the lab in Dallas."

A soft knock came to the conference room door.

"Come in," Mayor Reeves said.

The receptionist stuck her head in the door. "I'm sorry to interrupt, but there's an urgent phone call for you, Mr. Abbott. Someone from your office. Said it's important that he speak to you right away."

The mayor nodded, and Abbott got up from the table. He returned a few minutes later.

"Maybe now you all will believe me. My office received an anonymous tip about last night. The caller said he saw Brian Nichols sitting in his pickup truck in front of the Lawrence home not long before the fire started. He was at the scene of the crime. Now are you willing to believe he is guilty?"

***

It was almost noon before Rachel was able to take a break from seeing patients. She was grateful her practice was busy, even though most days were hectic.

When the last morning patient was gone, she went into her office and closed the door. She reached for her cell phone, surprised to find a voicemail from her sister. The message was brief. "Call me when you get a chance."

Nicole rarely phoned during the day. Although she didn't sound upset, Rachel hoped nothing was wrong. She pressed the call back button and was surprised when Nicole answered on the first ring.

"There you are. I wondered what took you so long to call me back."

Rachel frowned. "I was busy with patients. Is something wrong?"

"Nothing. Just wondered if you would like a visitor. Kevin is in Dallas all week for a conference, and he convinced me to come along. However, sitting in a hotel room all day isn't my idea of fun. And there's only so much shopping I can do. I'm already bored stiff."

"I would love to see you. But you'd be sitting around the house most of the day while I'm at work."

"Yes, but that's different. I don't get to see my big sister very often. We have a lot to catch up on. Besides, I haven't seen your new house."

Rachel smiled. Even with their age difference, she and Nicole were close—especially now that both of them were grown. "When can you get here?"

"This afternoon too soon? Say around five? Kevin told me to take the car. All the activities are here at the hotel, so he won't need it."

"Five is good. And I'll always make time for my little sister." Rachel glanced at her schedule. "I don't have a lot of patients this afternoon. I'll try to slip away early and be home before you arrive."

"Great! I'm looking forward to seeing you."

"Me, too," Rachel said.

***

When Matt returned to the police station, he went into his office and closed the door. He wasn't in the mood to talk to anyone right now. The smirk on Abbott's face when he relayed the news about a possible witness was enough to make Matt's blood boil.

If the witness was reliable, it put Brian near the scene of a fire. But if Brian was in that part of town, there had to be a reasonable explanation.

There was something about the call that disturbed Matt. Why did the call come to Abbott's office and not the hotline? The number had been flashed on the news a social media site for several days. Only a hermit would be unaware.

Someone tapped on his door. He looked up to see Agent Sikes and motioned him in.

"What's your take on Abbott's news about the witness?"

"I'm not even sure it's legit."

"You think Abbott would make this up?"

"No, but it just seemed too convenient. Why did this person call Abbott's office directly? Why not use the call line?"

"You think Abbott is lying?"

"No matter what I think about the man, he's not a liar. But a lot of people know how he feels about Brian. I think it's strange this anonymous caller decided to call Abbott's office directly."

"Whatever the case, I need to get Nichols back in here for questioning."

"I know. But this time I'm sitting in while you question him. I don't want there to be any more misunderstandings."

"A few days ago, you accused Abbott of not being objective. Now I wonder if you're the one who can't be open-minded about this."

Matt glared at the man sitting across from him. "I told you my department would cooperate. But I still think you're looking in the wrong direction."

"You have strong feelings about Brian's innocence."

"Enough to stake my career on it."

Sikes stood up to leave. When he reached Matt's office door, he turned back. "I know you want to believe your friend is innocent. For what it's worth, I hope you're right."

Chapter 17

"I was surprised to get your phone call," Rachel said to her sister. They had finished dinner and were now sitting in Rachel's den. "I'm glad you came."

"Like I said on the phone, I don't see my sister often enough."

"Guess we should do something about that."

"Austin isn't that far from Driscoll Lake. Kevin and I could easily come more frequently. But I'm glad we'll have these few days together alone. Gives us a chance to catch up. So, is there a man in your life?"

Rachel wasn't willing to discuss her relationship with Brian. "Not really. I've been too busy with my career, especially now that I bought the clinic. I don't have time to get too involved with anyone now."

"Rachel, come on. There's always time if you find someone you care about. And I don't need to remind you—"

"I know. I'm not getting any younger. I know. The right man will come along someday. Now, tell me about you. How does it feel to know you're going to become a mother in a few short months?"

Nicole sat back on the sofa and placed both hands on her still flat stomach. "It's the most wonderful feeling in the world. Just to know that inside me is a tiny little life. A life Kevin and I created together."

Rachel smiled. "I'm sure it is."

"Although I do have to admit it's a little scary knowing I'm going to be someone's mother. It's an awesome responsibility."

"Everything going okay? Any problems?"

"None. Except for the morning sickness. Well, it's not just morning sickness. It sometimes happens during the day. I swear it started when I was only three weeks along—before I even knew for sure I was pregnant. Leave it to me to be out of the ordinary."

"That happens with some women, although it most often starts around six weeks."

"I'm hoping it will end earlier. And no cravings except for chocolate ice cream."

"Speaking of which, would you like dessert?"

"Is it ice cream?"

"I even have chocolate."

"Then I'd love some."

Rachel got up from the sofa. "Sit still. I'll bring it to you." Once she was in the kitchen, she called back to her sister. "So how are Dad and Cecelia? Heard anything from Cade lately?"

"Dad and Mom are fine. Cade is busy. Excited about getting married."

"Have they set a date?"

"Nothing definite, but sometime early next summer. At least by that time, I won't be pregnant."

"That's a good thing. I imagine being pregnant during a hot Texas summer would be miserable." She looked back toward the den and saw Nicole had picked up a photo album of Stephanie's wedding. She had left it a few days ago for Rachel to look through.

"The photographer took a lot of candid shots," Stephanie had said. "There are several of you and Brian. Thought you'd want to see them. And if you want any copies, let me know, and I'll tell the photographer."

"Who got married?"

"My friend Stephanie. I was her maid of honor."

"Stephanie Harris? Isn't she the woman whose father was once thought to have murdered your mother?"

"That's her. It's funny how we spent so many years avoiding one another, and now we've become good friends. She came back to Driscoll Lake last year to settle her aunt's estate and found love." Rachel walked back in the room and handed a bowl of ice cream to her sister before sitting beside her.

Nicole took a bite of ice cream and turned back to the book. She came across one of the wedding party. "Tell me who everyone is."

"Except for the man on the far right, we all went to high school together. Stephanie and I moved away, but the others stayed here until they graduated. The woman on the left is Christine Lawrence. Stephanie's husband is Matt Bradford—he's our police chief."

"And who's the gorgeous hunk next to him?"

"Nicole, you're married! What would Kevin think if he heard you say that?"

"I'm married, not blind. But don't worry. Kevin is the only man for me."

"Glad to hear it." Rachel's voice was a little harsher than she intended.

"Oh, do I detect a bit of jealousy?" Nicole teased.

"No, of course not. Brian and I are friends. That's it."

"Brian huh? Is he married?"

"No."

"Then what's stopping you?"

"Nicole!"

"Can't blame me for trying. I confess. I'm a hopeless romantic."

"Yeah, you always were."

Nicole flipped through the book, stopping when she saw a candid shot taken of Brian and Rachel on the dance floor.

Rachel hadn't seen the photo before today, but there was no doubt in her mind the photographer took it during *the* dance. The one where she had momentarily forgotten her surroundings. Brian had pulled her close, and she had rested her head on his chest, her head tucked under his chin. "I didn't know someone took a photo of us."

"Whoa. Just friends huh?" Nicole teased. "Where did the two of you go after the wedding?"

"Really, Nicole. I came home—alone—after dropping Christine off at her house. I guess Brian went home, too."

"Did he bring a date?"

"No."

"I would hope not. The way the two of you were behaving on the dance floor, she would either be insanely jealous or too stupid to care."

"Nicole. I told you he and I are friends. That's it. Now, can we please change the subject?"

"Okay, but you're in denial, big sister."

***

Greg Sikes pinched the bridge of his nose, trying to ward off the beginning of a headache. Since the meeting with the mayor the day before, he had studied the notes on each of the suspected arson cases several times—hoping he would see something he had missed previously.

He had no doubt the key to the fires was Brian Nichols. But what was his motive? Abbott had made a good case for Nichols collecting insurance money, but that didn't fit with all the fires.

Greg's phone rang, and he picked up the receiver. "Agent Sikes."

"This is Etheridge."

"What do you have?"

Etheridge cleared his throat. "The arsonist is male, probably mid-thirties. Has some baggage from his past. A troubled childhood. Possibly comes from a broken home. Maybe even an abusive parent. Probably has a juvenile record, although nothing serious."

"That fits."

"Have a suspect in mind?"

"Yeah, but go on."

"If I were you, I would start looking for a common denominator for these fires. And I'm not just talking method or MO.

"Meaning?"

"Based on the information you sent me, I believe the fires are revenge-motivated."

"You think the perpetrator is targeting someone specific?"

"Could be several people, but more likely it's one person. I don't think he'll stop at anything to get what he wants. You've been lucky so far in that there haven't been any victims, but this guy won't stop at anything. There's a tie in somewhere. If I were you, I'd be looking for the connection and a reason someone wants revenge."

"That's one theory that has been tossed around."

"Also, the arsonist gets a thrill from setting fires. He waits around and watches the buildings go up in flames.

Another thing. I feel certain once he's finished with his current, shall I say task, he will go on to start more fires."

"Oh, yeah?"

"It's my opinion he's responsible for other arsons—not just the ones in Driscoll Lake. He'll continue until you catch him. My advice is that you find him soon."

"One question. All the fires have occurred within a short amount of time, but it was almost nine months from last year's fire until the one in Woodland Hills. What's your take on that?"

"As I said, this perp is likely responsible for fires in other areas. Need I remind you how many occurred in Texas during last year's drought? It didn't take much for someone to start fires and make them appear accidental. He could have been busy elsewhere. Now he's come back to Driscoll Lake to finish what he started."

"I see. Appreciate your help."

"I'll overnight a copy of my complete report."

Sikes hung up the phone, walked to Matt Bradford's office, and knocked on the door. "Got a minute?"

Matt waved him inside. "What's up?"

"Just heard back on the criminal profiler. He confirmed my suspicions. The fires, including the ones at the factory and Woodland Hills, are linked."

"You still consider Brian a suspect."

"I'm not ruling out any possibilities. It's time to question him about the fire at the Lawrence house."

***

This hadn't been Brian's best week. Someone had seen him near the Lawrence home the night of the fire, and Sikes questioned him again. Brian admitted to being in the vicinity, but after he told his side of the story, Sikes seemed to accept his explanation.

The following day, the rehab facility called to inform him the doctor would discharge his mother on Monday, which meant it was time for Brian to tell her about her new living arrangements. He picked one of her more lucid moments, thinking it would be best. He couldn't have been more wrong. She had not taken the news well.

"Why can't I go back to my apartment?"

"Mom, you're not able to care for yourself any longer. You need more nursing care than what you've been getting. Although you're finishing rehab, you've still got a way to go. The last thing you need is to fall again."

"I had one accident. Wasn't even in my room. Now you want to punish me. I know I'm forgetful sometimes, but I can still take care of myself.

Not for the first time, Brian wished he had other siblings to support him. "I'm not trying to punish you. I'd like to have you around a few more years. I—"

"Just go," she said. "I don't want to talk about this anymore."

Brian reluctantly left the rehab. He knew he was doing the right thing, but why did he suddenly feel like the evil son? One that didn't care. He'd known of people who put their relatives in a nursing home and never bothered to visit. Many of them died from sheer loneliness. But he wouldn't be that kind of person. He would be there for his mother up until the end.

Right now, he needed a friend. Someone to talk with. Someone who would understand. He needed Rachel.

***

"Would you see who's at the door?" Rachel called out from the kitchen.

"Sure," Nicole replied.

When Rachel recognized Brian's voice coming from the foyer, she hurried to greet him. "This is a surprise. What's up?"

"I needed to talk to you about something. Didn't know you had company."

"It's okay. This is my sister, Nicole. She's visiting this week while her husband is at a conference in Dallas. Nicole, this is my friend, Brian Nichols."

"Hi." Brian nodded in acknowledgment.

"Nice to meet you." Nicole smiled and then turned toward her sister.

Rachel didn't miss the impish look on her face and hoped that Brian hadn't seen it.

"I can come back at another time."

"It's okay," Nicole said. "I need to call Kevin. I'll leave you two to talk." Without waiting for either of them to answer, she turned and sprinted up the stairs.

"Come sit down." Rachel gestured toward the den. "Want something to drink?"

"No, thanks." Brian sat down on the sofa.

Rachel sat beside him. "What's up?"

"Mom is being discharged from the rehab facility next Monday. She's unable to stay in assisted living. I had to make a decision to move her."

Rachel nodded. "To skilled nursing?"

"Yeah. At least she can remain at Woodbine." Brian lowered his voice and scrubbed his hand over his face.

"But there's a problem."

"I had to tell her today. She didn't take the news well. In fact, she was so angry she told me to leave. I mean, what was I supposed to do? Mom can't take care of herself anymore."

"You're doing the right thing. In the short time since I've been rounding at Woodbine, I can see the changes in her condition. Your mother needs more extensive nursing care at this stage."

"I know I'm doing right, but how can I make her understand?"

"Give her time. Deep down, she probably knows it, but this move is another sign she has to give up her independence. It's not easy when people get older to admit they can no longer care for themselves."

"I don't want to hurt her. I gave her so much grief when I was a teenager. Guess I've spent a lot of my adult life trying to make up for that." Brian lowered his head.

"You are a devoted son. It's one of the things I lo—I admire about you. A lot of men would turn away. You haven't."

"Thank you for saying that."

"It's true. I'm here if you need me. If you'd want, I'd be willing to talk to her. Not as a doctor, but as a friend."

"I appreciate that. Guess I should be going and let you visit with your sister."

Rachel walked with him to the door. "I'm glad you stopped by. Don't worry about things with your mother. She'll come around."

"Yeah, I know. But sometimes it's hard."

"It'll be okay."

Brian looked at her and spoke softly. "You said the same thing a few nights ago. Right here at this very spot."

Rachel felt her face grow warm, remembering their night together. "Yeah, I did, didn't I?"

"What about us, Rachel? Where do we stand? Just friends?"

"We crossed that line, remember?"

"Yeah, I do." Brian put his arms around her waist, drew her close, and lowered his mouth to hers.

The kiss was long and slow—not passionate like ones they shared a few days ago, but neither was it chaste. It was warm, gentle, and it spoke volumes about their relationship. They pulled apart when they heard footsteps.

"Call me." Brian turned and walked out the door.

Rachel looked up to see Nicole standing at the bottom of the stairs. Her expression left Rachel no doubt she had witnessed the kiss.

"Just friends, huh?"

"Okay, so we're close friends."

"Are you sleeping with him?"

"That's none of your business." Rachel turned and stormed into the kitchen with Nicole close on her heels.

"I'm not asking to be nosy. I'm asking because I care about my sister. Answer my question."

"No, we're not sleeping together. Well, yes. Once."

"I guessed as much. It isn't hard to see that you're in love with him."

"I'm not—"

"Yeah, sure you're not. I know you're the older sister, but I'm going to give you some advice. Life is too short. You of all people should know that because of your mother. If you love him, let him know. Don't wait until it's too late." Nicole turned and left the room.

Rachel looked out the window. Rain had begun to fall, and she watched the drops splatter against the window pane. Replaying the conversation with Nicole, she whispered the words. "I'm not in love with him."

But even as she spoke, she knew the truth.

Chapter 18

Rachel was sad to see Nicole leave. She had enjoyed their visit together. Nicole was no longer the little kid following big sister around, spying on her and her boyfriends, trying to mimic her every move.

Rachel smiled wistfully. Her mother's death was tragic, but with it came the opportunity to know her siblings and her stepmother in a way that wouldn't have been possible had Madelyn lived. Both Cade and Nicole loved having their older sister around. Cecelia treated Rachel as if she was her biological child. She never attempted to take Madelyn's place, but Rachel knew Cecelia would always be there for her.

Not everyone was that lucky. Rachel had a friend in college whose stepmother resented her and did everything she could to come between her and her father. Cecelia was never that way.

"No, I got the evil stepfather," she said aloud as she walked into her clinic on Friday morning.

"What did you say?" the middle-aged woman sitting behind the counter asked.

Wendy Stiles had been with Dr. Jacobs for several years, serving in the capacity of a receptionist. She was a loyal and trustworthy employee. After the previous office manager retired, Wendy took over the position.

"Just talking to myself. What's my schedule look like today?"

"Full patient load all morning. A few openings in the afternoon, but somehow we always manage to have a few walk-ins on Fridays."

"Good. I like being busy."

"There are donuts and kolaches in the break room."

Rachel shook her head. "Thanks, but—"

"Some of the kolaches have jalapeños in them."

"Now you're talking."

In the break room, Rachel poured herself a cup of coffee. She grabbed one of the pastry-wrapped sausages, went into her private office, and closed the door, trying to keep her thoughts away from the conversation she had with Nicole the night before. She couldn't be angry with her sister for asking such personal questions, but she wasn't ready to deal with the answers.

It isn't hard to see you're in love with him. Let him know. Life is short.

Life was short, all right. Too short. Her thirty-fifth birthday was in a couple of months. It served as another reminder that her mother was only a few years older when she died.

Rachel shook her thoughts aside and drank the last sip of coffee before putting on her lab coat and walking toward an exam room to greet her first patient.

***

"I'm glad this day is over," Wendy said as she locked the clinic's front door.

Rachel nodded. "Amen to that."

"What's everyone doing tonight?" Katrina Sutter was a perky young nurse whom Rachel hired a few weeks earlier. She was good with patients and dedicated to her job.

"I'm going home, having a glass of wine, propping my feet up, and will probably fall asleep watching TV," Wendy said.

Katrina wrinkled her nose. "That's no fun. It's Friday night."

"I don't suppose you're going home."

"No way. I'm stopping off at my boyfriend's house to change clothes, and then we're going to Pinnacle."

Rachel frowned.

"It's a new club in Brewster."

Wendy shook her head. "Knock yourself out, kid."

"What about you, Dr. Jackson?" Katrina asked as Rachel walked into the room. "Got big plans for tonight?"

"First of all, its past office hours, so call me Rachel. And no, I don't have plans. I'll probably go home and go to bed early. Staying up late all week visiting with my sister has taken its toll."

"Oh, come on. You're too young to spend a Friday night at home alone. I'm willing to bet there's a special guy out there who would love to take you out. In fact, the rumor mill tells me you've been seen around town a few times with a tall, good-looking man."

Rachel tried to act indignant at first, but she was glad that both Katrina and Wendy had begun to open up more. Yes, they were her employees, but after work, it was okay to be less formal. She wanted them to develop a comfortable rapport. She smiled. "Is nothing sacred in this town? Brian is a friend."

Katrina grinned. "Oh, so she *does* know who I'm talking about."

"Katrina, don't you think you'd better leave well enough alone?" Wendy admonished her.

"It's okay, Wendy. But it's as I said—Brian is a friend, and no, we don't have plans for tonight." Rachel wondered how many times she would explain to people that Brian was only a friend. And just how many people had noticed them and thought there was more to their relationship.

"Can't blame me for trying." Kristina grinned.

A few minutes later, the three women left the office together. They were halfway to their cars when Wendy stopped.

"Something wrong?" Rachel asked.

"That car." Wendy nodded in the direction of a small white automobile parked across the street. "It's been sitting there for a while."

"Maybe they had car trouble. I wouldn't worry. It's probably nothing."

"I'm sure you're right."

Rachel smiled. "It's been a long day. Go home, rest, and enjoy the weekend. Katrina, try not to have too much fun tonight. I'll see you both on Monday."

***

He should have done a better job of hiding his car. It was obvious one of the women had noticed it sitting on the side of the street. From his vantage point, it was easy to see what was happening. Rachel had appeared to shrug it off. He had come today to look around and plan for his next fire. And he found a perfect spot to watch—a brick wall behind the office building across the street led to a wooded area. He could slip in and out quickly, and no one would see him.

Like the other fires, he would wait until dark, after people had gone home for the day. A rush of adrenaline enveloped him, but he needed to remain calm. Just a few more days.

***

Rachel got into her Corvette and pulled out of the parking lot. She smiled as she thought about Katrina. She might let down on the weekends, but she was a top-notch nurse, totally professional, and cared about her patients. Hard to imagine her dancing the night away in some club.

At least someone would be having a good time tonight. Rachel didn't look forward to going home to her once-again-empty house. Most of the time she thought of her home as a sanctuary. She never felt lonely there like she did when she lived in the family house. But Nicole's departure would leave a void. She turned on the car radio to a classic rock station. The song playing was unfamiliar to her but spoke of lost love. The melancholic tune and words weren't exactly what she needed to hear right now.

"That's worse than any crying-in-your-beer country song." She pressed the scan button for another station. After a few tries, she found an upbeat tune.

"That's more like it." The song made her think of Brian and wondered if he was playing with the band tonight. It was a Friday night, and she doubted he would be home. The truth was, she half expected him to call her today and couldn't help but feel a bit disappointed that he hadn't.

Sighing, she reached for her cell phone and dialed Christine.

"Hi, this is Christine. I can't take your call now, but leave a message."

Rachel hung up the phone. Nicole's words from the night before kept replaying in her head. *Are you in love with him?*

She needed a friend to talk with, but didn't dare bother Stephanie on a Friday night. And even if Christine had been home, Rachel wouldn't have told her anything. She probably wouldn't confide in anyone, although she knew Stephanie wouldn't betray a confidence—even though her husband was best friends with Brian. She would just have to suffer through this alone.

"Damn," she said aloud. "Why does life have to be so complicated?"

Rather than going home, she drove until she came to her favorite Mexican restaurant. She was lucky to be able to find a table right away, and when the waiter came, she ordered a margarita. She needed one tonight. Something to get her mind off Brian.

***

Two margaritas and one fajita salad later, Rachel still couldn't shake her melancholy mood. What was wrong with her? She usually kept her emotions in check, but tonight all she wanted to do was cry. And for the life of her, she couldn't figure out the reason. It wasn't sadness over her sister leaving town or the fact Nicole was happily married and pregnant. Maybe it was the conversation with Wendy and Katrina earlier.

You're much too young to spend a Friday night alone.

Or Nicole's words the night before.

It isn't hard to see you're in love with him.

Or maybe even Brian's words.

You said the same thing a few nights ago. What about us, Rachel? Where do we stand? Just friends?

"No," she said aloud. "We aren't just friends. That's not what I want."

Without conscious thought, Rachel drove through town, surprising herself that she ended up on Brian's street. She started to drive on by his house when she saw lights on inside. He was home. She pulled into his driveway, got out of the car, walked to the door, and rang the doorbell.

When Brian opened the door, he raised his eyebrows in surprise. "Rachel. Hi."

"Is this a bad time? I can come back—"

"It's okay. I just didn't expect to see you."

"Well, I'm here."

"Yeah."

She looked around, surprised he hadn't asked her to come inside. "Maybe this wasn't a good idea. I'd better go."

"No, wait. Why did you come?"

"I think you know."

Chapter 19

Rachel sat in Brian's kitchen the following morning, sipping a cup of coffee. She wore one of his t-shirts and a pair of sweats that were much too big for her, but she tied the drawstring tightly. Brian stood at the stove, preparing breakfast tacos, clad only in a pair of jeans

This time, there would be no turning back. If there had been any question about the crossing the lines of friendship before, there was little doubt now. She had stayed the night, at Brian's invitation. Today there was none of the awkwardness there had been two weeks earlier.

"The band is performing at that new club in Brewster tonight."

"Pinnacle? My nurse Katrina said she was going last night."

"That's the one. Want to come? Matt and Stephanie plan to be there."

"You bet. I've never heard you play before except when we were in the high-school band. And then there were two-hundred other members. I always wanted to hear you play."

"Oh, so you noticed me back then?" he teased.

Rachel's face grew warm. "You were such a rebel in those days. I always found it hard to believe you would dress in a band uniform, obey the director, and march with military-like precision."

Brian shrugged. "That was my way to connect with music. The uniform wasn't me. But you looked good in one. Especially when you became a majorette."

"Oh, so you noticed me back then?"

"Yeah. Your legs looked great in shorts, but when you didn't have to wear the marching uniform and put on those sequined things... Let's say I always wanted to be the one marching behind you."

Rachel laughed, enjoying the playful banter. "I had no idea. Why didn't you say anything?"

"I don't know. We were young. I wasn't exactly the kind of guy most parents would want their daughter to date. And I always thought you were—" Brian looked away and turned his attention to preparing breakfast.

"Thought I was what?"

Brian spoke softly. "Doesn't matter now. You moved away."

"Yeah, I did. But it wasn't by choice." Rachel lowered her head.

Brian rushed to her side and took her into his arms. "I'm sorry. I didn't mean to drag up painful memories for you."

She looked at him and smiled. "It's okay. Ever wonder what might have happened if I had stayed? Maybe you and I would have got together sooner."

"And maybe you would have decided I wasn't worth it."

"I would never think that."

"Never say never."

***

Rachel sat at a table with Stephanie and Matt, sipping ginger ale, and listening to the band perform. Brian was good. Real good. He kept in perfect rhythm. The drums enhanced the music, rather than distracted from it, even on a couple of hard rock pieces they did.

She kept her eyes on Brian as the song ended with a drum beat. He caught her eye, smiled, and winked. Rachel smiled in return.

Stephanie must have caught the interchange because she leaned close and whispered. "Want to tell me what's going on?"

"What makes you think there's anything to tell?" Rachel grinned.

"Come on. I'm not blind. I saw the look you and Brian just exchanged. And you're drinking ginger ale rather than your usual margarita. Is there something you're not telling me? Stephanie quirked an eyebrow.

"No. I've just decided that I won't drink when I'm around Brian."

"Oh, really. Why?"

"He doesn't drink, and I think it's best not to have the taste of alcohol in my mouth when he—" Rachel's face grew warm.

Stephanie's grin was mischievous. "When he does what? Come on, you can tell me."

Rachel glanced at Matt, who was listening to the music and seemed oblivious to their conversation. Taking a sip of her drink, Rachel said, "Okay, we're... I guess you can say we're dating."

"That's great! I knew something was going on between the two of you at our wedding."

Rachel cocked an eyebrow. "Really?"

"Yes. Especially when the two of you danced together."

Was there anyone who hadn't noticed? "Look, I know we—" Rachel glanced toward Brian, who was looking across the room with a scowl on his face. She turned to see what had his attention and saw Alan Davis making his way toward her table. "Oh, no. Why does he seem to turn up everywhere I am?"

"Who?" Stephanie asked.

"Alan Davis. I hope he's not coming over here. He never takes no for an answer."

Both Stephanie and Matt looked in Alan's direction.

"Rachel, pity you're here alone tonight. Would you like to dance?"

Rachel opened her mouth to explain she was with someone, but before she could say anything, Matt stood up.

"Actually, I was about to dance with Rachel." He looked at her. "Shall we?"

"Of course." Without acknowledging Alan, she got up and allowed Matt to lead her to the dance floor.

"Thought you needed rescuing," he said.

"Thanks. The man is incorrigible. Hope he doesn't corner Stephanie."

"She can hold her own with him. She'll put him in his place

"I thought I had done that, but apparently not. Maybe I need to get some tips from Stephanie."

"Wouldn't work."

"Why?"

"He isn't interested in Stephanie. And if I thought for a minute he was, I—"

"You would forget that you're the police chief and beat him within an inch of his life."

Matt laughed. "Probably. I have a feeling there's someone here who would do the same for you if he wasn't busy playing drums right now."

Rachel wasn't sure why his words caused her to blush. Maybe it was because she'd thought the same thing. When the song ended, they made their way back to the table. "Thanks again. I'm sorry you had to take time away from Stephanie."

"It's okay, she understands. Besides, I wanted to keep my friend out of trouble." Matt nodded toward Brian and grinned.

The band's leader announced they would take a short break and Brian quickly made his way to the table. He bent down, kissed Rachel lightly before sitting beside her, and draped his arm across the back of her chair.

"I don't have to guess what that means." Matt grinned.

Rachel looked at him and smiled. "No."

"When did this happen?"

Brian looked at Rachel. "Couple of weeks ago."

Matt took a sip of his beer. "About damn time. Maybe now you'll stop being so crabby."

"Hey, I wasn't that bad."

Rachel was a bit surprised at Matt's comment, given the recent disagreement between him and Brian.

"By the way, thanks, man." Brian glanced toward Rachel as he spoke, leaving little doubt he was referring to the dance between her and Matt.

"Anytime."

Rachel was glad to see the two friends talking again as if nothing had happened. "Want something to drink?" she asked Brian.

"No, thanks. I have some bottled water on stage. I try to stay away from anything carbonated when we're playing. Makes my throat dry."

"Hey," Stephanie said. "You guys are good. Do you ever sing lead?"

Brian shook his head. "Not yet, but I'm working on a couple of songs."

Rachel smiled "Guess I'm going to have to come to another show."

A slow song began to play. Brian leaned close to Rachel and whispered in her ear. "Want to dance?"

"Yes," she said.

Brian pulled her close.

"I think we should use a little discretion. Our escapade at Matt and Stephanie's wedding has caused quite a buzz."

"Oh, yeah? How?"

"Stephanie said something about it and so did my sister."

Brian frowned. "Your sister? How did she know about it?"

"Oh, I didn't show you the photo. It's a candid shot of us. Nicole saw it. Between that and the kiss we shared when you were leaving the other night, it didn't take her long to figure out we were more than friends."

Brian stiffened a bit. "Are you okay with that? Your family knowing we're seeing one another?"

"Why wouldn't I be?"

"I just thought…"

"Are you okay if your mother knows?"

"Of course."

"Then you have my answer."

***

Alan Davis watched the interaction between Brian and Rachel. No matter what she had said a few weeks ago, there was something more than friendship between them.

He glanced at his companion sitting across the table. "Looks like you have your work cut out for you."

Heather rolled her eyes. "I told you Brian isn't interested in anyone other than Rachel."

"But you're going to make sure it doesn't stay that way."

"Not that I wouldn't mind being his girl, but it's not going to work. I felt like a slut the day I walked into his office. I may be a lot of things, but that's not one of them." Heather stood up to leave, but Alan grabbed her wrist and pulled her back down.

"I don't care how you do it, but you will get him away from Rachel. You owe me, remember."

"Why are you so interested in a woman that obviously doesn't feel the same about you?"

"What makes you think she doesn't feel something for me?"

"If she did, you wouldn't need my help. And she certainly wouldn't be acting like she does with Brian."

"Heather, shut up before you say something we'll both regret."

***

After she had seen her last patient of the day on Wednesday, Rachel pulled out her cell phone to call Brian. He had said something about working late in the office.

"Hey there," she said as he answered the phone. "Still at work?"

"Yeah. Doing payroll. Again. Seems like it comes around often."

"Thought you were going to hire an office manager to do that stuff."

"Didn't have anyone apply that was capable. And I let the ad expire."

"Maybe you should rerun it."

He sounded tired. "Yeah, maybe."

"What about dinner?"

"I've got to finish here first. Sorry."

"It's okay. Why don't a pick up a pizza and come by there?"

"I'd like that. Thanks."

"I'll be there in half an hour."

Rachel ended the call just as Katrina popped her head in the door. "Wendy and I are getting ready to leave. How about you?"

"I need to finish up a couple of things first. No need to wait for me."

"Be careful. It's already getting dark outside."

"I'll be fine. See you tomorrow morning."

It was twenty minutes later when Rachel left the office by way of the back door. Although it was not yet six-o'clock, twilight had set in. Rachel was half way to her car when she felt a sudden chill. The evening wasn't cold, so she stopped to look around. It was more of a feeling of apprehension. Not seeing anything unusual, she walked faster and breathed a sigh of relief when she got into the car.

"What's wrong with me?"

She recalled the night Phillip hid in the back of her SUV and forced her to drive to the old factory. No chance of someone hiding in the two-seat Corvette, but she couldn't stop herself from glancing over her shoulder.

She took another look around the parking lot before starting the car and leaving a little faster than the posted speed limit allowed.

***

"Damn." The man said to himself as he watched Rachel's car exit the parking lot. "Too late."

Of course, he could still start the fire. That had been his plan, anyway. But when he saw Rachel leave, a new idea formed in his mind. He would bide his time. No need to give up easily. Another opportunity would arise.

Comforted by that thought, he got behind the wheel of his little white car and drove away.

Chapter 20

Rachel tapped on the door to Brian's office, a pizza box in one hand and a two-liter bottle of cola in the other. He jumped up from his desk when he saw her peering through the glass door and hurried to open it.

Brian took the pizza from her and placed a light kiss on her lips. "Hey there. Guess I should make you a key. After all, you are my partner." He grinned.

"In more ways than one." Rachel winked at him and then walked to the small break area. She took a couple of plastic cups and filled them with ice while Brian grabbed some paper plates. They sat down at a small table.

She placed a slice of pizza on a paper plate but didn't take a bite.

"Are you okay?"

"Long day. Guess I'm paranoid, but I had a strange feeling when I left the office earlier.

"Were you alone?"

"Yes. Katrina and Wendy had already left."

"What happened?"

"I'm sure it's nothing, but I felt like someone was watching me."

"Did you see anyone hanging around? Anything unusual?"

"No. When I got to the car, I couldn't help but think about last year when Phillip hid in the back seat of my SUV. He must have been watching me for a few days to see where I parked and the time I would leave each evening."

Brian took her hand. "Babe, you don't have to worry about Phillip anymore."

"I know. But something felt weird tonight. I even glanced over my shoulder. Silly. The car doesn't have a back seat. That was probably one of my reasons for buying it. I don't think I could go through what happened last year again." Tears came to her eyes.

Brian stood up, walked around the table to Rachel, then pulled her into his arms. "You don't have to worry. Phillip can't hurt you now."

She wiped the tears and looked up at Brian. "I know. I'm usually not like this."

"It's okay. What you went through couldn't have been easy."

"It wasn't. But hey, that's in the past." Rachel smiled. "Come on. We should eat the pizza before it gets cold."

Once they finished eating, Rachel gathered the paper plates and cups and took them to the trash.

When she walked back to his office, she saw a pack of cigarettes lying on Brian's desk. Rachel frowned. She knew Brian once smoked in high school, but since they became reacquainted, she'd never seen him with a cigarette. Sometimes there was a smell of smoke on his clothes, but only after he had played or practiced with the band. "Where did those come from?" she asked, pointing to the Marlboros.

Brian frowned. "Sorry. Didn't intend for you to see them."

"You started smoking again?"

"On occasion. With everything going on with the arson investigation... Sometimes nothing else will do but a cigarette. And yes, I know smoking isn't good for me, but I know better than to resort to using alcohol."

"I'm not going to lecture you. Just curious. Guess I'd better get out of here and let you finish up."

Brian walked her to the car and waited until she opened the door before drawing her into his arms to kiss her.

Rachel responded—the kiss a little too long for a simple goodbye. When they finally broke apart, she said in a low voice, "I should go. Otherwise, you won't get your work done."

"Yeah. See you tomorrow night?"

"Stephanie and I are meeting for a late lunch, but I'll be home in the evening. Why don't you come by the house?"

"I'll be there."

***

His eyes grew wide as he looked at the man and woman embracing in the parking lot. Cozy little scene. Oh, yes, there was definitely more than friendship between those two. He'd been right about checking out Rachel's office. Now he knew for sure the next target he'd planned was the right one. If there had been any doubt as to the relationship between her and Nichols before, their actions tonight confirmed they were much more than friends.

The stakes had been raised. It was time to put a little fear in Rachel.

***

"Glad we could get together," Stephanie said as Rachel got in the car.

"Me too. We haven't had a chance to talk much. That is, without the men around."

"So how are things with you and Brian? Matt and I are so happy the two of you finally got together."

"There are times when I thought it would never happen. I mean, we were friends and all. Reminded me of a movie I once saw. The two main characters kept denying their true feelings for years. Finally, they admitted they loved one another."

"At least it didn't take you and Brian that long."

"Yeah, well. We haven't got to that point yet." Rachel turned her head and looked out the window. Neither one of them had mentioned love. Just a mutual physical attraction.

"Hope you don't mind, but I need to stop off to see Matt before we go to lunch."

"No problem."

Stephanie slowed the car and parked in front of the police station. "Shouldn't take more than a few minutes unless he's busy. Want to come in or wait out here?"

Rachel shrugged. "I'll go with you."

**

Greg Sikes tapped lightly on Matt's office door. "Got a minute?"

"Sure, come in and have a seat."

Sikes walked into the office, not bothering to close the door.

Matt hoped Greg would have some good news regarding the ongoing arson investigations. Many of Driscoll Lake's residents were getting edgy, wondering if their home or business would be next. The last fire at the empty house of Curtis Lawrence had everyone wanting answers. "Any new leads?"

Greg shook his head. "The DNA evidence collected at the Tippet house was inconclusive."

"Damn." Matt pounded his fist on the desk. "I was hoping..."

"Me too. Haven't heard back from the samples collected at the Lawrence house. Hell, even if we had got a good profile, we wouldn't be able to get a match unless the person is in the database. Even then there are over nine-million records there. Finding a match without a having a suspect would be nearly impossible."

"True."

"However, having a DNA profile on the perp would be ideal. This guy is careful. He's also calculating. Plans his targets well. Sooner or later, he's going to make a mistake. When he does, we'll nail him."

"Wish we had more."

"We know this. The arsonist likes Marlboro cigarettes. Investigators found the same brand of cigarette at both locations."

"A lot of people smoke that brand."

"But not everyone who smokes that brand is a serial arsonist."

Matt looked to see Stephanie and Rachel standing at the door.

"Oh, I'm sorry," Stephanie said. "I had no idea you were with someone."

Greg stood up. "It's okay. I was just leaving."

"Agent Sikes, this is my wife Stephanie and her friend, Rachel Jackson."

Greg stood up to greet them. "Greg Sikes. I'm with the ATF. Nice to meet you both."

"Likewise," Stephanie said.

Rachel nodded.

Greg nodded at Matt. "Catch you later."

***

Katrina stuck her head in the door of Rachel's office. "Hey, Rachel. Wendy and I are ready to leave for the day. Are you coming?"

"Not yet. I have a couple of things to do first."

"You're going to stay here alone? It's almost dark outside."

"I'll be okay. It's not like this is a bad part of town or anything. Brian is coming by later."

"Hot date?"

"Katrina!"

"Can't help it. I think the two of you are perfect for one another."

"Then you'll be happy to know we are going out tonight."

"I knew it. The last few weeks, you've acted differently."

"Have I?"

Wendy called out from the back door. "Katrina, I'm leaving now if you want to walk out together."

"Coming."

"Take care. I'll see you on Monday."

Rachel waited until she heard them leave before turning her attention to the computer. She decided to listen to a couple of online webinars while waiting for Brian. A quick glance at her watch indicated she would have time to watch at least one before he arrived.

After Rachel finished the second webinar, she glanced at the clock to see more than an hour had passed. Brian should have been here by now. Thinking she heard a noise at the back, she got up from her desk and walked to the back door. "Brian?"

No one answered. She stood there for a minute, listening, but there was only silence.

"Must be hearing things." She turned and went back to her desk when her cell phone rang. "Hello."

"Hey, it's me," Brian said. "I'm at the front. Want to let me in?"

"I'll be right there."

"Hi," Brian said as she opened the door.

Rachel reached up to place a light kiss on his lips before turning back toward her private office.

"That's the only greeting I get?"

"Later. I listened to a couple of webinars, and I need to finish an online test to get the CME credits."

"You need what?"

"Continuing medical education. I need a certain number of credits to maintain my medical license."

"Makes me glad I'm not a doctor."

"How's your mom?"

"Okay."

Brian followed her to the office. Ignoring the chairs, he sat on the corner of her desk. Rachel turned her attention to the computer.

"So, do you want me to take you to dinner?" Brian asked.

"What?"

"Want to go out to eat?"

"That's fine." Suppressing a smile, she said beneath her breath. "For starters."

"You have something else in mind?"

"We'll discuss it later."

"You're going to make me wait?"

She looked up at him and smiled. "Yes." Then she continued to take the online test.

Brian got up and walked around the room. Rachel watched as he turned his attention to the diplomas on the wall. She was proud of them—each one an achievement—from her undergraduate studies, medical school, and completion of residency.

He turned to look a collage of photographs on another wall. It contained several family photos, including one with her mother. They stood together on the front steps of their home. Rachel wore her high school band uniform. Someone must have taken it before a football game. Both were smiling. Other photos were her father, step-mother, and siblings. It would be nice to add a picture of Brian or one of the two of them together. Maybe even that candid shot of them dancing.

Rachel wasn't sure if Brian sensed her watching him, but he turned to her and smiled. She quickly looked back at the computer, but he walked to stand behind her and began to massage her neck and shoulders.

She leaned back in the chair, temporarily forgetting about the test. The things he could do with his hands. The man could have been a masseuse. "That's nice."

"You like?"

"I like."

Brian brushed her hair to the side and started to kiss her on the neck.

But before they lost control, she sat up straight in the chair. "However, if you don't stop, I'll never finish this thing. And the sooner I'm through, the sooner we can leave."

"Is that a promise?"

Rachel turned to look at him. "Yes."

"Then I'll keep my hands to myself."

Five minutes later, Rachel finished the final question and powered down her computer. Whirling around in her chair, she turned to Brian. "Now, about dinner."

He stood, reached for her hands, and pulled her close. "For starters?"

"How about this first?" Rachel pressed her lips to his.

"Oh, yeah." Brian kissed her again, and her lips parted as he deepened the kiss.

She pulled back, breathless. "Why don't we get out of here?"

"Good idea." Brian stepped away from her while she gathered her purse and cell phone.

When they walked into the hallway, Rachel suddenly stopped. "Do you smell smoke?"

Brian frowned. "Yeah, I do. I'd better—"

His words were interrupted by someone pounding on the front door. "Hello? Is anyone inside? There's a fire behind the building. You need to get out now."

Chapter 21

"You're lucky Rachel," Fire Chief Stan Gardner said. "If someone hadn't come along when they did, the entire building could have gone up in flames."

Rachel stood in the parking lot, staring into the alley behind her office. "Then why don't I feel lucky? Until someone catches this lunatic, everyone in this town is on pins and needles."

"I know. Agent Sikes is one of the best. He'll do what it takes, including pulling in more people if necessary. But we'll catch the guy."

"I hope its sooner rather than later."

"Don't we all? I'd better get back to work."

Rachel leaned against the trunk of her Corvette and watched as the firemen packed up their equipment. The fire started directly behind the building. The back door and wall sustained minor damage, but fortunately, someone saw the flames and was quick to call the fire department.

She felt numb. If this was arson, was she the target? Or was Brian? Did the arsonist know of their association? Had someone been watching and knew he was with her in the office? She thought back to a couple of nights earlier when she had the "uneasy" feeling while leaving the building.

Rachel glanced around the parking lot and saw Brian standing with Matt and Carlos Gonzales. A fourth man joined them. Rachel recognized the ATF agent she met in Matt's office a few days ago.

Brian looked at her, nodded, and said something to the agent. Together, they walked toward her.

"Agent Greg Sikes, this is Dr. Rachel Jackson. She owns this clinic." He gestured to the building.

Rachel smiled at Brian's use of her title. "I didn't expect to see you again so soon."

At Brian's look of surprise, she added, "Stephanie and I stopped at Matt's office yesterday, and Agent Sikes was there."

Greg nodded. "Dr. Jackson. Wish it could be under more pleasant circumstances."

Brian moved beside Rachel and put his arm around her waist. Was he jealous?

"I understand both of you were inside when the fire broke out."

"That's correct. We were about to leave when we smelled smoke, and then someone started banging on the front door and told us to get out."

"I'll need to get your statements."

Rachel shuddered. Memories flooded back to a year earlier at the warehouse.

Brian must have sensed something was wrong because he tightened his grip and pulled her closer. "It's okay. We're safe."

Rachel nodded and reached to wipe the tear that escaped. "I'm sorry. Just thinking about what could have happened."

Sikes softened his stance. "Look, we don't have to do this tonight. It's getting late, and you've been through a harrowing experience. Can you both come to the police station in the morning?"

Rachel nodded.

"We'll both be there," Brian said.

"Ten o'clock?"

Rachel looked at Brian who nodded in agreement. "That will be fine."

"I'll see you both then." Sikes nodded before walking away.

"You okay?"

"Not really. After last year, I never thought I'd have to go through something like this again. We could have been hurt. Or worse."

Brian pulled her into his arms. "We're safe honey. Nothing happened."

"But what if this madman isn't finished? Everything so far has been targeted at you or involves you somehow."

Brian touched his fingers to her lips. "Stop worrying. They're going to catch this guy. Everything will be okay."

"I hope so."

"It will. I promise." He kissed her lightly.

"I don't want to be alone tonight. Stay with me."

***

Rachel's hands shook. She couldn't remember being this anxious after the ordeal with Phillip. She had been running on pure adrenaline that night. First, she had to deal with Kyle's injury and subsequent death. When they'd realized the building was on fire, survival instinct kicked in. After everyone had made it outside, she'd rushed to help Matt, who had been suffering from smoke inhalation.

She didn't have time to think then. Tonight was a different matter.

Matt walked over to where she and Brian stood. "Why don't you take Rachel home. "I'll drive your truck back to police headquarters. "It will be safe there, and you can get it tomorrow."

"Good idea. Thanks buddy."

"No problem. Take care of Rachel. If Stephanie and I can help, let us know."

Brian first stopped off at his house to pick up a change of clothes. After everything that happened, neither of them felt like eating dinner, so they went straight to Rachel's house.

Around midnight, they shared a snack of chips and salsa before falling asleep on the sofa. They woke up around two and went upstairs to bed, falling asleep almost immediately.

Although she rested only a few hours, Rachel woke up early the following morning. She lay in bed for a while, hoping to doze back off. The bedside clock indicated it was only six o'clock. She had plenty of time before the meeting with Sikes.

He was still asleep. She eased out of bed so as not to awaken him and went into the bathroom to shower. Emerging a few minutes later, she found Brian still sleeping. The morning was chilly, and she dressed in jeans and her favorite Longhorn sweatshirt.

Downstairs, she selected a French vanilla coffee pod and popped it in the Keurig. A minute later, a steaming mug of coffee in hand, she went into the den and sat down on the sofa. Spending the morning talking with an arson investigator and contacting her insurance agency wasn't her idea of a fun Saturday morning. But for now, she didn't want to think about the fire. She just wanted to enjoy the moment.

It wasn't long before she heard the shower running. Before long, Brian came downstairs, his hair still damp.

"Good morning." Rachel said.

He sat beside her on the sofa, put his arms around her, then drew her mouth to his. "It is a good morning when I began the day like this."

When the broke apart, she said, "Want some coffee?"

"As long as you don't tell me to help myself before I see myself out."

Rachel picked up a pillow and threw it at him. "I wouldn't do that again."

"In that case, I'll take a cup. Stay here. I'll get it." He flashed her a brilliant smile.

"Are you hungry? Since we didn't eat dinner, I thought you might want some breakfast," she called out.

"Sure."

She got up from the sofa and walked into the kitchen. "I've got the ingredients to make omelets. Mushroom and sausage okay?"

"Sounds good. Need any help?"

"I've got it covered, but you can keep me company."

"I can do that." Brian smiled and sat on a bar stool facing the kitchen island. "Are you okay this morning?"

"Not really. I need to contact my insurance company, and then I should go to the building and take another look at it. Guess they'll allow me to go inside today."

"I don't see why not. The damage was minimal."

"Hopefully the place isn't reeking with the smell of smoke. Then there's this meeting with Sikes... Dammit, I forgot to call Wendy and Katrina." Rachel slammed her fist on the kitchen counter.

Brian stood up, hurried to Rachel, and drew her into his arms. "I'll help. You're not in this alone. I'm with you every step of the way."

***

Rachel and Brian arrived at the police station ten minutes early. Although Brian seemed to be late for almost everything these days, he had been ready to go a good half-hour before Rachel. When they walked into the building, Matt was there as well as Carlos Gonzales. Both looked weary. Apparently, they had worked most of the night.

Matt greeted them. "Hey. How's it going?"

"As well as can be expected," Brian said.

"Still a little shaken, but I've been through worse things." Rachel crossed her arms and rubbed them together.

"Cold?" Brian asked.

She shook her head. "Nervous."

"Don't be. Remember what I said earlier." Brian put his arm around her waist.

"Come on," Matt said. "I'll tell Sikes you're here."

They followed him down the hall to the office Sikes occupied. Rachel didn't expect to be back so soon after her last visit, and she certainly didn't expect to be questioned about another fire. She and Brian waited for Matt to announce their arrival.

"Rachel, he wants to talk to you first. Brian, you can wait in my office?"

Straightening her shoulders, Rachel took a deep breath and walked to Sikes' office door.

"Come in." He stood to shake her hand. "Please, have a seat."

"Thanks." She took the chair closest to the door.

"I won't take too much of your time. Just need to ask you a few questions about last night."

"Sure."

"I understand you and Nichols were the only ones in the building when the fire broke out."

"That's correct. My office manager and nurse had already left for the day. I spoke to them this morning. Both said they would be glad to answer any questions, although neither one claims to have seen anything unusual. I have their names and telephone numbers." Rachel took a piece of paper from her purse and handed it to Sikes.

"Thank you. Tell me what happened."

"I stayed to work on a few things before Brian arrived."

"Then you were there alone for a while?"

"About an hour."

"Then it wasn't until after Brian arrived that you became aware of the fire. How long was he there?"

Rachel shrugged. "I don't know. Maybe twenty minutes. We were leaving when we both smelled smoke, and that's when someone pounded on the front door to warn us."

"Did Nichols enter through the front or the back door?"

Why all the questions about Brian? After what happened last night, why would Sikes still consider him a suspect? "The front. I had to let him in."

"Does he often come to your office?"

"No, we planned to meet there before going out to dinner."

"And what time did you plan to meet?"

"Around six. Brian was running late and didn't arrive until after seven."

"Why was he late?"

"Probably with his mother at the nursing home. He stops to see her most evenings. She isn't in good health, so sometimes the visits take longer than anticipated."

"How long have you known Nichols?"

"Since high school. We lost touch with one another when I moved away, but have been—" Rachel hesitated. The exact nature of her relationship with Brian wasn't any of Sikes' business. "We've become good friends since I moved back here."

"I see. Do you know of anyone who might have a grievance with you? Want revenge for something? Maybe a disgruntled former employee?"

"Not that I'm aware of. I recently took over the practice from another physician who retired. I offered jobs to all the former staff members. A couple of them decided to resign, but as far as I know, there wasn't any animosity."

"I see. No one else comes to mind?"

Rachel shook her head. "Will that be all?"

"I have a couple of questions regarding the fire last year at the factory. I understand both you and Nichols were there that night.

"Yes, along with a few other people."

"Your stepfather forced you to drive to the site, correct?"

"My mother's husband. I never refer to him as my stepfather. But yes, he forced me to drive there."

"Maybe there's something you forgot about that night. I've looked at your statement from last year, but is there a chance that Denton started the fire?"

"No. From the time we got to the factory until Judge Lawrence killed him, Phillip never left me alone. As much as I'd like to blame it on him, someone else started that fire. I can promise you it wasn't Denton."

***

Brian entered the office and sat down opposite Sikes. He didn't like the man. Didn't understand why he had been so quick to agree with Abbott. But Brian would do anything to help catch the arsonist. Especially if Rachel was in danger.

"I understand you went to Dr. Jackson's office last night to meet her and shortly after that, the fire started."

"That's correct. We were about to leave when it happened."

"Do you go often go to her office after hours?"

Brian shook his head. "No."

"Why were you there last night?"

"We planned to go out for dinner. Rachel needed to stay after the clinic closed, so I agreed to meet her there."

"Did you use the back or front door?"

"I parked in front of the office. Rachel unlocked the door for me."

"You never went to the back of the building?"

"No."

"Didn't see anything unusual?"

"Nothing."

"What is the nature of your relationship with Dr. Jackson?'

"What does that have to do with anything?"

"Just trying to get all the facts."

"I don't see why my relationship with Rachel has any bearing on your investigation."

"You don't care to answer?"

"It's no secret. Rachel and I have known one another since before high school. We became reacquainted when she moved back to Driscoll Lake last year."

"That's what she said. Then you're what some would say, good friends?"

"You could say that. She is also my business partner." Brian didn't miss the flicker of surprise in the agent's face. However, Sikes was quick to recover.

"Business partners? I see."

"She provided financing for the project at the old factory site."

"Interesting. Do you have a backup plan?"

"What do you mean?"

"Many times business partners have life insurance policies on one another. That way, if something happens to one, the other one isn't left with a financial burden."

Brian shook his head. "No, we don't have anything like that. As I said, Rachel provided financing for the project. She's not involved in any of the planning and development."

"Sweet setup."

Brian seethed at the agent's words but tried to remain calm. "It works for us. Anything else you want to ask me?"

"Nothing."

"Good. Then I'll see myself out."

Chapter 22

Greg Sikes paced back and forth within the small office he occupied at the Driscoll Lake Police Department. Three weeks into this investigation, he was no closer to solving the case than when he began. His original theory about Brian Nichols wasn't panning out. Why was Abbott so adamant? And why had he listened to the man who apparently had an ax to grind?

But no matter what, he couldn't help but believe Brian was the key to this series of fires.

Although some evidence had come to light, the arsonist continued to evade them. Greg was not one to voice his frustrations often, but in a meeting with Matt Bradford, he admitted the investigation was at a standstill. "Maybe we should bring in more people."

"You're the lead investigator. Do what you think is best," Matt said. "I'll support you, and I'm sure the mayor will too."

"I had hoped we would be further along by this time."

"Learn anything new from the last fire?"

Greg shook his head. "Not really. No one saw anything. This guy is careful, but he'll make a mistake one day. When he does, we'll be there to catch him. I just hope it's not too late when we do."

"Meaning what?"

"I believe, as does the profiler, he will become desperate. He won't stop at anything. Sooner or later lives could be in danger. The fire at the clinic on Friday was evidence of that. The perp had to know someone was inside."

"Seems to me I was right about Brian. He's the target, not the perpetrator."

"I'm convinced he's the link. And if you're right, the people he's closest to could also be in danger."

***

The damage to Rachel's clinic was minimal and limited to the back exterior of the structure. After their meeting with Sikes on Saturday, Brian insisted upon accompanying Rachel to view the building.

After inspecting the place, Brian offered to do the repairs. "I can get this done in a couple of days. There's not enough damage to meet your insurance deductible. Your only expense would be materials, which I get at a discount."

"Go for it. That's one less thing for me to worry about."

Rachel had a full patient load on Monday, stopping only long enough for a quick lunch. By the time she closed the clinic at five, she was exhausted. She was a little apprehensive about leaving the building that evening, fearful the arsonist might make another attempt to destroy the place. But Matt told her the police would step up patrol in that area, and that gave her some assurance.

She made sure to walk outside with Katrina and Wendy. No sense in being caught alone. Once she got into her car, she phoned Brian. "Hey, I'm finished for the day and thought I would grab a bite to eat. I'm too tired to cook tonight. Want to meet somewhere?"

"Wish I could, but I'm still in Brewster. Got tied up with an issue on a job here. It's going to be late when I get back home."

"I understand. See you tomorrow?"

"You can count on it."

Rachel ended the call, pulled out of the parking lot, and drove to a favorite local restaurant. The place was crowded when she arrived, and the hostess informed her it would be at least thirty minutes before a seat would become available.

"We do have a few tables near the bar if you don't want to wait."

"Okay by me," Rachel said and followed the hostess to a small table. She ordered a glass of wine and opened the menu.

***

After learning he would have to wait a long time, Alan decided to leave the restaurant. He was already in his car when he saw Rachel enter the building alone. Curious to see if Brian joined her, Alan decided to linger for a while. According to Heather, the scuttlebutt had it that he had spent a few nights at Rachel's house. Likewise, Rachel had stayed overnight with Brian on occasion.

They weren't even trying to hide the fact they had become lovers. Alan also heard Brian was with her in the office on Friday when the fire broke out.

He would have to work a bit harder to get what he wanted. Heather's information about Rachel's business partnership with Brian had been a surprise. However, it might turn out to be the best thing to happen.

He would have to change his tactics a bit. If Rachel had refused his invitations while claiming to be "only friends" with Brian, she wouldn't be receptive now.

He drummed his fingers on the steering wheel. Maybe he should forget the whole thing, give up, and go home. But he'd made a promise to someone, and it was a promise he intended to keep.

That's when the idea struck him. Reaching into his pocket, he pulled out his cell phone and turned it to silent. He knew how much Rachel detested the interruptions. No sense in setting her off right away.

He got out of the car and walked into the restaurant. After a quick glance around, he found Rachel seated in the bar area. Alone.

When the hostess greeted him, he said, "I changed my mind. I'll sit at the bar."

Alan walked casually to the stool closest to Rachel's table. He would pretend surprise. Maybe luck would be on his side. He would talk to her long enough for someone else to occupy the seat he intended to take. Since there were no available tables, she might allow him to sit with her.

"Rachel, I'm surprised to see you here. How are you?"

***

Rachel looked up at the sound of her name and tried not to roll her eyes when she saw Alan Davis. She felt like telling him to take a hike, but she didn't want to act rude in public. Okay."

"I heard about the fire at your office building. Tough break."

"Yeah. Could have been worse."

"Sorry that it happened. I guess until authorities catch the person responsible, we should all be cautious. Homes, businesses. The arsonist doesn't care."

"Guess you're right."

"I don't want to keep you. I'm sure you're waiting for someone."

Rachel didn't respond.

Alan looked toward the bar where someone had just taken the last available seat. "I should have taken that space when I had the chance. It's crowded in here tonight. Guess I'll find somewhere else to eat."

"Wait. I'm here alone. You can sit here. Rachel regretted her words as soon as she said them. This man irritated her like no one else, but she determined not to allow him to get to her. Besides, she and Brian were together now. She had no problem setting Alan straight.

"If you're sure."

Rachel gestured to the vacant chair. "It's okay. Go ahead."

Alan sat down opposite her. When a waiter came by, he ordered a glass of white wine and glanced at the menu. "Have you ordered?"

"Not yet. I was about to when you walked up."

The waiter returned with Alan's wine. "Are you ready to order?"

Rachel ordered a Mushroom-Swiss burger while Alan selected Chicken Alfredo.

After the waiter left, Alan spoke. "I owe you an apology. I've acted obnoxious around you the past few months. You are an attractive woman, but I should have realized you belong to someone else."

Rachel couldn't have been more surprised at his words. "You're right. I care a lot for Brian."

"I could tell the night I saw you at Pinnacle. At first, I thought you were just there to hear the band perform, but then I saw the two of you dancing together. I should have known when I saw you at Matt and Stephanie's wedding. Can't blame a guy for trying."

"Okay, who are you and what have you done with Alan Davis?"

"I deserve that. Hope there are no hard feelings."

Rachel smiled. "Of course not."

The food arrived, and after they began to eat, Alan said, "Speaking of Brian, I hear he was with you the night of the fire. Must have been a scary time for both of you."

"You know, it happened so fast, neither of us had time to think until it was over."

Alan shook his head. "Strange that most of the fires have involved him in some way."

Rachel frowned. "What's that supposed to mean?"

"Oh, forget I said anything. It's just that I happened to be driving by your office not too long before the fire. I had business nearby and happened to see Brian walking in the alley behind your building."

"You saw what?"

"I thought it was a bit strange, but I figured he was going to the back door."

"Brian parked in front of the clinic. He never went to the back."

"I'm probably mistaken, then. Forget I said anything."

Rachel frowned. "But you saw someone?"

"Yes, I did."

"Did you tell the police?"

"No, why?"

"You may have seen the arsonist."

"Didn't think about that."

"Alan, you should talk to investigators."

He shifted in his chair and adverted his eyes.

"Is something wrong?"

"Uh, no. You're right. I should tell someone what I saw. I'll do that tomorrow."

***

Brian phoned Rachel early the next morning. "Want to go out of town this weekend? Radical is performing at an annual music festival near Waco, and I thought you might want to go with me."

"Sounds like fun. Getting away from this place is the best idea I've heard in a while."

"The concert is Saturday night, but I thought we could drive down on Friday and have most of Saturday to spend together. I have a friend who has a cabin overlooking the Brazos River. He's offered to let us stay there."

"What about the other band members?"

"Most of them plan to drive down on Saturday morning. We'll need to practice for a while that afternoon. Otherwise, I'm free until that evening. If you'd rather not attend, you can hang out at the cabin."

"No, I want to hear you play."

Brian smiled. "Good. I want you to be there. We can come back home Sunday afternoon. With everything that's been happening, we need some time away. We can leave Friday after you've seen your last patient. Will that work?"

"Absolutely. In fact, I'll ask Wendy to make sure I don't have anyone scheduled past two. That way we can get to Waco before dark."

"I'm looking forward to it."

"Me too."

***

Rachel spent Thursday afternoon visiting patients at Woodbine. Dorothy Nichols was her last patient of the day. Rachel enjoyed talking with Dorothy on her "good" days. Today was one of them.

"Brian tells me the two of you have been seeing one another."

Rachel wasn't sure if Brian had told his mother about their relationship. "Yes, we have."

"I think it's wonderful. I've seen a change in him the past few months. He's had a hard time overcoming his past. I know part of that is his own doing. Most people don't care about the things he did as a teenager. But when you live in a small town, there are always those who dwell on the negative."

"Yeah, Brian seems to be pretty sensitive about that period of his life."

"A lot of it of is his father's fault. You do know that my husband was an alcoholic?"

"Yes, Brian told me."

"He was a good man until the bottle got the best of him. He was hard on Brian."

Rachel took Dorothy's hand. "You care a lot about your son."

"Yes, I do." Dorothy shook her head. "I admit there was a time when I wondered if he'd make it in the world. He went through those rebellious teenage years. Gave me my share of grief."

"Yes, he's told me. He regrets it, you know."

"You're good for him. I've been telling him it's time he settled down and found a wife. I'm not getting any younger, and I would like to live long enough to have grandchildren."

"Mrs. Nichols, it hasn't been that long since Brian and I started dating. We haven't discussed marriage or children."

"I can hope, can't I?"

Rachel smiled.

"By the way, when is the last time you saw him?"

"Yesterday when he came to my office to install a new door. Fire damaged the old one."

"Yes, I heard. Terrible thing about all those fires." Dorothy shook her head.

"Hope they catch the person responsible."

"So, how is my son? Wish he had time to see me. Can't remember the last time he stopped by."

Rachel couldn't help but feel a little guilty. She and Brian had been spending a lot of time together, but she also knew he still made a point to visit his mother often. It made her a little sad that Dorothy seemed to have forgotten those times. "He's been busy with the factory project. Now that he's playing in a band, practice takes up a lot of his free time. But I know for sure he was here last Friday."

Rachel heard a slight knock and looked to see an aide standing in the doorway. The young woman smiled apologetically, but Rachel nodded for her to come in.

"Friday?"

"The night of the fire at my office. He visited with you first. That's why he was late."

Dorothy raised her voice in agitation. "You're wrong. He told me he was coming, but he never made it that night."

"Mrs. Nichols, I'm sure you're mistaken."

"He didn't come. Susan can tell you." Dorothy nodded to the aide.

"No, ma'am. I'm certain her son didn't come on Friday. I was on duty all evening and she was quite upset over the fact he wasn't here. In fact, I tried to reach him several times at both his office and on his cell phone."

Rachel shook her head. Hadn't Brian told her he planned to visit his mom? Or did she just assume that was the reason for him being late in meeting her?

Chapter 23

After she left the nursing home, Rachel drove to a local Mexican restaurant to meet Brian for dinner. She didn't want to dwell on her visit with Dorothy. Brian was right. The memory lapses had gotten worse. The conversation began normally. Rachel was sure Dorothy was coherent. But now she was starting to forget Brian's visits. Or had she forgotten?

Brian was already sitting at a booth when Rachel arrived. He stood and placed a light kiss on her cheek "I hope you take note that for once I wasn't late. Never say I can't get somewhere before you."

Rachel slid into the booth. "Sorry. I got tied up at the nursing home."

He smiled. "Honestly, I just got here myself."

When the waitress came to take their drink order, Rachel was quick to answer. "Margarita on the rocks."

"Iced tea for me."

"I'll have those right out."

Brian looked at Rachel. "Rough day?"

"You could say that. Why?"

"I've noticed you haven't been drinking anything alcoholic of late. Not even wine."

"Yeah, well maybe I need something stronger today."

"You said you went to the nursing home."

Rachel nodded her head, hating that he brought up the subject.

"Did you see Mom?"

"Yeah."

"How was she?"

"When I first arrived, she seemed okay. Acted as if nothing was wrong. Then she..." Rachel shook her head.

"She what?"

"It's not that important."

"Tell me."

"She wanted to know when I last saw you. Said you hadn't visited in a while. She didn't even remember your visit from last Friday."

"That's because I wasn't there."

"You weren't? You were late meeting me. I thought you said you had visited."

"No, you asked me how she was doing, and I told you she was okay. I never said I had been to see her."

"But you planned to go. If I had known you could have met me earlier, I wouldn't have stayed at the clinic."

Brian frowned. "So what if I was late? Everyone isn't like you. Always on time. What's the big deal?"

The waitress returned with their drinks and asked if they were ready to order.

"Give us a few minutes," Brian said. When she walked away, he turned back to Rachel. "You were saying?"

"It seems like it happens more often. You were late the night we had dinner with Stephanie and Matt. It all started last summer when we were supposed to meet at the park."

"You're keeping count? There have been plenty of other times when I arrived on time. Even early."

"I know. Guess I'm too much of a stickler for punctuality."

"Then I'll work on being on time more often."

"Deal." She smiled.

"Probably the easiest one I've ever made."

Rachel shook her head. "Guess I overreacted, but all this business with the arsons, I... Seems like every time you've been late meeting me, there's been a fire."

Brian's eyes narrowed. "What are you saying?"

"Nothing. It's just coincidence. I told Alan he was wrong about seeing you at the back of my office building last Friday."

"Alan Davis? When did you talk to him? And why would you believe anything he has to say?"

"He saw someone behind my office shortly before the fire started. Said he thought it was you, but I told him he was mistaken. I think he may have seen the arsonist."

"Did he talk to the police?"

"I guess. Told him he should." Rachel lowered her eyes and shifted in her seat.

"What are you not telling me?"

"Right before you called to say you were at the front door, I heard a noise at the back of the building. I thought it might have been you."

"You think I started the fire?"

"No! I would never believe you would do anything like that."

"Then what are you thinking?"

"Nothing. After talking with Alan, I remembered hearing the noise. That's all. At any rate, even if you had been at the back, it doesn't mean you started the fire. Just coincidence." Rachel regretted the words as soon as she said them. She couldn't quite decipher the look on Brian's face. Hurt? Anger?

"How could you—" He shook his head.

"I'm sorry, I shouldn't have said that."

"I could take it when Matt questioned me. He was only doing his job. But I thought we had something special together. All those times you've said you believed in me. But they were just empty words."

"No that's not true. I meant what I said."

"Which time? When you said you cared for me or just now. You practically accused me of being an arsonist. If you can't trust me, there's nothing more to say."

"Brian, I'm sorry. Please listen."

"I've heard enough." He stood up from the table, pulled out his wallet, and threw some bills on the table.

"Where are you going?"

"I should have known better than to believe we could ever have a relationship."

"We do."

"Oh, yeah?" He smirked. "Have a good life." He turned and left.

Rachel watched him walk out of the door. He couldn't be leaving. Not after what they had shared. Why had she even brought up the conversation with Alan? She knew Brian wasn't responsible for the fires. But she had just destroyed the trust he'd felt for her.

She looked at the margarita, wishing it was a straight shot of tequila or bourbon. But no amount of alcohol could dull the ache she felt in her heart. With tears in her eyes, she got up from the table and left the restaurant, her untouched drink on the table.

***

Heather Stevens watched from across the room as Brian stormed out of the restaurant. It didn't take much to see he and Rachel disagreed about something. When Rachel left a few minutes later, Heather couldn't help but notice she had tears in her eyes. This wasn't a minor disagreement. It was something big.

Talk about being in the right place at the right time. Heather reached for her cell phone.

"I've got news," she said.

"This had better be good, Heather. You haven't been doing your job lately. I've come to believe I don't need you anymore."

"Oh, you'll need me all right. I can be there to pick up the broken pieces."

"What are you talking about?"

"There's trouble in paradise."

"Rachel and Brian?"

"Yes. Big time trouble if what I witnessed was any indication."

"That's good news."

"I've done my part. The rest is up to you."

***

Rachel hoped Brian would call Friday morning. Once he had a chance to think things over, he would realize she didn't blame him. After all, he and Matt had settled their differences on more than one occasion.

But as the morning went on and she didn't hear from him, she called his cell phone. The call went to voicemail. Just before she was scheduled to see her last patient of the day, she tried to reach Brian again on both his cell and office phone. "Brian, this is Rachel. We need to talk. It was all a big misunderstanding. Please, call me."

She rubbed her eyes, trying to ignore a growing headache. Her two o'clock appointment was a regular patient who loved to talk. Rachel usually enjoyed listening to the elderly woman, realizing she was lonely. But today Rachel wasn't in the mood for idle conversation. She couldn't help but think about their planned weekend away—something she had looked forward to. But it seemed as if it wouldn't happen. Brian wasn't going to call.

Taking a deep breath, Rachel knocked lightly on the exam room door and walked inside. The woman was busy chatting with Katrina. "How are you today, Mrs. Anderson?"

"Oh, pretty good. I was just telling that sweet nurse of yours about my new great-grandson. He started walking last week, and he's only ten and a half months old."

The woman continued to talk while Rachel washed her hands, but she tuned out the words. She opened her tablet to look at Katrina's notes. Putting on her best smile, she turned to the patient. "I see your vitals are good. Blood pressure is under control. You've maintained your weight. No recent falls. No complaints of pain. We'll get the results of your lab work back next week, and as long as those are good, I don't see any reason for you to return sooner than six months."

"Well, I do try to take care of myself. Now about my little grandson, I couldn't be prouder of him. Do you have children, Dr. Jackson?"

Rachel focused her attention on making notes in the patient's medical record and tuned out Mrs. Anderson's words. But when the woman tapped her on the arm, she was forced to pay attention.

"You didn't hear a word I said."

"I'm sorry, what?"

"I asked if you had any children."

"Uh. No. I'm not married."

"Oh. Well, that doesn't stop some people these days, although I can't see that happening to you. I'm sure you'll find the right man someday and settle down."

Why of all days did Mrs. Anderson bring up the subject of a husband and children? Her words only served as a reminder of what she had lost. Rachel managed to put on a smile. "Perhaps. As long as you don't have any problems, I'll see you in six months."

"Honey, what's wrong? You're not yourself today."

"I'm sorry. I have a headache. You take care of yourself, Mrs. Anderson. Katrina will walk you to the front desk." Rachel left the room, hurried to her private office, and checked her cell phone for any missed calls. Nothing. There was no use in hoping. Brian wasn't going to call. Gathering her things, she went to the front and spoke to Wendy and Katrina. "Can the two of you lock up and set the alarm? I'm out of here."

"Of course," Wendy said.

"Ready for that trip, I suppose?" Katrina's eyes were warm and bright.

"I'll see you both on Monday." Fighting back the tears, Rachel turned and walked out the door.

***

Brian pulled his cell phone from his pocket, checking for any missed calls or voicemails. He expected Rachel would phone again. She had called a half-dozen times on Friday. Maybe it was his headstrong nature. Perhaps it was pride. But he would not call her back. Her words had hurt him, and some wounds were too deep to heal quickly. If ever.

He thought Rachel was different, but now he knew she was just another one of those people who considered him to be like the "good for nothing" teenager he'd once been. She was probably calling only to appease her conscience. Rachel couldn't possibly feel anything for him. Not after the things she said on Thursday. Why was it the people he cared about the most were the ones who often hurt him?

You'll never amount to anything.

You want to be a rock star? Ha! You'd better think of something else because you're not good enough.

Why do you waste so much time on music? If you were any good at it, I would understand.

Brian flinched as he remembered the words spoken to him. They were as clear as if they had been said yesterday. He had tried to put that part of his life out of his memory, but of late old wounds had surfaced.

He managed to make it through the practice session with the band, even though he'd lain awake most of the night. A night he was supposed to spend with Rachel. Away from Driscoll Lake. Away from thoughts about fires and arsonists and business. Just the two of them. But that didn't happen.

Putting his cell phone back into his pocket, he resigned himself to the fact his relationship with Rachel was over.

"Brian, I thought you might want to rehearse that new number again," Danny Evans, the band leader, said. "After that, let's call it quits and get some rest before tonight."

"I'm not doing the song. I don't think I'm ready." The song was something he planned knowing Rachel would be in the audience. It would be too painful now, and the last thing he wanted to do was to break down on stage.

"Why not? You sounded great when we practiced a few nights ago."

"I said I'm not doing it."

"But you—"

"No. If you want me to sing another song, okay. If you don't want me to sing at all, that's fine too."

"Relax man, chill out. You can do something else." Danny turned to the rest of the band members and said, "Okay, that's it for now. Let's meet back here at six."

Brian grabbed his leather jacket and headed for the door before anyone could stop him. However, he wasn't fast enough. Danny caught him in the parking lot.

"You okay man?"

"I'm fine."

"Seem a bit edgy today. Something going on?"

"Nothing I care to discuss."

Danny put both hands in the air. "Hey, just trying to help."

"Don't worry. It won't interfere with my playing tonight. I'll throw myself into the performance one-hundred percent." Brian got in his pickup and spun out of the parking lot.

One thing in his life was certain. Music had always been his outlet—a place of refuge during some of the darkest moments of his life. And once again, he would seek its shelter to get him through what would undoubtedly be the most challenging road he'd had to face.

***

Two days had passed since Brian had walked out of the restaurant and Rachel's life. She called him several times. Left voicemails. Apologizing. Even drove to his house a couple of times only to find he wasn't home. He hadn't returned any of the calls.

Her words, spoken in haste, were wrong. Didn't Brian know how much she cared for him? He hadn't even given her a chance to explain.

If her office staff noticed anything, they didn't ask. Several times she'd caught Wendy and Katrina watching her. And although she'd put on concealer and used eye drops, it was hard to hide red puffy eyes.

When her phone rang late Saturday afternoon, she hurried to answer without checking the caller ID. "Hello? Brian?"

"Expecting someone else, huh?"

Rachel detected a bit of humor in her stepmother's voice. "Cecelia. I didn't pay attention to the caller ID. Good to hear from you."

"You probably would have been happier if I had been the person you were expecting. Who is this mysterious man? Something your father and I should know?"

"No. He's just a friend." She was back to using that terminology again. After Thursday, she doubted they were even that.

"I called to invite you for Thanksgiving. Cade is bringing his fiancée, Melissa. Nicole and Kevin will be here. Why don't you come and bring your friend? Did you say his name was Brian?"

"I doubt he would want to spend the holiday with me. Like I said, we're just friends. In fact, I won't be able to make it this year."

"We were hoping you could come since you don't have to worry about being on call at the hospital. Won't you close your clinic on Friday?"

"Yes."

"Then you'll have four days. So why not come?"

"I have a lot going on. Maybe next year."

"Your dad will be disappointed. If you can't come for Thanksgiving, how about Christmas?"

"I'll see."

"Is everything all right"

Rachel paused. Although Cecelia didn't give birth to her, she had that mother's intuition. "Everything is fine. Just busy. And a little tired."

"If you're sure."

"I am."

"Okay honey. Promise you'll call if you need anything."

"I will. And give Dad my love." Rachel ended the call. She hated lying to Cecelia, but she wasn't ready to tell her family about Brian. After all, what was there to say? It was apparent he no longer wanted to be a part of her life.

Chapter 24

The band's performance had gone well. As promised, Brian threw himself into the music, temporarily forgetting about Rachel and his other woes. Well, maybe not forgetting, but at least he didn't have time to dwell on things.

During intermission, Brian overheard several people remark how much better Radical was with their new drummer. And when they finished with a rousing performance of "Life in the Fast Lane," followed by another upbeat tune, they received a standing ovation. Although he wasn't in a stadium with fifty-thousand people in attendance, it still felt good.

"Take that, Dad," Brian said as he walked off stage at the end of the show.

He decided to drive back to Driscoll Lake after the band finished playing. He knew he wouldn't go to sleep right away. Might as well be at home in his own bed. Alone. What was supposed to be a special weekend had been a disaster.

An hour outside of Waco, he started to feel drowsy, so he found a convenience store and purchased a cup of coffee. Revived by the caffeine and the cold night air, he climbed back in his truck and switched on the radio. The music would help to keep him awake, and he sang along with several of the songs.

After a while, a familiar tune began to play. The same song had played the night he and Rachel went into Brewster to celebrate her new practice. His thoughts drifted back to the conversation they had on the drive home.

Who broke your heart? Was it your ex-wife?

Who said I'd had my heart broken?

I'm sorry, I shouldn't be asking you such personal questions.

Angie and I parted by mutual consent. And no one else has broken my heart.

It had been easy to say those words then. Ironic in a way. The very person who asked was the one who ended up hurting him the most.

***

Rachel was happy the weekend was over, but she didn't look forward to going into the office on Monday morning. Katrina would have questions about her trip, and Rachel wasn't ready to discuss the matter. Sometimes Katrina got a little too personal, but Rachel supposed it was her fault. She had encouraged familiarity outside of working hours. It was a little late to stop things now.

She entered through the back, taking notice of the new door Brian installed last week. So much had changed since then. Rachel wasn't sure if she and Brian could ever repair their relationship. If she had only kept her mouth shut.

It was no excuse, but she had been so discouraged after the visit with Dorothy. Speculating, or instead voicing her thoughts aloud, had been a mistake. Brian was sensitive about some subjects, but she would never have guessed he wouldn't take time to hear her out.

Taking a deep breath, she walked into the break room where Wendy and Katrina were already drinking coffee. She walked straight to the coffee pot and poured a cup before turning to them.

Wendy spoke first. "Good morning."

Rachel plastered a smile on her face. "Hello."

"Can't believe it's Monday already," Katrina said. "Bet you didn't want the weekend to end. Not that I would blame you."

"Actually, I was more than ready for today. I hope we'll be busy."

"Uh-oh. I take it your trip didn't go well."

Might as well get this over. Katrina wouldn't give up until she learned the truth. "I didn't go. And before you ask, it's not likely I'll be planning any more trips with Brian."

"What?"

"No way."

Wendy and Katrina spoke in unison, and they both stood for a moment, as if unable to say anything else. Katrina recovered first. "What happened?"

Rachel held up her hand. "We're not together anymore. But that's all I'm going to say about the matter."

She walked out of the break room, went into her private office, put her head on her desk, and wept.

***

Brian tried to ignore the incessant ringing of his phone. "Go away." He wasn't ready to face the world just yet. For that matter, who would be calling so early? He turned away from the offensive sound and pulled the covers over his head.

A short time later, the phone rang again. Brian pounded his fist into his pillow, opened one eye, and reached to answer. He recognized the number of his lead carpenter, Jack Richards.

"Hello?"

"Brian, this is Jack."

"What do you want this early in the morning?" Brian's words came out a bit harsher than he intended and he tried to calm his voice. Jack had done an excellent job with the factory project. With the first phase of the job nearing completion, the last thing he wanted was to anger the middle-aged man. Workers like him were hard to come by these days. "I'm sorry, Jack. Didn't expect you to call this early."

"It's almost nine, and you're usually on the job long before this time."

"What?" Brian sat up and looked at the clock. Had he slept this late?

"I called because something has happened at the factory site and I thought you'd want to get over here. I've already phoned the police."

"Please tell me it's not another fire."

"No, it's not that. There's been a break-in. Someone cut through the chain-link fence at the back of the building and went into the old factory section. As far as we can tell, they didn't take anything, but we're waiting for police to arrive."

"I'll be right there." Brian ended the call and jumped out of bed. He went into the bathroom and splashed some cold water on his face before pulling on a pair of jeans, a long-sleeved Henley shirt, and boots. After grabbing his phone and keys, he rushed out the door.

By the time he arrived at the factory, both Matt and Carlos Gonzales were at there. Brian hurried to talk to Matt. "What happened?"

"Someone broke into the building. Jack's inside now. We've asked the workers to stay away until we can dust for prints and look to see if there's any other evidence."

Brian shook his head. "One more thing to go wrong. I'm beginning to think this entire thing was a mistake."

"Could have been worse. A year ago, you weren't sure you'd ever be able to get the project off the ground."

"Maybe I shouldn't have tried."

"Hey, don't give up. You're so close to finishing now."

"What of it? I wished I'd never bought the place. The sooner I get this behind me, the better. Why did I think I could take on something as big as this and make it a success? At any rate, I'm not sure I'm going to keep the building."

"What gives? This doesn't sound like you. You've dreamed about this for years."

"Things change. And people aren't always what they seem."

"Something else wrong?"

"Nothing I want to talk about."

"Rachel doing okay?"

"How should I know?"

"You mean she didn't go with you this weekend?"

"That's another subject not open for discussion." Brian didn't want to talk about Rachel right now, not even to his best friend. Besides, this was hardly the time. When he looked to see Carlos and Jack come from the building, it provided the perfect opportunity to change the subject.

"Find anything?"

"Everything seems okay. I don't think anything is missing," Jack said.

Carlos looked at Brian. "I guess the person or persons got scared and ran off. You don't have an alarm system?"

Brian shook his head. "Too many workers coming and going. You don't think someone was trying to start another fire, do you?"

"No, but with everything going on, it might not be a bad idea to hire a security guard."

"I agree," Matt said. "You've got too much to lose."

"What difference does it make?" Brian turned and walked away.

***

Matt sat in his office, drumming his fingers on his desk. Something was wrong with Brian, he could sense it. Rachel was a part of the reason, but he suspected there was a more significant problem.

Matt had seen the look in Brian's eyes. One that hadn't been there in years. And there was the almost defeatist attitude, something that was often present when they were teenagers. It hadn't surfaced in a while, only on occasion. As far as Matt knew, the last time was years ago.

It was hard for Matt to understand how someone could have such a strong hold on another person, even from the grave. Brian had fought those demons before and won.

Matt shook his head. Maybe he should call his father. No, not yet. At any rate, it wasn't his place to call. Brian would do that if and when the need arose.

Instead, he looked at his watch. He hated to disturb Stephanie—they had an understanding not to call one another during the time she set aside for writing—but he had to talk to someone.

He called her cell phone. "Hey," he said when she answered. "Sorry to bother you."

"It's okay. I finished early today. What's up?"

"Have you talked to Rachel?"

"Not since last week. I'm sure she's busy today. She and Brian probably didn't get home until late last night."

"I don't think she went with him."

"What makes you say that? She was looking forward to the trip."

"Something has happened. Brian's not talking, but he's upset."

"Did they break up?"

"Not sure. Thought you might know something." Matt looked up when someone knocked. Carlos was standing outside his office door. "I have to go. Carlos is here. If you do talk to Rachel, don't say I told you anything."

***

Brian stared at the computer screen, trying to make sense of the open spreadsheet. His mind kept wandering, making it difficult to concentrate. How could he have been stupid enough to become involved with Rachel?

Not only had he allowed her in his personal life, but allowing her to become a business partner was not a wise move. Brian wished he could turn back the clock. He would have never allowed her to become more than a casual friend. But he had, and it cost him.

The personal relationship was over. Dissolving the business partnership would be harder, but not impossible. He just needed to formulate a proposal to his banker. It might take time, but he had an excellent credit rating.

Of course, the easiest thing would be to sell the building. He wished he had talked to that realtor in greater detail. Instead, he listened to Rachel, who had encouraged him to keep the place because she didn't want to see it fall into the wrong hands.

If she felt that strongly about a couple of buildings and a piece of land, why did she sell it to him in the first place? But now he couldn't sell it without her consent.

Brian rubbed the bridge of his nose. For the second time today, he wished he had never started this project.

You can't do anything right. One would think you'd be able to do a simple project. But even that's too hard for you. You're worthless.

The phone rang, bringing a welcome respite from his thoughts. After all these years, the wounds were still deep. He wasn't sure if they would ever heal.

Frowning, he looked at the caller ID. He wasn't one to believe in coincidence, but the number was from the real estate office in Brewster. "Brian Nichols."

"Mr. Nichols. This is Kimberly Eves. You may recall we spoke a few weeks back."

"Yes, I do."

"I wanted you to know that my client is still interested in the property. They're also interested in mineral rights, but I gather you don't own them."

"No, I don't. Ownership remains with Ra—the Cameron heir retained those. I'm not sure she will sell."

"Let me worry about that. My client is prepared to make her a generous offer."

Brian frowned, realization dawning. These people weren't interested in the buildings, but what might lie beneath the ground. With recent changes in drilling techniques and the discovery of a significant natural gas field in Tarrant County, investors were scrambling to buy up all the oil and gas royalties they could.

"Would this sell be dependent upon your client's ability to purchase the mineral rights?"

"Not necessarily. I know you weren't interested in selling when we last spoke, but if you think there's a chance, I'll contact my client and have them make an offer."

"Actually, I am interested. However, I've made some significant improvements to the buildings since their last offer. Phase one of my project is over ninety-five percent complete, and we've just started on phase two."

"I'll talk to my client and get back to you."

Brian hung up the phone, not believing his luck. If this deal went through, he would be able to sell the property and make a decent profit. More importantly, he would be able to dissolve his last tie to Rachel.

It was time for him to move on with his life. A life without her.

Chapter 25

Rachel managed to make it through the past couple of days on autopilot without answering many questions. After she spoke to Katrina and Wendy on Monday morning, neither of them had mentioned Brian's name again.

Stephanie had phoned that evening. Rachel detected the concern in her voice. She couldn't help but wonder if Brian had talked to Matt who in turn told his wife.

Rachel appreciated the fact Stephanie hadn't been inquisitive, secure in their friendship. Sometimes things were best left unspoken. Stephanie would be there whenever Rachel was ready to talk. And Rachel knew she would eventually have to talk to her.

Brian may not have talked to Matt. He had a habit of clamming up about certain things. Regardless, Matt and Stephanie needed to know. Rachel didn't want to put either of them in an awkward position.

She swallowed the lump in her throat, remembering the wedding, the dinner Matt and Stephanie hosted, and the night at Pinnacle. Stephanie would always be Rachel's friend. The bond they shared was too strong to allow anything to come between them. Matt and Brian would remain friends. However, the times when the four of them did something together was a thing of the past.

Rachel glanced at her watch. It was just after two. She had time to call Stephanie before her next patient. She reached for her cell phone when it rang. Brian's number appeared on the caller ID.

Her pulse quickened, and she closed her eyes and took a deep breath. "Hello?"

Brian's words were quick and to the point. "I received an offer today from someone who wants to buy the factory. I've decided to sell."

"What? You can't do that."

"Can't? I can and I will."

"Brian, the factory was your dream. You're so close to completing the project. I would hate to see you do something you'll later regret."

"Spare me your concern. Since you have a vested interest, you'll have to agree to the sell. And don't worry, you'll get every cent of your money and then some."

"I don't care about the money. You know the place means a lot to me."

"Then you should have kept it. If it was that important to you, why did you agree to sell it to me?"

"Because I thought you…" Her voice broke.

"I hope you won't try to stop me. It's better this way. After the sale is final, you'll be rid of me for the last time."

"Who says I—"

"Don't go there. You said enough the other night."

Rachel sighed. There was no sense in trying to talk to him. He'd made up his mind. "Whatever. But I still think you're making a big mistake." She pressed the button to end the call.

Propping her elbow on her desk, she rubbed her forehead. How did they get to this point after what they had shared the past few weeks? Didn't their relationship mean anything to him? A soft knock at the door disturbed her thoughts, and she looked up to see Wendy standing in the doorway.

"Are you okay?"

"I'm fine."

"You sure? You haven't acted like yourself the past few days."

"A little more tired than usual. That's it."

"Katrina and I have been concerned."

"That's kind of you."

"Dr. Jackson, I don't know what happened, and I'm not trying to pry, but if you need to talk to someone, I'm a good listener."

"I appreciate the offer."

"I understand. If you change your mind, I'm available."

"Thanks. That means a lot to me. Did you need something else?"

"Yes. I wanted to remind you about the cancer research fundraiser on Friday. One of the organizers called today to confirm your attendance. They're finalizing seating arrangements."

"Is that this Friday?"

"Yes."

"I'd forgotten all about it. Guess I should go. Call back and tell them I'll be there."

***

Brian sat his phone on the desk when he heard the line click dead. The conversation had gone better than he expected. Rachel hadn't put up much of an argument. He thought she might attempt to appeal to his sentimental side since she was so attached to the place. However, she didn't even inquire as to the identity of the buyer.

When the real estate agent phoned today, Brian was surprised at the generous offer. Of course, he knew better than to accept right away, merely telling the agent he would give the matter serious consideration. Might even negotiate for more. If these investors wanted the property bad enough, they would come through.

What makes you think you could do something like that?

The unwelcome thought invaded his mind, and he quickly pushed it aside. The last thing he wanted was to drag up old memories. Things that were best left buried in the past. Too many of those memories had surfaced of late, but right now Brian had more important things to do.

A substantial profit would have significant tax implications. Although Matt's father had retired, he still provided Brian with tax advice. It was time to give him a call.

Dan Bradford's voice was cheerful when he answered the phone. "Good to hear from you. It's been a while."

"Yeah, I've been busy. Sorry. Sounds like I'm trying to make excuses."

"Don't worry about it. Nell and I have been on the road a lot since Matt's wedding."

"I wonder if I might come by the house and talk with you."

"You don't need to ask. You're welcome here anytime."

"I know that."

"Something troubling you?"

"No. Not really. I need some tax advice."

"I'm glad to help. Why don't you stop by this evening around seven? Nell has a women's event and won't be here."

Brian closed his eyes. He knew that by mentioning Nell's absence, Dan was saying it would be okay to talk about anything. But even though Dan Bradford had been more like a father than his own, Brian wasn't ready to open up. "It isn't necessary for her to be away, but seven works for me."

***

Dan Bradford closed the computer program, sat back in his chair, and smiled at the young man sitting opposite him. In many ways, Dan was almost as close to Brian as he was to his own son. It was hard to imagine the well-respected business owner was once a troubled and rebellious teenager.

He recalled the day Dorothy Nichols had called him in tears. "I don't know what to do with him anymore. He's smoking, drinking, and I'm afraid if something doesn't change, he'll resort to using drugs. A couple of weeks ago, Kyle Lawrence brought him home. Brian was passed out drunk. Couldn't remember anything the next day. Dan, I don't want him to turn into a carbon copy of his father."

"You know I'd like to help, but he has to be willing to listen."

"I know, but I'm at my wit's end. All this business with Cameron. People are saying the plant may have to close and if it does, I won't have a job, and you know I can't depend on Thomas anymore. He's part of the problem with Brian."

"Relax, Dorothy. If you lose your job, you'll have one with me. And try not to worry about Brian. I'll do whatever I can."

At first, Brian hadn't been the easiest person to deal with. He was reluctant to talk and seemed proud of his "bad boy" image. Dan thanked God his own son, though not perfect, had never given him any grief. Eventually, Brian began to open up. He told Dan he had already stopped messing with alcohol. "I quit cold turkey," he said. "Something happened that helped me see where I was heading. I don't want to be like my father."

Dan soon realized behind the tough exterior was an emotionally troubled teenager. Both physical and verbal abuse leave scars, but often those left by verbal abuse take the longest to heal. They fester and grow. Hidden to the outside world. Sometimes they surface, often to reappear months or years later.

Dan was determined to make Brian see his self-worth. When he discovered Brian was nearly at the top of his class academically, Dan encouraged him to get a college degree. He already knew Brian was a talented musician.

"I don't care about college. I keep my grades up so I can stay in the high school band. That's about the only time I get to play."

Dan wanted to ask what he meant by that statement but decided to let Brian open up about it when he was ready.

"Music is my life. Someday I'll use it to get away from Driscoll Lake."

"Away from the town or something else?"

"It doesn't matter. My dream is to become a rock star. Not much chance of that happening around here."

"From what I've seen, you certainly have the talent. I won't discourage you if that's what you want, but Brian, you're smart. A college degree could take you far in life. Much farther than a musical career."

As time progressed, Dan and Nell often invited Brian into their home. Somewhere along the way, Brian and Matt became good friends. Brian began to share more about his home life and the problems with his father. As Dan suspected, Brian was a victim of intense verbal abuse.

Thomas Nichols was not only a drunk, but he took every available opportunity to belittle his son, telling Brian he was worthless and criticizing both this musical and academic talents. It was almost as if he wanted to drive Brian to a life of alcohol or drug abuse.

Dan could never understand why someone could be so cruel. And on the one occasion where Thomas resorted to physical violence, and Brian retaliated, it was all Dan could do not to beat some sense into the man. But he knew to do so would be stooping to the same level. He had quietly gone to Thomas and convinced him not to press charges against Brian. "You've done your best to destroy his self-esteem. Don't do something that will follow him the rest of his life."

When Thomas died from alcohol poisoning shortly after Brian graduated from high school, the news came almost as a relief to both Brian and his mother.

"Well, what do you think?" Brian's words jarred Dan back to the present.

"You'll have some extra tax debt due to capital gains, but nothing you can't handle. And even after paying off the debt incurred, you'll still be in good shape financially."

"That's good to know."

"Why are you doing this son?"

"What do you mean?"

"Why are you selling the factory? For years, you've dreamed of turning that place into something useful for the town. Why stop now?"

"I don't think I have to tell you the fire last year delayed things and put me in a bit of a financial strain for a while."

"It's not that way anymore. Besides, you have a partner who's more than willing to help you see this project through."

"Yeah, well, Rachel and I don't seem to agree on a lot of things."

"But you told me she's only a financial partner."

"True, but… I don't think I can…" Brian shook his head. "Let's just say it's best to sell now and allow the buyer to decide if they want to continue the second phase."

"Don't let him win."

"Who are you talking about?"

"Your father. If you give up now, he'll win."

***

Rachel walked into the crowded banquet hall for the annual fundraiser. More than once she considered not coming and instead making a generous donation, but since her social life was lacking these days, she decided to attend.

"Good evening, Dr. Jackson. Glad you could join us tonight." The young woman seated at the greeter's table smiled as she spoke.

Rachel recognized Kara Mitchel from the public affairs office at Memorial Hospital in Brewster.

"Thank you, Kara," Rachel said looking around the crowded room. "Looks like you have a good attendance."

"Yes, it is. Should be a special night. We have some great entertainment lined up. You're at table eleven, the second row from the stage."

Rachel took the program from her and walked into the banquet room. Many of the people in attendance were physicians she recognized from her days on staff at Memorial.

Soft music played over the intercom as she made her way to her assigned table. She stopped short when she saw who else sat there. She recognized Dalton McRae, a lawyer from Brewster and his wife Liz, along with Michael Barnett, a physician Rachel knew from her days of being on staff at Brewster Memorial.

Sitting next to the only vacant seat was Alan Davis. She stopped, about to turn and leave when Alan spotted her.

"Rachel, I was beginning to think you weren't going to make it." He stood and held the empty chair.

"Thank you," she said forcing a smile.

"I believe you know everyone here."

Rachel nodded to the others. She had the utmost respect for Dr. Barnett, had interacted with his wife Jackie at social events, and found both of them to be quite amiable.

However, she despised Dalton McRae. He was supposed to be a top-notch trial lawyer, but Rachel thought he was arrogant and condescending. His wife Liz was not only snobbish but known to indulge in gossip whenever she could use the information to her advantage.

The dinner conversation was pleasant even though Liz McRae complained about the food. "One would think they could do better than this given the price we're paying for the meal."

"I happened to think the food is delicious," Rachel said.

Liz merely rolled her eyes and turned her attention to the young woman on stage. Abby Marsh was a resident of Brewster, in her early twenties, and an incredibly talented vocalist and guitarist.

When she finished her performance, Kara Mitchell came on stage. "Thank you for that spectacular performance, Abby. I think everyone will agree this area has a lot of talent."

A round of applause went up as Kara addressed the crowd. "I want to thank you all for coming tonight to support such a worthy cause. Don't forget to have all bids for tonight's silent auction placed by nine.

"And now, are you ready for some more local talent? Let's give a round of applause to Driscoll Lake's popular band, Radical."

Rachel's jaw dropped. She had no idea Brian would be here tonight. If she had bothered to look at the program, she would have seen it and been able to make an exit before they took the stage. But to leave right now would give some people cause for speculation.

"You looked surprised, Rachel," Liz raised her eyebrows. "I would have thought you knew who would be here tonight. It's no secret you and the band's drummer are an item. How come you didn't know he was going to be here?"

Rachel glared at her.

"Give it up Liz," Jackie Bennett said. "Rachel's private life is none of your concern."

Sending a look of gratitude to Jackie, Rachel watched as Brian took his place behind the drums and the band began to play a lively number. He always seemed the most relaxed when he played. Music came naturally to him. He could have easily made it in the music world. Rachel was glad he chose to stay in Driscoll Lake.

For all the good it did. Brian might as well be on the road touring with a rock band. He made it clear a few days ago the two of them didn't have a future together. Rachel looked away from him. From the corner of her eye, she caught Alan studying her. She looked down, not wanting him to see any hint of the sadness she felt. She certainly didn't want him to know her relationship with Brian was over.

But she couldn't hide it long. Driscoll Lake was too small. Alan would either overhear somewhere or figure it out on his own if he didn't already know.

Somehow, Rachel managed to make it through the band singing several numbers without falling apart. As far as she knew, Brian had not looked in her direction, so she allowed herself to listen to the music and enjoy being able to see him. Most of the audience seemed to like the music, and several couples moved onto the dance floor.

Rachel didn't realize Alan had moved closer to her and slipped his arm around the back of her chair.

"Want to dance?" he asked.

"Don't even go there. And kindly remove your arm from the back of my chair." She turned to look back, and the stage and her eyes met Brian's. He quickly looked away, and it was hard for Rachel to discern his emotion.

Liz McRae took that moment to speak up. "Well, aren't we touchy tonight? I don't think Rachel cares much for you, Alan. Of course, Rachel, anyone can't help but notice you haven't taken your eyes off that drummer. Like mother, like daughter. Choosing men beneath your social status."

Rachel bristled at her tone. Liz was known to flaunt her husband's career and wealth. She would never associate herself with someone she considered to be "beneath her." Rachel wasn't like that, and to see Liz look down at Brian made her angry. However, she managed to hold her tongue, not wanting to cause a scene.

"Liz, do you ever say anything nice?" Jackie Bennett said.

"Come now. Everyone knows Ron Jackson didn't have two pennies to rub together when he married Madelyn. I always thought he was after her money."

"How dare you say that about my father?"

Michael Bennett was quick to speak up. "Back off, Liz. A lot of physicians worked their way through medical school, including me. There's no shame in that. Rachel's father is one of the most respected surgeons in Austin."

Rachel decided it was time to leave. She wasn't going to sit and listen to Liz's condescending words. When she started to stand up, the lead singer of the band began to speak.

"How many of you like the Eagles?"

Rachel turned her attention back to the stage as several members of the audience voiced their affirmation.

"For our next number, drummer Brian Nichols takes the lead on one of their tunes."

There was another round of applause, and Rachel couldn't help but smile. She never got the chance to hear him sing lead. Not surprising he would pick an Eagles' song. Before the music began to play, she wondered which tune he would sing.

Rachel half-hoped it would be what Don Henley once described as their "anti-politically correct song." She would love to see Dalton and Liz McRae react to the line about lawyers. And the thought of making Alan uncomfortable caused her to smile inwardly.

No, Brian might be a rebel, but he wouldn't sing that song at an event like this. Probably something fun and peppy like "Take it Easy." But when the music began, it wasn't what she expected. Her eyes misted with tears as she listened to him sing the words to "The Best of My

Love." The words of the song seem to parallel their own lives.

His eyes met hers, and this time he didn't turn away. There wasn't any sign of anger but a look of sadness. Of hurt. It was if he was singing the song to her.

When the song ended, Jackie put her hand on Rachel's arm. "Are you okay?"

Rachel suddenly felt nauseous. The room seemed too warm. "I don't feel well. Excuse me."

She practically ran to the restroom, barely making it to one of the stalls, emptying the contents of her stomach in the toilet.

Chapter 26

Rachel stood at the sink and looked at her reflection in the mirror. She rarely got sick. Maybe Liz McRae had been right about the food. Or was it something else? She quickly pushed that thought aside, not wanting to consider the possibility. Taking some paper towels, she wet them with cold water and touched them to her throat.

Still feeling a little nauseous, she discarded the towels in a trash can. Fresh air would help, so she made her way outside into the chilly November night.

A few people mingled near the door, but Rachel didn't want to become involved in a conversation with anyone. There were some park benches beneath a large oak tree a few yards away, and no one was sitting on them. It would be a good place to relax for a while. Hopefully, the nausea would soon pass, then she would go back inside for her purse and then could leave.

Recalling the incident at her office a few weeks back, she felt a little apprehensive. However, enough people were nearby. No reason to be afraid. She was almost to the bench when she saw a man leaning against the tree. He wore a black leather jacket as protection against the night air. It was Brian.

A lit cigarette was in his hand. He must be smoking more often.

Rachel wanted to turn back before he saw her. He'd made it plain he didn't want anything to do with her, but she couldn't forget the look in his eyes on that last song. She watched as he took a drag from the cigarette before tossing it to the ground and grinding it beneath the heel of his boot.

He looked up to see her standing there.

"What are you doing here? Follow me outside?"

"No, I...I wasn't feeling well. Thought the fresh air might help."

"Help yourself." He started to walk away.

"Brian, we need to talk."

"About what?"

"About us. I know this isn't the time or the place but—"

"There will never be a time or place. Besides, there isn't an 'us.' You made that pretty clear when you voiced your doubts about me regarding those fires."

"I wasn't accusing you."

"Save it. Anyway, didn't take you long to move on."

"What's that supposed to mean?"

"Alan Davis."

"I'm not here with him. I came for the fundraiser, and somehow the organizers stuck me at the same table with him."

"Yeah, right. You expect me to believe that?"

Rachel clasped her hands across her stomach as another wave of nausea swept over her.

"What's wrong?" Eve with the animosity between them, there was no mistaking the concern in his voice.

Taking a deep breath of air, she said, "It's nothing. Probably something I ate. I'll be fine. The queasiness seems to have subsided."

"Are you sure? You look pale."

She nodded and opened her mouth to speak when Alan walked up and put his hand on her arm.

"Liz said you weren't feeling good. Want me to take you home now? We can leave early."

Rachel turned to see Brian's lips curl. His eyes were cold as he turned and walked away.

Rachel jerked away from Alan. "How dare you? Get your hands off me. And don't ever come near me again."

***

Alan watched Rachel walk away. He had succeeded in the sense that Brian believed he and Rachel were involved. But he had also failed. Heather had been right. Rachel wasn't interested in him. Her breakup with Brian didn't make a difference.

It wouldn't matter if he waited six days or six years. Rachel wasn't likely to change her mind. He hated to admit it, but the time had come for a different tactic. Or maybe it was time to give it up altogether. The promise he'd made was foolish. He thought back to a particular conversation from a year ago.

"Everything is out of my hands now. It's up to you."

"Don't you think it's time to put it behind you and move forward? Isn't what you lost, your own flesh and blood, worth more than a piece of land? If you keep going, someone else could get hurt."

"I want what is rightfully mine. One of the Cameron ancestors stole it from my family. My great-grandfather couldn't prove it, but I know how those Camerons operate. Now it's up to you."

"What do you expect from me?"

"I don't care how you do it, but I trust you can take care of Rachel Jackson. Promise me that."

"I'll do what I can."

The sound of a car door jolted Alan back to the present. A promise was a promise. He needed to visit someone and make one last attempt to persuade him to change his mind. And if he was unsuccessful, come Monday morning, he'd put his other plan into action.

***

Brian finished loading his drums into the truck. The rest of the band members had already stowed all their instruments. They stood together in the parking lot, talking about the show.

"Good event," the lead guitarist said.

Danny Evans agreed. "Yeah. I don't mind donating our time to a worthwhile cause such as this one. Besides, it's good publicity. Had a couple of people approach me about the possibility of doing a few parties during the holidays."

"As long as they don't interfere with family events, I'm good with it," the keyboard player said.

Danny looked at Brian. "What about you? You game?"

"Don't have much family. I'm good." Brian reached into his pocket for a cigarette and lit it. He was smoking too many of them. Years after kicking the habit, he'd allowed himself to pick it up again. Cigarettes had once helped perpetuate his "bad boy" image. He didn't need the perception or the cigarettes now. He'd only thought he needed them as a teenager.

So now you've taken up smoking those damned things? Don't you know nicotine is addictive? But why doesn't it surprise me that you'd need a crutch?

That's rich. Coming from someone who can't control his dependence on the bottle.

Danny's voice brought Brian back to the present. "It's getting cold out here. Why don't we go to the Red Barn for a few drinks and talk about it there?"

The last place Brian wanted to be tonight was a bar. It would be too easy to give into temptation. "No, thanks. I'm going home. Talk you guys later."

"Hey, man. You okay?" Danny said.

Brian crushed the half-smoked cigarette beneath his boot. Shame to waste it. "I'll unwind at home. Whatever you guys decide about the holidays, is fine with me." He got into his truck and drove out of the parking lot.

Rachel consumed his thoughts on the drive home. He should have considered the possibility she would be at the event. Had he known, he would have never sung that Eagles' song. Especially since she was there with Alan. But it had been a request from one of the event organizers, so it wouldn't have looked good for him to have back out.

He was glad there was an intermission right after he finished singing. He couldn't get out of the building fast enough. But then he saw Rachel. Talking to her was almost his undoing. She said she wasn't feeling well but shrugged it off. He couldn't help but notice her pale color. If the dark circles under her eyes were any indication, she hadn't been getting a lot of rest. He could relate to that. More than a week had passed since he'd had a decent night's sleep. He'd almost reached out to her.

Then Alan had shown up. And her denial of being with him went out the window when he asked if she needed to leave early. The fact that she had turned to Alan was the final nail in the coffin He had managed to convince her that being with him was worthwhile. And that left Brian out in the cold.

A few weeks ago, Rachel claimed to have detested Alan. But Brian thought about most of the audience tonight. Doctors, lawyers, business executives. Not lowly building contractors who played with a rock band on the side. Rachel was with the type of people she was accustomed to. The more he thought of, the more he realized he'd been a fool to think they could have had a future together.

***

Rachel parked her Corvette and waited for the garage door to close. She went into the house through the utility room entrance, slamming the door behind her. Pausing to take a few deep breaths, she walked to the kitchen for a glass of water.

Alan had gone too far this time. Yes, he made his comment appear innocent enough, but anyone who didn't know would assume they had gone to the benefit together. Rachel didn't doubt he did it to anger Brian and to further drive a wedge between them.

Not that it wasn't deep enough already. Rachel wasn't sure if they would ever be able to repair the rift between them. She had hurt Brian deeply. And even that all started because of a comment from Alan.

Rachel sat the empty glass on the kitchen counter a little harder than she intended. She picked it up to make sure it didn't crack as it met with the hard granite surface. Satisfied, she turned and stormed up the stairs to her bedroom, slamming doors and dresser drawers as she went about getting undressed.

She opened the door of her walk-in closet and stepped out of the sequined dress, tossing it aside without bothering to place it on a hanger. Kicking her silver pumps off, she slipped on her favorite nightshirt and then walked into the bathroom to remove her make-up. She glanced at her reflection in the mirror. Her hazel eyes looked as if they could slice through a thick plate of steel. What her father once described as, "Never make Rachel angry unless you want to suffer the consequences" look.

She rarely got this livid. Even the drive home wasn't long enough for her to cool down. Rachel had little doubt that Alan cajoled the event organizers into placing her at his table—and in clear view of the stage. He knew Brian would be there, and he carefully orchestrated things to make it appear as if they came together.

Too much to be a coincidence. The occasion when he leaned close to whisper in her ear, placing his arm on her chair, and then showing up outside just as Brian started to open up. It was apparent Alan was trying to make Brian believe there was something between the two of them.

Rachel knew now that Alan had been lying to her when he said he understood he could never take Brian's place. That was a bald face lie. What else had he lied about?

"Crap. I bet he lied about seeing Brian behind my office that night, too." Rachel had a sickening feeling, and it wasn't related to the bout of nausea she had earlier. If Alan lied about that, was there any validity to the other things he had said?

Why had she been so quick to believe him? Had it not been for everything else—Brian's lateness on several occasions, someone seeing him near Curtis Lawrence's home, cigarettes being found at each scene. But deep down she knew Brian wasn't responsible. How could she have doubted him so quickly?

***

Alan looked around the room. Hospital visits always depressed him, but coming here was less likely to raise questions than visiting his friend anywhere else.

"I told you never to visit me. You're taking a big chance."

"Is there anything wrong with a lawyer visiting his client?"

"Nothing, except you weren't my defense counsel."

"No, but I could be the one handling your estate. With your situation as it is, estate planning isn't unreasonable."

"What's the real reason you came?"

"Well," Alan said, drawing out his response. "You know that property you've always wanted? I may have found a way to make it happen."

"The old Cameron place? Thought that was out of the picture."

"It was, but, there have been some new developments. I'm fairly certain Nichols will sell."

"What sort of changes?"

"The rumor mill has it that he's the prime suspect in a series of arsons. If he's arrested and charged, he'll need a lawyer. Good defense attorneys aren't cheap. He'll need the money."

"So?"

"He's already received a lucrative offer. According to the realtor, he's considering the sell."

"You don't get it, do you? I don't give a damn about what's above the ground. The oil and mineral rights are where the real money lies. And Rachel Jackson has control of those."

"She might be convinced to reconsider."

"How's that?"

"You leave it up to me. I'll take care of Rachel Jackson. And Brian Nichols."

Chapter 27

"Dr. Jackson?"

Rachel looked up to see Wendy standing in the doorway of her private office. "Yes Wendy?"

"Is everything okay? You're still not acting like yourself."

"I'm still a little tired but otherwise okay." That wasn't entirely true. Rachel had been sick on and off since Friday. She first thought it might have been something she ate at the fundraiser. However, she was able to eat and hold food down the following day. A stomach bug likely wouldn't have lasted more than twenty-four hours.

It's not a stomach bug, and you know it. She became lost in thought and forgot Wendy was still standing at her door. "I'm sorry, Wendy. Was there something else?"

"Yes." She held an envelope in her hand. "This came for you. Certified mail. I thought it might be important, so I decided to bring it to you now."

"Thanks. I'll take it."

After handing the envelope to Rachel, Wendy turned and left the room.

Rachel started to put the letter aside when the return address caught her eye. Why would an attorney in Florida contact her, and what was so important to send certified mail? Curious, she tore open the envelope and began to read.

My name is Donald Roberts. I am an attorney representing a firm interested in purchasing oil and mineral interests in the State of Texas. Our records indicate you are the holder of such rights on property in and around Driscoll Lake, Texas. Specifically, the company is interested in the property located at 705 Industry Drive.

Rachel read the remainder of the letter. Industry Drive was the location of the old factory. Why would someone only be interested in that particular area? She owned the mineral rights to much more extensive tracts of land. When she sold the Cameron homestead, she retained the rights to almost two-hundred acres. The factory location was somewhere around twenty acres. Didn't make sense. The letter continued with contact instructions if she was interested in their rather generous offer.

At any rate, she had no intention to sell her interests, no matter what Brian decided to do with the property. She tossed the letter aside. Lunch break was over, and she had patients to see. When she stood up from her desk, she felt a little dizzy and a bit nauseous.

"Not again."

"What's wrong?" Katrina stood in the doorway.

"Nothing. Just a little dizzy."

"Are you sure you don't have anything contagious? Should you be seeing patients?"

"No. It's not like I'm unable to eat. It comes and goes." Rachel stood still for a few minutes until the nausea passed. "See, I'm fine now. Let's go see our next patient."

"Okay, but if this keeps up, promise me you'll get checked out."

Rachel knew Katrina's concern was genuine. "Thanks. I will."

***

Brian received another call from the real estate agent on Wednesday morning. "Mr. Nichols, Kimberly Eves here. I wondered if you've considered the offer to buy your property. My client is anxious to hear from you."

"I'm considering the offer, but there are a couple of details I need to work out first."

"I see. When can I expect to hear from you?"

Brian sighed. He was making excuses. Rachel hadn't contacted him since their last conversation. He needed her okay if he decided to sell. There was no reason to keep the place. Whatever plans and dreams he'd had didn't seem important. Besides, the offer was more than generous.

But before he could answer, he'd have to talk to Rachel again. Why had he ever agreed to her proposition? He'd known of too many friendships destroyed because of a business partnership. Not to mention when your business partner was also your ex-lover.

"Mr. Nichols?"

"Sorry. Just thinking. It's Thanksgiving week. I'll make a decision and get back to you early next Monday."

"If that's as soon as you can give me your answer, I guess my client will have to live with that. But I must tell you they are most anxious to close this deal. I can't promise the offer will remain open if you wait much longer to decide."

"If they want the property bad enough, they'll wait. If they decide to withdraw the offer, so be it." Brian ended the call. He didn't like the idea of being pressured into making a decision. A few days ago, when the offer first came, he thought it was the perfect way out of a difficult situation. But yesterday, he'd gone to the site. Now that the first part was near completion, some of the workers had expressed their eagerness to get started on the second phase. And even he had to admit that seeing the old brick building reignited his passion for wanting the job completed.

He had allowed his emotions over dealing with Rachel cloud his decision. There had to be an alternative. Some way he could keep the property but at the same time dissolve his business partnership with Rachel. When the tenants began to occupy the building, he would have additional income. And although he might have to cut a few corners, he would use every last cent of rental income to pay Rachel back.

She had been right about one thing. The Cameron place had been his dream. Why should he allow their dispute destroy that? Or was the disagreement with Rachel the real reason he considered selling? Brian knew it wasn't.

His father's words kept replaying in his mind.

You'll never amount to anything. You'll always be a loser.

Brian slammed his fist on the desk. "No, Dad. You're not going to win this time."

He picked up his phone to call the real estate agent but stopped before he pressed the call button. He'd already said he would give his decision the following week. No need to rush things. Let them sweat a bit. Monday morning, he would call and decline the offer.

***

Rachel stepped out of her 'Vette and took a deep breath. The crisp autumn air was refreshing. Reaching into the car, she grabbed the sack containing a six-pack of ginger ale and box of crackers.

She locked the car and hurried into the office where Wendy and Katrina had already gathered in the break room.

"Good morning." Rachel removed a can from the plastic ring and placed the rest in the refrigerator. She filled a glass with ice and poured the ginger ale.

"I stopped by the bakery this morning. Bought a variety of goodies. Cinnamon rolls, cream cheese Danish, and even a couple of chocolate eclairs." Katrina lifted the lid on the still warm box of pastries.

The delicious aroma permeated the air. Something Rachel usually found enticing. But not today. The minute she got a whiff of cinnamon, her stomach began to feel queasy. "I think I'm going to be sick." Rachel sat the glass on the counter and hurried from the room.

A few minutes later, Rachel sat behind her desk, clutching damp paper towels to her throat. Something had to give. She was rarely sick, and this little bout of illness had gone on long enough. When she heard a soft knock on her door, she looked up to see Wendy standing there with the glass of soda in her hand.

"Thought you might want this."

"Thanks." Rachel motioned for her to come into the office.

"Do I need to call and cancel the rest of today's appointments? A couple of patients are already in the waiting room, but I still have time to notify the others."

"No, I'm okay now. This has been coming and going for a few days, but I'll be fine. The ginger ale helps."

"I understand. It was one of the few things that helped settle my stomach when I had morning sickness." Wendy's face colored. "I'm sorry, I didn't mean to insinuate anything. I mean, it helped with nausea, and I'm not often sick."

"It's okay. I've had a lot going on, and I'm just a little run down. Nothing a few days of rest won't cure."

"Guess I'd better get back to the front desk." Wendy turned and left the room, closing the door behind her.

Rachel had decided to close the clinic at noon. Having Thanksgiving Day and the Friday after off would give her four days to recover from whatever was causing this sickness. She needed the downtime.

Once she was alone, Rachel reached for her phone to look at her calendar. No use in putting it off anymore. It had been six weeks since her last period. As much as she wanted to deny the possibility of being pregnant, she knew she was carrying Brian's child.

***

After the clinic closed for the long Thanksgiving weekend, Rachel drove to a drugstore in Brewster. She could have purchased a home pregnancy test in Driscoll Lake, but the town had too many sets of eyes and ears. No reason to become the newest subject of the rumor mill. If she were pregnant, her friends would know soon enough. But Rachel would tell them in her own time, on her terms.

When she arrived home, she went upstairs and changed clothes, taking the kit with her. Might as well find out now.

A few minutes later, Rachel sat down on the bed to wait for the results. Three minutes seemed like an eternity. When the appointed time was up, she held her breath and turned the stick over to see the results.

Positive. Maybe there was a mistake. She and Brian had been careful. Except for the first time. The time when he wanted to wait. The time she assured him everything would be okay. And it should have been. But even then, she knew there was a chance this could have happened.

Of course, there was the outside possibility the test result was wrong. Maybe she would be in the less than one percent of women with a false positive. As much as she wanted to deny it, her body told her otherwise.

"I'm going to be a mother," she whispered. Part of her wanted to jump with joy. After all, she wanted a child for a long time. But not like this. Although Rachel had dreamed of having Brian's baby someday, she didn't want to be a single mother. The pregnancy couldn't have come at a worse time. Their relationship was probably beyond repair.

"What am I going to do?" Rachel put her head in her hands and wept.

When the tears subsided a few minutes later, she got up from the bed, walked to the bathroom sink, and splashed cold water on her face. Getting upset wouldn't be good for the baby. No matter what happened, she was going to raise this child. But right now, she needed someone to talk to.

She went back to the bedroom, picked up her phone, and called Stephanie.

"Hello?"

"Hi, it's Rachel. Hope I'm not disturbing you. I know tomorrow is Thanksgiving and you're probably busy."

"I'm not doing anything. Matt and I are going to his parent's house tomorrow, and Nell insists on doing the entire meal. I've finished writing for the day."

"Is Matt there?"

"No, he won't be home for at least a couple of hours."

"Good. I need to talk to you alone. Can I come over?"

"Of course. Are you okay?"

"Yes. No. I don't know. I'll explain when I get there."

***

Rachel took a deep breath and exhaled slowly before ringing the doorbell. She wasn't especially nervous about talking to Stephanie, but she was still a little apprehensive about sharing her news. Regardless, she needed to speak with someone. And Stephanie was the only person she felt comfortable confiding in.

She wasn't ready to let her family know. She could only imagine their reaction if she told them over the phone. "Hi Dad and Cecilia, I'm calling to wish you a Happy Thanksgiving. By the way, I'm pregnant, but the baby's father and I aren't on speaking terms."

That wasn't the way. Maybe she would take a few days during Christmas to visit them and break the news.

Stephanie opened the door. "Okay, what's going on? Is something wrong?"

"I'm sorry. Didn't intend to alarm you. I mean, I'm okay, but..." Rachel's voice trailed off.

"But what? Come inside and tell me what this is all about."

Rachel took a seat on the sofa.

Stephanie sat down next to her. After a few minutes of silence, she said, "I'm waiting."

Rachel stood up and began to pace the floor, clutching her arms. "I'm pregnant."

"You're what?"

"You heard right. I'm going to have a baby."

Stephanie jumped up from the sofa and rushed to embrace Rachel. Stepping back, she said, "I'm so happy for you. I'll bet Brian is excited."

Rachel turned away and looked out the window. "He doesn't know."

"You came to me before you talked to him?"

"I took a home pregnancy test. I didn't intend to get pregnant. It's my fault."

"Well, the last time I checked, it takes two."

"Yeah. But the first time we didn't use protection. Brian wanted to wait, but I insisted it would be okay. I feel so stupid. After all, I'm a doctor. Of all people, I should have known better. He's not to blame."

"Stop beating yourself up. No matter what you say, Brian was a willing participant. He's partially responsible. Maybe the two of you didn't plan for this to happen, but I'm sure he'll be happy."

"I don't want to tell him."

"Why not? He has a right to know."

"Brian and I aren't together anymore. We're barely speaking to one another. We wouldn't even communicate if it wasn't for our business partnership."

Stephanie sighed. "I was afraid of that. Matt mentioned that Brian was acting strangely a few days ago. Want to talk about it?"

"Not really. I said some things I shouldn't have said. Brian is sensitive about certain subjects, and I hurt him."

"I'm sure you two can work it out. You love him, don't you?"

"Of course, I do."

"Then talk to him. It's obvious he loves you."

"Maybe he once did, but not anymore He's lost whatever trust he had in me. Believe me. It's over between us."

Chapter 28

"Dammit!"

Matt jumped at the sound of his wife's words. He had been trying to watch a football game but had fallen asleep on the sofa. Stephanie was at her desk in the loft, having turned down his mother's offer to go shopping.

"What's wrong?" Matt called out.

"I hit my head again," Stephanie yelled back.

"Sorry. Are you okay?"

"I will be. You'd think after three months I would be used to the low ceiling. This is like being in an attic. There's just not a lot of room to move around." Her voice drew closer as she descended the stairs.

Matt stood up from the couch, pulled her into his embrace, and placed a light kiss on her lips. "You need a bigger space. Why don't we turn one of the extra bedrooms into your office?"

Stephanie turned away. "We've talked about that before. You know why it wouldn't work."

"There are three bedrooms. We'd still have an extra one."

"But if we... What would we do for a guest room? I realize your parents live here, and I don't expect Mom and

David to visit often, but now that I've sold the cottage, our options are limited if we have overnight guests."

Matt forced himself not to sigh. He and Stephanie had briefly discussed the possibility of having a baby, but they both agreed to wait at least six months after the wedding before trying.

Although nothing would make him happier than for Stephanie to have his child, he didn't want to go through what happened with his first wife, Tara. Her inability to conceive had put an enormous strain on their marriage that ultimately led to her death.

Matt would much rather remain childless and have Stephanie in his life. They had been separated for too many years, and he didn't want anything to come between them. But something had been bothering Stephanie for the past couple of days. Something she wasn't willing to talk about.

"Honey, we'll cross that bridge when we get there. We can always add on or move to a bigger place."

Stephanie turned and smiled. "You're right. I'm just frustrated. Having a hard time with writing this morning, and I have a two-week deadline with my publisher."

Matt picked up the remote and switched off the TV. "This is probably distracting you. How about if I get out of the house for a while. Maybe I'll talk to Brian. He'll have some ideas on what we can do."

"Don't you think that's a bit premature?"

"It's okay. I'd like to talk with him, anyway. Haven't seen him in a few days. He usually comes to my parent's house for Thanksgiving. Don't know why he decided not to come this year. Last time I saw him, he had a lot on his mind."

"If he only knew…"

"Knew what?"

"Never mind."

"Know something I don't?"

"Brian and Rachel are having troubles. That's all."

"Yeah, I know. Not sure what's going on, but he's stubborn. I'm still going to talk to him. Give you some time alone. I'll be back in a couple of hours."

***

Stephanie waited until Matt left before going upstairs. She had almost let Rachel's news slip out. She disliked keeping secrets from her husband but vowed to keep her promise to Rachel. It was Rachel's news to share, anyway.

She sat down at her desk, making sure not to bang her head on the angled ceiling, and opened her computer. Emotions were a powerful tool that often drove her writing, so she might as well make the most of it. She could always delete whatever turned out to be junk.

The trouble was, she wasn't sure what she was feeling today. Sadness for her friends and their failed relationship, anger at their stubbornness, and hurt for the tiny life that would be affected by his or her parents' choices.

Stephanie put her fingers on the keyboard and started to type. When she next looked at the clock, almost two hours had passed. After a few minutes of free writing, she had turned her attention back to the manuscript. Pleased with the day's progress, she closed the laptop and walked downstairs to the kitchen for a bottle of water.

Matt still wasn't home. She hoped he was able to talk with Brian. Although neither of them knew about the baby, she hoped Matt could persuade Brian to talk with Rachel about their differences. Whatever the disagreement was, Rachel seemed resolved to the fact a reconciliation wasn't possible.

Stephanie felt a little guilty about not checking on Rachel yesterday. Other than saying she didn't plan to spend Thanksgiving at her father's house in Austin, Rachel hadn't spoken of her plans. She probably spent the day alone, and right now she needed the support of friends.

Picking up her phone, she pressed the button to call Rachel's number. "Hey," she said when Rachel answered. "I've been thinking about you. How are you today?"

"I'm all right. Still trying to come to terms with the fact I'm going to be a mother in a few months."

"I can only imagine the feeling of excitement. I'm sorry. Maybe I should have put it another way."

"It is exciting. I mean, I've wanted a baby for a long time. I wanted Brian's child."

"Have you reconsidered talking to him?"

"No. He knows where to find me."

"Rachel, no matter what happened, I know the two of you care for one another a lot."

"I thought he cared."

"Believe me, he does. Promise me you'll think about trying to resolve your differences. You don't have to mention the baby right away."

"No."

"But—"

"But, nothing. Stephanie, I'm not having this conversation with you right now."

"Rachel, please reconsider. Brian is the baby's father. He has a right to know. Don't hang up—" The line clicked dead. Stephanie laid the phone on the counter when she heard a noise. Turning around, she saw Matt and Brian standing at the kitchen door.

She hoped they hadn't overheard her conversation but the look on their faces said otherwise. "Matt. Brian. Sorry, I didn't hear you come in."

"You were talking to Rachel?" Brian asked.

"Yes. I didn't know you were here."

"Obviously not." Brian turned to Matt. "Did you know?"

Matt shook his head.

"When did she plan to tell me?"

"Brian, you need to ask her that question."

"I'll do that." He turned, walked out the door, got into his truck, and drove away.

"I've messed things up now. Rachel didn't want to tell him."

"So, it's true? She's pregnant?"

"Yes. She told me Wednesday. Made me promise not to say anything. She didn't want me to tell you for fear the news might accidentally get back to Brian."

"If he's the father, what's the big deal?"

"Rachel said they aren't even speaking to one another."

"Maybe so, but if I know Brian, he's on his way to Rachel's house as we speak."

Stephanie reached for her phone. "I need to tell her."

***

Darkness was his friend. The cover of the night brought a lot of possibilities, and therefore he always waited until dark. Maybe that's why he liked fall and winter so much. Shorter days meant longer nights. Longer nights meant more time to set a fire—maybe even two or more in one night.

He would do that soon, but this one would be a solo event. It was too vital for him to be distracted by the possibility of setting a second one. Twilight had descended on the neighborhood. Not much longer and it would be entirely dark.

A smile came to his face. Gated community. It was almost laughable. All those rich folks thinking they were safe behind secured gates when all he had to do was to slip over a fence, go through some woods, and he was near her backyard. The vacant wooded lot across the street was the perfect place to hide out. Once he started the fire, he could watch from here and still slip away unseen.

He had awakened early this morning in anticipation of what was soon to come. This was the night. He called his boss to say he was sick and wouldn't be at work. His job tonight was to set a fire. The biggest one yet in terms of excitement. He had failed to get Rachel Jackson before, but this time he would be successful. He could watch all the action. And now that she and Brian were at odds with one another, the investigators would likely blame Brian.

At first, he feared she might not be home, but he saw her through the front windows. His heart began to race, and he took some deep breaths to calm himself. This job called for patience. It would happen soon enough.

He frowned when a pickup turn into her driveway. He hadn't counted on her having company. But the frown turned into a smile when he saw Brian Nichols exit the vehicle and walk to her front door.

***

Rachel wasn't surprised to see Stephanie's number appear on her phone. She was wrong to be angry with her friend, but she didn't want to discuss Brian today. He would know about the baby eventually, but she wasn't ready to tell him. Stephanie's insistence angered her.

After her voicemail picked up the call, she settled back on the sofa. She would call Stephanie tomorrow. Right now, she wasn't in the mood. Rachel had spent most of the day sitting around the house, not brooding, but thinking about her child. She knew a lot of single mothers who had successfully raised children, and most of them didn't have the resources she did. In that aspect, she was lucky.

The ringing of the doorbell surprised her. It was too soon for Stephanie. Getting up from the sofa, she went to the foyer and looked out the peephole to see Brian standing at the door. What had brought him here? He was the last person she needed to see today.

Easy enough to deal with. She wouldn't answer the door.

He rang the bell again, and Rachel ignored it. Brian was persistent, ringing the bell a third time as well as knocking. "Rachel, I know you're there. Open the door. We need to talk. This can't wait."

What was so important? Their stupid business partnership? Selling the property? Something else?

"Rachel, please. It's important."

She couldn't hold back forever. Whatever was on Brian's mind, he apparently needed to talk about it today. It may not be about business. Maybe his mother had taken a turn for the worse.

After a quick look in the hallway mirror, she took a deep breath and opened the door. Figuring the best defense is a good offense, she said, "What's so important that you needed to see me today?"

Brian didn't say a word but walked through the open door and into the den.

"Come in Brian. Thank you, I will." Rachel's voice dripped with sarcasm.

Brian stood in front of the French doors, arms folded, and his gaze narrowed. This was a side of him she didn't see often, but she could tell by his demeanor the reason for his visit was serious. After a couple of minutes, he spoke. "When were you planning to tell me you're pregnant?"

"What? How did you—"

"It must be true if you aren't bothering to deny it."

Rachel threw her hands in the air. "You heard it from Matt, didn't you? I should have known Stephanie would tell him, and of course, he couldn't keep the news from his best friend."

"Stephanie didn't say anything to him. He was just as surprised as I was when he happened to walk in on her conversation with you a few minutes ago."

"Oh."

"Then you didn't plan to tell me? Why?"

"Because you walked away from me and our relationship."

"Relationships are built on trust. You don't trust me."

"I do trust you. Look, I made a mistake, okay."

"I was a mistake? Or do you mean getting pregnant?"

"I didn't think it would happen our first time."

Brian snorted. "You're a doctor Rachel. It isn't hard to figure out how to prevent getting pregnant. But you've talked about wanting a baby for a while now. You got what you wanted. What was I to you, just the sperm donor?"

Without giving it a second thought, Rachel drew her hand up and slapped him across the face. "How dare you say that? Even think that. Get out."

Chapter 29

Rachel stood in the foyer and listened as Brian slammed the door of his truck and peeled out of the driveway. She shouldn't have slapped him, but his words cut deep. How could he believe her feelings for him didn't go deeper than a means for her to have a child? Hadn't they shared something special? When had they gotten to the point where all they did was to hurt one another?

She had every intention of telling Brian about the baby, but not until after she had made an appointment with the OB/GYN. No matter how bad things were between the two of them, she never had any intention of keeping him from his child. She would leave it to him to decide how much he wanted to be involved.

Rachel hoped they would eventually be able to resolve their differences. But now, with more words spoken in anger, they had drifted further apart.

Walking back into the den, she spotted her cell phone lying on the coffee table. She picked it up and saw the missed call and voicemail from Stephanie. Right now, she needed a friend. She hit the call back button.

Stephanie answered on the first ring. "Rachel? Is Brian there?"

"He was."

"I take it things didn't go well."

"No."

"I'm so sorry he found out that way. I didn't know he and Matt were standing in the kitchen. I never intended for him to hear the news from me."

"I know you didn't. I could use a friend right now."

"I'll be right there.

***

He watched Brian leave Rachel's house. By all indications, things weren't right between them. Whatever the case, he would be able to carry out his original plans. The timing wasn't good unless he started the fire now. But there was still too much light to risk it.

If only darkness would come. He'd never been good at waiting, but he couldn't take a chance on being seen. He'd been too careful with the other fires. No reason to risk being caught now. He took a deep breath and waited.

It wasn't long before another car turned into Rachel's driveway. He watched the tall brunette woman get out of her car and walk to the front door. He immediately recognized Stephanie Harris, Chief Bradford's wife. Rachel opened the front door, and Stephanie went inside.

It wasn't supposed to happen this way. Stephanie's arrival thwarted his plans. No way would he start a fire if she was inside the house.

Frustrated, he turned and made his way through the woods back to where he had left his car. He had to start a fire tonight. The temptation was just too great. Undaunted, he got into his car and drove toward Brewster. Even if the location had nothing to do with Brian, tonight something would go up in flames.

***

Brian drove aimlessly around town. He should have waited before confronting Rachel and allowed himself time to get his emotions under control. He wasn't sure if he was angry or hurt because she hadn't told him about the baby. If Stephanie had been correct, Rachel hadn't planned to tell him anytime soon.

He thought about driving to the factory site. It seemed he always ended up there when needed a place to think. But he couldn't bring himself to go there tonight. Instead, he decided to drive to Casey's, a popular restaurant and bar in Driscoll Lake.

The first place he and Rachel had dinner together. It hadn't even been a date. They had just happened to end up at the restaurant at the same time on a busy evening, and she asked him to sit with her.

Was that only a little more than a year ago? So much had happened since then. If he had to pinpoint a turning point in their relationship, it was that night. He opened up to her a bit, sharing his reasons for not drinking alcohol. Rachel was considerate of his feelings, asking if he minded her having a glass of wine.

When he told her about his disagreement with Matt regarding Stephanie's accident, she had been able to look at things with an open mind, pointing out that Matt had been acting upon emotion. She also voiced her belief in him. If Matt does think you're involved, he's got a thing or two to learn about people. The Brian Nichols I know wouldn't do anything like that.

After he almost lost her at the hands of Phillip Denton, their friendship deepened. They would call one another on occasion and meet somewhere for dinner or an occasional movie. Neither of them called it dating, just a casual outing between friends. Somewhere along the way, Brian knew she meant much more to him than a friend, even though he thought he would never be good enough for her.

But Rachel didn't seem to care about the differences in their backgrounds. Taking their relationship to the next level had been easy. They were good together. Good for one another. Until the night she voiced her doubts about him. How could she even think he was responsible for the fires?

Seems like every time you've been late meeting me, there's been a fire.

She hadn't exactly accused him.

Now that Brian had time to think about things, he should have considered the fact it was only a few days after the fire at her office. It was the second time in a year she had been inside a burning building. The experience had set him on edge. He could only imagine what it was like for Rachel.

She hadn't wanted to be alone that night. "Just hold me," she had said.

They talked that night—about the fire, about the ordeal from a year earlier, about how Rachel's life had changed upon her mother's death. Although neither of them said the words, it was as if by unspoken agreement they would always be there for one another.

But in a few days, things changed between them.

It's just coincidence. I told Alan he was mistaken.

Alan Davis. The man kept turning up like a bad penny. Brian didn't doubt that Alan wanted Rachel for himself. And he kept feeding her lies. Placing doubt. The man was fast becoming the bane of Brian's existence.

Rachel had never said she didn't believe in him. She supported him last year through the disagreement with

Matt as well as this year when he came to her about the ATF agent's questions and subsequent dispute with Matt.

You think I'm hiding something? So now you also doubt me?

No, of course not. All I'm saying is because you're innocent, it shouldn't matter what Matt says. Anyway, he's not the type to sell you out. He wouldn't do that to his best friend.

Rachel was right. He had been wrong again, allowing his sensitivity to overrule logical thinking. Once again, she encouraged him to reconcile with Matt.

It sounds to me like you're as much a victim as anyone.

Rachel said those words the night they first made love. The night she conceived their child. How could he ever have thought she believed he was responsible for the fires? Why did he say those hateful words to her tonight? No matter what happened, he had probably damaged their relationship beyond repair.

"Damn you, Brian. You've really done it this time," he said aloud as he pulled into the parking lot.

Whatever his reasons for choosing this particular restaurant, he needed a place to think. Or commiserate. Or both. Getting out of his pickup, he walked into the restaurant and went straight to the bar.

"What'll you have tonight?" the bartender asked.

Brian started to order a beer, but tonight called for something stronger. Over twenty years had passed since he took his last drink of alcohol. "Double bourbon, straight."

***

Christine Lawrence sat at the table with three other teachers from her school, exhausted after a long day of shopping. Why she allowed them to talk her into going to almost every Black Friday sale within a fifty-mile radius was beyond her. But she was lonely and the three colleagues, although younger, were single.

Christine cherished her friendship with Stephanie and Rachel, but now Stephanie was married to Matt. Rachel and Brian were together. Christine didn't want to feel like a fifth wheel.

Kyle had been dead a little more than a year now. Although the pain of losing him was still somewhat fresh, she found herself wondering what it would be like to date again. She and Kyle started dating their junior year of high school and married in college. The whole dating scene would be like a new experience.

When the three women suggested they get a drink and a bite to eat at a local bar and restaurant, Christine agreed. It wasn't like she had to hurry back to Emily. Her daughter had asked to spend the weekend with a friend, and Christine didn't look forward to going home to an empty house.

She took a sip of her daiquiri and listened as one of her colleagues told an amusing story of something that happened in the classroom earlier this week. It wasn't how she liked to spend a Friday night, but what else was there to do? Sighing, she reached for a nacho and listened to another dull story from another co-worker when she saw Brian Nichols walk up to the bar.

"Double bourbon, straight."

He sat down at a booth, swirling the amber liquid in the glass. It was almost as if he debated drinking it. After a couple of minutes, he picked up the glass and tossed back a large swallow. She had never known him to drink alcohol since they were teenagers. Kyle always said Brian feared he would turn into an alcoholic like his father.

Oh, well. Things change. She assumed he was meeting Rachel here. One of her companions said something, drawing her attention back to them.

A half hour later, she glanced in Brian's direction. He was still alone, and another shot of bourbon sat on the table. She watched as he downed the drink in one swallow. This couldn't be good.

"Christine, you didn't hear a word I said."

She turned back to her colleagues, but her gaze kept straying toward Brian. "Sorry."

The three women seated with her all looked to see what had her attention.

"So that's what, or maybe I should say who has you preoccupied. Can't say that I blame you."

Christine turned away, allowing her thoughts to drift back several years. There was a time in high school when she had been attracted to Brian. Probably because of his rebellious side. She'd always been one of the good girls but secretly envied those who were a little wilder.

She had been hesitant about becoming involved with Kyle at first because of his father, but once they started dating, she lost interest in any other boys. And even now that Kyle was dead, Christine wasn't interested in Brian. At any rate, he belonged with Rachel. If she had any doubts, it became apparent the night of Stephanie's wedding.

"Christine? What gives? Wishing he would hit you up for a date?"

"No, of course not. He's my friend's..." She paused, not sure how to describe the relationship between Brian and Rachel. Certainly, more than friends but using the term boyfriend to describe a man in his mid-thirties didn't seem right. "He's my friend Rachel's significant other."

She glanced at Brian and saw that he had asked for another drink. Something wasn't right. Brian was also a friend, and she didn't want to see him get into trouble. Turning back her companions, she said, "Will you excuse me for a minute? I need to make a phone call, and it's too loud in here."

She got up from the table and reached for her cell phone. Not paying attention to where she was going, she bumped into someone. "Sorry."

"Christine?"

Vince Green stood in front of her. She hadn't seen the handsome FBI agent since Stephanie's wedding. Then again, she had no reason to see him. "I apologize. I wasn't paying attention to where I was going."

"It's okay. Are you here alone?"

"No, I'm with some coworkers, but right now I'm concerned about a friend." Her gaze drifted toward Brian.

Vince frowned. "Isn't that Brian Nichols?"

"Yes. And he usually doesn't drink. Something must be wrong. I was on my way outside to call Rachel Jackson. He doesn't need to drive."

"How can I help?"

"Stay until someone arrives?"

"Sure."

Christine stepped outside and hit the speed dial button for Rachel's cell phone. "Rachel, this is Christine. You need to come to Casey's right away."

Chapter 30

Brian opened his eyes, only to close them again. Pale light filtered into the living room, but even that was too much for his pounding head. What happened? He turned on his side and tried to stretch his legs. A sofa was no place for someone with a six-foot, three-inch frame. And why was he even sleeping on his couch?

He couldn't remember coming home. He'd been at Rachel's house. They had argued. He'd said some cruel things, and he couldn't blame her for throwing him out.

No wait, he left there and drove around town. A sickening feeling came over him as he remembered ending up at Casey's.

How many shots of bourbon did he have? And why did he give in to the temptation? One thing was sure. It was the same as the night with Kyle many years ago. He couldn't remember a thing.

He raised up and propped himself up on one elbow. Someone had placed a pillow under his head and covered him with a quilt. Who? Looking around the room, he found the answer to his question. Rachel lay curled up, asleep on the love seat.

After everything he had put her through, after all the hateful words he had said, she was here.

Brian swung his feet off the couch and sat up, ignoring the pounding sensation in his head. He was still wearing the jeans and t-shirt from the night before. Rachel must have heard him because she turned over and opened her eyes.

"I see you're awake," she said.

"Barely. I need coffee." He started to get up.

"Stay there. I'll take care of it." Rachel went into the kitchen. She came back a few minutes later with a sports drink in her hand.

"This isn't coffee."

"No, but it will be better for you. You need hydration right now, and caffeine will make you more dehydrated."

"Whatever." His head hurt too much for him to argue. He took a sip of the drink and rested his head on the back of the sofa. After a few minutes, he said, "Why are you here?"

"I brought you home."

"You came to Casey's?"

"After Christine called to tell me you weren't in any shape to drive."

"I don't remember. Did I cause a scene?"

Rachel shook her head. "You were quite mellow. Stephanie, Christine, and Vince Green helped get you to your truck."

"The FBI agent? That's rich."

"Christine asked him to help until Stephanie and I arrived."

"How did Stephanie get involved?"

"She was at my house when Christine called. She's the one who drove me to the bar. You managed to get in the house, but you passed out on the sofa."

"Damn." Brian shook his head. Too late he realized his mistake and rubbed his forehead to ease the pain. "Why are you still here?"

"Because you needed someone. What else was I supposed to do?"

"You didn't have to come. In fact, I wouldn't blame you if you hadn't. Not after the way I've acted toward you."

"Yeah, well, in spite of all that, you are still my baby's father. I couldn't stand by and do nothing." Rachel turned away and looked out the window.

"Your baby's father is a jerk."

"Don't say that."

"It's true. There are a lot of things we need to talk about."

"Yes, but we can wait until you're feeling better. Why don't you get a shower and I'll make breakfast?"

"I don't feel much like eating, but somehow I don't think you're going to take no for an answer."

"Got that right. Grab a shower while I cook. You're right. We have a lot of things to discuss."

***

Matt walked into the police station early Saturday morning. He hadn't planned on going in, but Stephanie had buried herself at her computer, lost to the world of writing. He had gone for an early morning run around the lake, enjoying the fresh autumn air, then decided the morning would be an excellent time to catch up on some paperwork at the office.

When he arrived at the station, Agent Greg Sikes was already at his desk, talking on the phone. He motioned Matt inside.

"Chief Bradford is here, so I'm going to put you on speaker," Greg said to the caller as Matt entered the room. "It's Abbott," he said to Matt.

"Thought you'd want to know there was a fire at a house in Brewster last night. The MO was the same as the Driscoll Lake fires. Pretty sure it's the same suspect."

"Yeah? I'd like to take a look at the scene."

"Thought as much. It's 1104 Camden Road."

"Be there as soon as I can." Greg hung up the phone. "Want to come along?"

"Sure," Matt said and followed Sikes out the door.

Twenty minutes later, Greg and Matt arrived at the burned-out shell that had been someone's home. Abbott's team was already sifting through the evidence.

"What time did the fire start?" Greg asked as he approached Abbott.

"The call came in around eight. A neighbor saw flames and called 9-1-1. As you can see, it was too late to prevent major damage."

"I gather no one was home at the time?"

Abbott shook his head. "Out to dinner with friends."

"What can you tell me about them?"

"They're a retired couple who moved here from California about six months ago."

"Interesting."

"I haven't spoken to them yet. Do you want to question Brian, or should I?"

Matt, who had stood by and listened to the conversation between the two men, spoke up. "Whoa, wait a minute. You can't be serious?"

"I am," Abbott said.

"Well, you're wrong. If the fire started around eight, Brian has an alibi."

"Yeah, right. Let me guess, Rachel Jackson."

"Along with my wife, Christine Lawrence, and an FBI agent. Good enough for you?"

"Well, I'm sure there's some explanation. I said someone reported the fire around eight. It could have started earlier."

"Give it up, Abbott. You're grasping at straws. There's no way you can pin this one on Brian. And if the person responsible for this fire is the same one who started the ones in Driscoll Lake, your theory about him has just been proved wrong."

Abbott's shoulders dropped, and he broke eye contact with Matt.

"He's right," Sikes said. "But I had already come to that conclusion. Nichols doesn't fit the profile. We need to concentrate our efforts elsewhere. It's your crime scene, Abbott, but mind if I look around?"

"Go ahead."

Sikes walked away, leaving Matt standing with Richard Abbott.

"I was so sure Brian was responsible. You know he was a bit of a loose cannon as a teenager."

Matt spoke softly. "That was a long time ago. People change. I know you still blame Brian for a lot of things that went wrong in your son's life. Did you ever stop to think Clay made his share of mistakes?"

"He was a good kid until he got involved with drugs."

"It's not too late for him. I seriously doubt he's still using, although we both know there are ways to get drugs in prison."

Sikes looked surprised. "I think he's clean. At least now. But I can't help but worry since—"

Their conversation was interrupted when Sikes returned. "Just talked to a neighbor. He reported seeing a white Honda in the area around seven."

Matt glanced at Abbott, puzzled by the look he saw in the man's eyes.

"A white Honda?' Abbott asked.

"Yes. A neighbor reported a similar car in the neighborhood before the Tippet home burned. Rachel Jackson's office manager stated she'd seen a white car near the office in the days leading up to the fire there. I'd say the person who started this fire is the same person responsible for those in Driscoll Lake, and he drives a small white car."

***

Rachel sat on the sofa in Brian's living room, absently flipping through the pages of a magazine. After she had made breakfast, of which Brian ate very little, she suggested he lie down for a while. He tried to convince her to go home. She insisted upon staying, telling him he could drive her home once he felt better. She napped for a while on the sofa, having gotten little sleep the night before.

When her cell phone rang, she wasn't surprised to see Stephanie's number.

"How is Brian?"

"Doing okay. Sleeping now."

"You're still with him? Does that mean everything is okay between the two of you?"

"We still have some issues to deal with."

"But you're making progress?"

"Yeah, I think so. Thanks for being there last night."

"That's what friends are for. I'm available if you need me."

Rachel ended the call. She started to pick up the magazine again, but it held no interest for her. She debated on calling Stephanie back and asking if she would pick her up. Maybe this wasn't the time to talk with Brian since the memories of last night were still fresh on her mind. But she told him she would stay, and she wouldn't go back on that promise now. It was almost eleven when she looked up to see him standing in the hallway.

"You're still here?"

"Told you I would be. Feeling better?"

"Yeah. I guess we need to talk." Brian sat down on the love seat opposite Rachel.

"Why did you do it?" she asked.

"Go out and get drunk? I wish I could answer that. There have been times when I've been tempted to 'drown my sorrows' so to speak, but I've always resisted because of my father."

"Yeah, I know. What made this time different?"

Brian rubbed his face. "Because I hurt the person that I care about the most. Because I chose to believe voices from the past rather than seeing the truth. I jumped to conclusions—the wrong conclusions."

"We're all guilty of doing that sometimes."

"I've done it too many times. With Matt. With you. I know you weren't accusing me of being the arsonist."

"You did take me by surprise, but I probably didn't make myself clear. With everything happening and the fire at the office, I guess it got to me more than I realized."

"And I should have been there to support you."

"It's okay."

"No, it isn't. I can't keep hurting the people who mean the most to me." Brian got up from the sofa and stood by a window. "Do you remember the night I told you about stabbing my father?"

"Yes."

"You asked me if that was the first time he had been physically abusive?"

"I remember."

"There are other kinds of abuse. Verbal abuse is the worst of all."

"Your father?"

Brian nodded. "I was never good enough in his eyes. Everything I did, he belittled me. My music, my schoolwork, my carpentry skills. Which, I might add, he taught me."

"I didn't know."

"Yeah, well, I never talked about it. You know the real reason I didn't pursue a musical career? I wanted to stay and prove to myself I could be a better builder than he was. That I could run my own business. It was too late to show him, but I would at least have the satisfaction of knowing."

"You *are* successful. Don't you think it's time to put your father's ghost to rest?"

"I shouldn't say this, but I'm not sorry he died. I only wish he'd lived long enough to see me what I've become. It's not always easy to leave the past behind."

"It helps to surround yourself with people who care about you."

"Yeah, if I don't keep driving them away. Rachel, I'm sorry. Sorry for how I turned you away. Sorry for the things I said last night. I'd like to think what he had was special."

She noticed his use of past tense. Did he think it was over? No matter what happened, now there would always be a connection—their child. "And I'm sorry for the way I acted."

The empty sound of silence filled the room. After a few minutes, Brian spoke. "So, what now?"

Rachel took a deep breath. "I had every intention of telling you about the baby. I only found out Wednesday when I took a home pregnancy test, although I suspected I was pregnant for a while. With everything that happened, I needed a friend and called Stephanie."

"Then you haven't seen a doctor? I mean you're a doctor, but—"

"But I'm not an OB, and no I haven't seen one. I'm going to make an appointment first thing Monday. I planned on talking to you after that."

"You mean there's a chance the test could have been wrong?"

"Is that what you want? Do you hope the test was a false positive?"

He walked to stand in front of her, held out his hands, and pulled her to him. "No. I don't want it to be wrong."

Rachel put her arms around his waist and laid her head against his chest. "It's my fault. I knew there was a possibility I would get pregnant that night. I mean, I thought we were in the clear, but there's always a chance. I'm sorry."

"Wait, stop right there. I had a part in this too. Thinking about what we might have done differently now doesn't matter. We're in this together."

Chapter 31

When Brian entered his office on Monday morning, he went into the break area to make coffee. Then, looking at his desk, he saw the stack of paperwork he'd allowed to accumulate. For the first time in a couple of weeks, he felt like tackling the task at hand.

After pouring himself a cup of coffee, he walked back to his office, taking notice of the pack of cigarettes lying on his desk. He picked them up and tossed them in the trash. He didn't need to pick up that nasty habit again. Whatever curves life threw at him, he needed to face them head-on.

The past was the past, his father was dead and buried, and there was no reason to allow his harsh words to dictate the future. A future Brian hoped to spend with Rachel. They had managed to talk through a lot of issues, and their relationship was getting back on track.

Brian sat down at his desk. The first order of business was to call the real estate agent in Brewster. When the receptionist answered, he asked to speak to the realtor.

Kimberly Eves' voice was cheerful. Almost too sunny for this early in the day. "Good morning, Mr. Nichols. I was hoping you would call. My client is anxious to hear from you. In fact, a representative has already contacted me this morning."

So early? Once again, Brian wondered why this company was so eager to get their hands on his property. The agent also seemed impatient. And although he'd never met her, there was something about Kimberly Eves that set Brian on edge. Maybe that's the reason he refused to allow her to rush him about the matter and why he toyed with her a bit this morning.

"So early? It's just after eight. They must be in a different time zone."

"I'm always in the office by seven."

Why is she so evasive? Oh well, enough of this. It was time to put Kimberly Eves and her client behind him. "I have reached a decision, and the answer is no. I'm not selling."

There was silence on the other end before the agent found her voice. "I see. I didn't expect you to turn down such a generous offer. Are you sure you won't reconsider?"

"There are a lot of things in life more important than money. I'm sure your client will find another suitable piece of property."

"I suppose."

Brian smiled upon hearing her tone. Not hard to detect her disappointment. She would have made an excellent commission had the sell gone through. "By the way, just who is this client? You never told me the name."

"I guess it's no secret. It's a firm out of Florida. C. R. Investments. Are you familiar with them?"

"No, I'm not. I won't take any more of your time. Goodbye, Ms. Eves." Brian hung up the phone, confident he had made the right decision.

***

Rachel arrived at her clinic a little after eight on Monday. She was beginning to get a hold of the morning sickness. It was still there but waking up earlier allowed for most of the nausea to pass before she had to go to the office. She'd discovered that by accident when she was at Brian's house on Saturday.

At least he didn't have to see her sick that morning. Sickness made her feel weak, and she had wanted to be strong when they faced the issues between them. They were working things out, but now that there was a baby on the way, the dynamics had changed.

She walked into the breakroom to find Katrina and Wendy already there. "Tell me someone brought donuts this morning."

Wendy smiled. "And kolaches."

"That's even better." Rachel reached for one of the sausage stuffed pastries.

"You must be feeling better," Katrina said.

"I am." Rachel and Brian agreed not to tell anyone besides Matt and Stephanie about the baby until she'd visited her OB.

"Coffee?" Wendy asked.

"Not today." Rachel didn't miss the look of surprise as she reached into the refrigerator for a bottle of water. "I'm sure we have a full schedule this morning. I need to make a couple of phone calls first." She turned and left the room.

Once inside her private office, she closed the door and sat down at her desk. Finding the number for her OB, she placed the call.

"Good morning, this is Rachel Jackson. I need to make an appointment."

"Of course, let me pull up your records. Can you confirm your date of birth?"

Rachel gave the information. She could hear the click of a keyboard while waiting.

"You're not due for your annual exam. Are you having any problems?"

"No, I'm not. I need to confirm the results of a home pregnancy test."

"Oh, I see. I assume you'll want to see Dr. Aldridge at the first available opportunity."

"Yes, I would"

"Okay, let me look to see what we have available." There were a few more clicks of the keyboard before the scheduler spoke again. "We have a cancellation tomorrow afternoon at three. Would you be able to come then?"

"The sooner, the better. Tomorrow is fine." Rachel ended the call and stood up to leave when Wendy buzzed her on the intercom.

"Sorry to bother you, but there's a Mr. Roberts on the line for you. He says it's important."

"I don't know anyone by that name, but put the call through."

"Okay."

Rachel spoke into the phone. "This is Dr. Jackson. How may I help you, Mr. Roberts?"

"A few weeks ago, I contacted you by letter about the possibility of purchasing the oil and mineral rights to your property. I wanted to you if you'd given any consideration to the offer."

"I received the letter, but I'm not interested."

"You aren't? Was the offer not enough? Did someone else offer you more money?"

"Mr. Roberts, I've received a lot of offers over the years, and each time the answer has been no. I have no intention of selling these rights to anyone."

"May I ask why? You're the last Cameron heir, and I wouldn't think—"

"My reasons are my own, and you have no right to ask. If you're that interested in obtaining mineral rights to property in this area, I suggest you look elsewhere. This conversation is over." Rachel slammed the receiver to end the call.

The audacity of the man. What did her being the last Cameron heir have to do with anything? She already thought there was something strange about the offer and the phone call proved that. However, there wasn't time to think about it now—she had patients to see.

***

Matt looked at the man sitting across from his desk. Greg Sikes must have worked all weekend, even late into the night, if his looks were any indication. The man looked exhausted.

"I've gone over all the files on each arson," Greg said. "Wanted to see if I'd missed anything important. Hoping I would find something else that would lead me to the perp, but I've come up empty."

"When did you stop considering Brian as a suspect?"

"Pretty much after the fire at Rachel Jackson's clinic. The fire in Brewster proves he isn't the one."

Matt wanted to say, "I told you so," but he remained silent. Sikes was here to do a job, and Matt could see his frustration in not being able to solve the crime. "So, what do we have now?"

"No eyewitnesses to any of the fires. No conclusive DNA evidence. Sightings of a small white car in the areas of several of the fires, but no license number, and no good description of the driver. This guy is good. I'll give him that."

"Any thoughts on the theory that Brian is a target?"

"I've considered that. However, there isn't any way to connect him with the house in Brewster. Unless..." Greg's voice trailed away.

"What?"

"Unless our guy has moved on. The profiler thinks he'll continue setting fires once he's finished here."

"Do you believe that's the case?"

"I'm not sure, but—" Greg's words were cut short by the ringing of Matt's phone.

Matt frowned. "It's the dispatcher. Mind if I take this?"

"Go ahead."

"Sorry to interrupt, Chief, but there's a Mr. Jim Davenport online one that says he may have some information related to the fires. I know Agent Sikes is in with you."

"Put the call through Sandra." He turned to Sikes. "Someone claims to have information that may help with the arsons."

Greg instantly looked more alert. "Put him on speaker."

"Mr. Davenport, this is Chief Bradford. I have Agent Greg Sikes with the ATF in my office. My dispatcher says you may have some information."

"Yes, I do. I live on Hudson Road. Last Friday, sometime around six in the evening, I was driving home when I saw a white Honda parked along the side of the road. The hood was up, so I figured someone had car trouble. I slowed to see if anyone was inside, thinking they might need assistance. No one was around, so I left. Didn't think anything about it until I read the newspaper story about that fire in Brewster."

Greg nodded at Matt. "Go on, Mr. Davenport."

"When I read you are looking for information about a small white car in connection with the Driscoll Lake fires, I thought I should call. Since the fire was in Brewster, this may not be related, but I couldn't keep silent."

"You did the right thing by calling. By chance did you get a license number?"

"No. At the time, the thought never crossed my mind."

"Understood. We appreciate your call."

"Hope I was of some help."

Matt ended the call and turned to Greg. "What do you think?"

"I don't know. It's a long shot. If Nichols is his target, the suspect has already failed in his attempt to destroy Rachel Jackson's clinic. Unless the person saw Brian enter the building that night, his target was Rachel. Her car was in plain sight in the parking lot."

"Are you saying because Rachel and Brian are involved, she might still be in danger?"

"That's exactly what I'm saying. Where does Rachel live?"

"In a gated community called Lakeview Estates. Hudson Road runs right behind the area."

"Is security pretty tight there?"

"Yes. I live in the same area. However, it's on the outskirts of town. Lots of wooded areas surrounding it, so it wouldn't be hard for someone to slip in unnoticed."

"Does Nichols live with her?"

"No. He owns a house in a subdivision here in town."

"Does he have any other family members here?

Matt shook his head. "Only child. His mother is in a nursing home."

"What about Rachel's family?"

"They live in Austin."

"Probably no need for them to worry, but I do think she and Brian may be in danger. Adding additional surveillance of their homes, as well as their businesses, isn't a bad idea."

"I can have my people patrol the areas around their offices as well as Brian's house. Rachel's house isn't in the city limits, but I know the head of security at Lakeview. He'll help."

"Good. Do you want to be the one to talk to them, or should I?"

"Why don't we do it together? Brian isn't too fond of you."

"Can't say that I blame him. I hope he will realize I was only trying to do my job."

"Once he hears all the facts, he'll come around. And if he thinks Rachel is in danger, he'll do anything to protect her."

***

He was optimistic this would be the week he would finally be the owner of the former Cameron Manufacturing property. However, Kimberly Eves phoned him before lunch, dashing his hopes and dreams.

"He said no."

"What? Nichols doesn't want to sell? A week ago, you assured me he was on the verge of accepting the offer."

"That's what I thought, but apparently I was wrong."

"It's not over yet."

"I don't think he's likely to back down. Mr. Nichols seemed adamant in his decision. However, if you're interested in other investments, I can help. In fact, we have several commercial properties listed in the Brewster area."

"I don't want any other places. I want that property. Tell Nichols I'll offer another quarter of a million."

"I'll do what I can, but I don't think he'll change his mind. I'll let you know."

The line clicked dead.

Alan sat back in his chair and rubbed his forehead. "Damn!" Brian Nichols was all but defeated last week. What happened to make him change his mind?

Okay, it was time to regroup. Not all was lost. If he couldn't get his hands on the physical property, he could at least control the oil and gas interests. He flipped through his contact list, picked up the phone, and punched in the number for Donald Roberts.

"Any word from Rachel Jackson?"

"I'm glad you called. Since she didn't respond to the letter, I decided to call her this morning. She's not selling."

"Offer more money." Sources said the gas field below Driscoll Lake was more significant than the one in Tarrant County. He stood to make a small fortune if he could acquire the rights.

"I don't think that will do any good. Not after her comments this morning about some things being more important than money. It's not like she needs it, anyway."

"I know she doesn't need the money, but maybe if presented with other options, she might change her mind. Everyone has a price."

"You'll have to find another way. She ended our conversation rather abruptly, and I don't think she wants to hear from me again. Sorry, but I've done all I can do."

"Thanks for nothing." He ended the call and walked to the small private liquor cabinet in his office. It was still early in the day, and he didn't often indulge, but right now he needed a good, stiff drink. He poured a shot of bourbon and chugged it down in one swallow. Somehow, he had to tell his partner they had lost again. And he wasn't looking forward to the encounter.

Chapter 32

Rachel smiled as she pulled into Brian's driveway. He had called earlier to say he was working late, so she volunteered to pick up a pizza. It was like old times before their disagreement. The past two weeks without Brian had been hell—something Rachel didn't want to repeat.

Getting out of the car, she hurried to the front door and rang the bell. He was on his cell phone when he opened the door. Rachel didn't know who Brian was talking to, but she could tell he wasn't happy with the person. His lips pursed, and he rubbed the back of his neck. He looked up and smiled at Rachel briefly before turning his attention back to the caller.

Rachel took the pizza into the kitchen but could still hear Brian's side of the conversation.

"Look, Ms. Eves. Let's cut the chase. I gave you my answer this morning. If your client can't be satisfied with that, I'm sorry. Deal with them, but leave me out of it. The property is not for sale. You're wasting both my time and yours by continuing to pursue the matter. Goodbye."

Brian ended the call and walked into the kitchen. He put his arms around Rachel and pressed his lips to hers. "Seeing you is the best part of my day."

"Tough one?" Rachel turned away to pour two glasses of cola and sat them on the counter.

"Not really, but that's the last time I'll forward my office phone to my cell. Dealing with a persistent real estate agent. I called her first thing this morning to inform her I was not going to sell the property. Thought I'd made myself clear, but she called back to say her client was willing to offer more money."

"Oh, really?"

"Yeah. The first offer was already more than fair market value. Now the people upped the offer. These people must think they can make a profit if they're willing to shell out that much money." Brian sat down and reached for a slice of pizza.

"Do you know who the client is?"

"I didn't until this morning. The agent said it's a firm out of Florida. C. R. Development or something like that."

Rachel looked at him in surprise. "C. R. Investments?"

"Yeah, that's the name."

"That's the same company who made an offer last year before I sold the property to you. It wasn't the first time they approached me about buying it. The first time I was in medical school, and they made another offer during my residency."

"That is strange."

"Funny thing. Each time they wanted to purchase both the property and the mineral rights."

"The agent mentioned that, but I told her you retained those. She said it wouldn't be a problem."

"Okay, wait. This is too weird. A couple of weeks ago, I received a letter from someone inquiring about purchasing mineral rights in this area. This morning, the man called me to see if I was interested in selling them. Funny thing, they only wanted the rights at the factory site. Never asked about the ones on the old homestead. I still own those, and it's a much larger tract of land."

"They must know something we don't."

"Can't imagine what. I know there are new drilling methods in place, but I haven't heard from any oil company about wanting to drill in this area. If they did, it would make sense for an investor to obtain all the oil and gas interests they could buy."

Brian nodded his head. "I agree. There must be another reason why this company wants their hands on that particular property."

"I don't think it's a coincidence that someone offered to buy your place and someone else asks me about the oil and mineral interests."

"You're probably right. Is there a way to find out who owns C. R. Investments?"

"Might take a while, but I know someone who can. I'll call first thing tomorrow. If for no other reason than to satisfy my curiosity."

When Brian's cell phone rang, he glanced at the caller ID. "It's Matt," he said before answering. "Yeah. Rachel's with me. We're at my house. Why?"

Rachel looked at Brian and raised her eyebrows in question.

"You want to talk to both of us? When? Let me check with her." He placed the phone on mute. "Matt and Agent Sikes need to talk to both of us. You okay if they come by now?"

"Yeah, sure. Have they learned something about the fire at my office?"

"That's my guess."

"I'm eager to know if they have any news. Tell him now is fine."

**

By the time the doorbell rang a half hour later, Brian and Rachel had already cleaned up the kitchen and put away the leftover pizza.

Rachel went into the living room and sat down on the love seat while Brian went to the door.

"Hello, Matt. Agent Sikes."

"Thanks for letting us come by on such short notice," Matt said.

"Not a problem. Come in." Brian motioned them toward the living room.

Matt sat in a chair, while Sikes took a seat on the sofa. Brian sat down beside Rachel and took her hand in his. Words weren't necessary. No matter what Matt and Sikes had come to say, they were together and would support one another.

Sikes seemed nervous, his expression pensive, and he kept rubbing the back of his neck. His actions were a far cry from the arrogant, self-assured agent from a few weeks ago. Brian couldn't help but wonder what had changed. While it was true he disliked the guy, Brian knew Sikes had a job to do—learn the identity of a serial arsonist. Too bad the agent had been so quick to believe Richard Abbott. If he'd remained impartial, he might be further along in his investigation.

Rachel spoke first. "So, what's this all about? Did you learn anything about the fire at my office?"

"Yes and no," Sikes said. "There was another fire last Friday night at a residence in Brewster. Started sometime around seven o'clock. We're still investigating but are reasonably certain it's the same arsonist."

The corner of Brian's mouth twitched. "Let me guess. It was a house I built."

"No. In fact, we couldn't find any connection to you."

"So how do you plan to pin this one on me?"

"I'm not. I have it on good authority that you had an alibi for that time."

Brian winced. Yeah, he had an alibi and plenty of witnesses. Too bad he couldn't remember much about Friday night. How much did Greg Sikes know? He looked at Matt, who must have guessed what he thought because he shook his head.

"I gather since you're under the belief the same person is responsible for all the fires, you no longer consider Brian a suspect?" Rachel said.

"No, I don't. I had my doubts since the fire at your office. However, Brian, except for the fire in Brewster, I still believe there is a connection to you."

"I don't understand."

"Do you have any enemies? Someone who would want to hurt you and make it appear you're the guilty party? Disgruntled former employees?"

"Like most employers, I've had to let some people go for various reasons, but I can't think of anyone in particular who is that devious."

"It may not be a former employee, but I do think someone is out to get you. The fact that you and Dr. Jackson are involved also makes her a target. And believe me when I say this guy isn't finished. If my theory is correct, he won't stop until he's achieved his goal to destroy you."

***

Alan entered the hospital room and looked at the man lying in bed. It was hard to imagine this was the same arrogant, self-serving person he'd once been. One year can make a huge difference. But despite the man's weakened state, he still managed to project an air of arrogance and authority. Cold, hard eyes glared at him as he neared the bedside.

"I thought I told you not to come here."

"You did."

"What happens if word gets around you've been to see me twice?"

"People will assume I'm here to handle changes to your estate."

"I may be sick, but no one is going to believe you're here for that reason. Especially since you waited until evening to visit and not during the day. Why did you come?"

"To tell you Nichols turned down the offer."

"Thought you said he was about to give in, that he'd lost interest in the place."

"That's when he didn't have Rachel. Apparently, they're back together."

"How do you know?"

"I have my sources." Alan paused and looked out the window. "Rachel also turned down my offer."

"Your offer for what? What are you talking about?"

"Tried to purchase the oil and mineral rights. I thought that's what you always wanted."

"You told her?"

"No, of course not. She doesn't even know I'm the one who made the offer. I had someone contact her on the pretense of representing a firm interested in buying oil and mineral rights in Texas."

"That's not very smart. But why should I expect any different from you? Can't imagine how I had two sons who never could do anything right. Kyle always disappointed me as well."

Alan jerked his head. It was unusual for the old man to acknowledge him as a son. It was one of those dark secrets his father wanted hidden. He suddenly empathized with his half-brother. "He did his best. Even you admitted you had been too hard on him."

"Doesn't change the fact that he made poor choices in life. Now you've failed me. You couldn't make Rachel Jackson interested in you, either. But it doesn't matter anymore. It's too late now."

"You don't know that."

"We both know it's true. The doctors haven't said it, but I know I'm dying."

"I tried to get the property for your sake. I don't give a damn about the place. It means nothing to me. You were the one who wanted it."

"Yes, because it's rightfully mine. It should have never fallen into Rachel Jackson's hands. My ancestors would have had that property first, if not for that scheming Levi Cameron. Made it all legal and there wasn't a damn thing my family could do about it. His son Lucas was worse. Always rubbed it in my family's face. The high and mighty Cameron family became the town's elite, while my ancestors were always in their shadow."

"I'm sorry." Alan lowered his head and was silent for a few minutes, trying to gather his composure. He was never one to let emotions rule his life or his decisions. At least, he used to be that way. He'd stuck his neck out to obtain a piece of property that he neither wanted nor needed. All in an attempt to gain his father's approval.

While the possibility of making money from the mineral interests was intriguing, he wasn't the same ruthless person as his father. At least, he didn't use to be. But what he had done over the past few months made him no better than the man lying in the hospital bed.

Experience should have taught him that no matter what he did or didn't do, nothing would ever be good enough. He cleared this throat in an attempt to regain his composure. The last thing he wanted was to allow his emotions to show. Feelings were a sign of weakness, and he'd be damned if he let himself to look weak in front of his father.

When he spoke again, Alan said the first thing that came to mind, knowing it would anger his father. But he didn't care. He was tired of the older man continually belittling him. "Must have been hell knowing you were always second best."

Then he turned and left the room, denying his father the satisfaction of a reply.

Chapter 33

It was after eleven when Rachel left Brian's house. She hadn't planned to stay late, but after the visit from Matt and Greg Sikes, she and Brian needed to discuss several things.

He asked her to stay with him, saying he wouldn't fear for her safety as much if she was nearby, but she declined. Not that she wanted to leave, but she didn't have a change of clothes suitable for the office. After assuring him she had a state of the art security system and would take extra precautions, she went home.

Neither of them wanted to believe they might be in danger, although Rachel had thought weeks ago someone was trying to make Brian look guilty. But who would want revenge on him so much they would stoop to arson and attempted murder? She and Brian could have died if they had been trapped in her office.

Maybe the entire thing was a coincidence, and the arsonist picked random targets of which Brian happened to have some association. Like that was possible. Perhaps one or two fires, but six out of seven? No way.

And then there was the issue of that same company offering to buy the old factory site. Rachel wished she had made more of an attempt to learn something about them a year ago.

What was strange was the fact they had always insisted upon purchasing the oil and mineral rights. This time they made the offer to Brian for the land only. Did someone know he didn't own them? Anyone could easily access the information through public records, but Rachel couldn't shake the feeling there was more to the story. And was the sudden offer to purchase them from her related? There had to be some connection. It was just too coincidental.

She was still pondering the situation when she arrived at her office the following morning. As ludicrous as it might be, Rachel couldn't help but wonder if the offer to buy Brian's property was somehow related to the fires. Was the person trying to destroy Brian so that he wouldn't have any choice but to sell?

The first thing she did was to phone Hamilton Realty and ask to speak to the agent she worked with last year. "Debbie, this is Rachel Jackson."

"Good morning. How can I help you today?"

"Do you recall last year when a firm in Florida asked about buying some of my property? They were interested in obtaining mineral rights."

"Rings a bell. Why?"

"This same company contacted Brian Nichols through a realtor in Brewster. The name is C. R. Investments. Based in Orlando. You told me last year you knew someone who might be able to give you some information on them."

"I have some contacts there. I'm sure they would be able to tell me something."

"Can you call them? I hate to ask, but it's important."

"No problem. I'll get back to you as soon as possible."

"Thanks. I appreciate your help."

Rachel managed to keep her mind off the fires while seeing patients, but when lunchtime approached, it was foremost on her mind. When she arrived at the office that morning, she had instructed Wendy to order food delivered from a local deli and asked that she and Katrina remain at the clinic during lunch.

Rachel didn't want to alarm them, but they needed to know what Sikes had said about the fires. After all, if the arsonist decided to hit the clinic again, they would be affected. Agent Sikes didn't want his latest theory made public knowledge, but Wendy and Katrina would keep silent about the matter.

How did everything get to be such a mess? She thought life in Driscoll Lake would be more laid back than in the city. In most aspects it was, but no one could say living here was dull. However, this kind of excitement wasn't something she needed.

Last year it was the deal with Stephanie and Phillip Denton. This year the fires. Nothing of this magnitude happened when she lived in Austin or Dallas. But Rachel knew she wouldn't trade being here, owning a private practice, and having Brian in her life for anything in the world.

Rising from her desk, she made her way into the break room to talk with her staff.

***

The feeling of restlessness threatened to overtake him. He increasingly found it difficult to concentrate on his job. He had a few close calls, and he couldn't afford to mess up again.

Yes, he had recklessly driven to Brewster last Friday and randomly picked a target. But he took no satisfaction in it. Didn't even wait around to see the house go up in flames.

His anger over not being able to finish the job at Rachel's home clouded his judgment.

The past few days, he replayed the incident in his mind. He hadn't taken as much care as usual and couldn't help but shake the feeling he'd made a crucial mistake. Something that could lead to his discovery. He'd come too close to achieving his goal to mess up now.

Maybe it was time for a slight change of plans. Instead of going after Rachel again, he would change things around a bit. There was someone else Brian was close to. It would take some careful planning, but he could do it. So what if other people got hurt?

"Oh, yes. This is going to be good." He laughed. Suddenly, his outlook became brighter. In a few days, all would be right with the world.

***

After her appointment with Dr. Aldridge, Rachel walked to the parking lot and got into her car before calling Brian to tell him the news.

She debated on waiting to talk to him in person, but he knew about her appointment and would want to hear the outcome. However, she got his voice mail and decided to leave a message. "Hey, it's Rachel. Give me a call when you can."

Rachel drove to the mall. Her sister's birthday was coming up, not to mention Christmas. Might as well do some shopping. The parking lot was crowded, but she managed to find a spot near the main entrance.

Once inside, she went to the food court. Right now, nothing sounded better than a strawberry-banana smoothie. She placed her order and, upon receiving it, sat down at one of the many tables. Relaxation first. And she wanted time to reflect on her doctor's visit.

"Congratulations, Rachel. You're going to be a mother. Based on the information you've given me, your due date is sometime around July tenth." After confirming the pregnancy, the doctor went on to assure her that everything was progressing normally and answered Rachel's questions.

Rachel took a sip of her smoothie. She was going to be a mother. It wasn't exactly how she envisioned it happening. She'd always expected to get married first. Then again, she hadn't anticipated being almost thirty-five and still single. But she couldn't imagine anyone other than Brian being the father of her child.

He had said he was happy about the baby, but would he still be excited once he learned the tests results were correct? Would he turn away? Maybe he'd never wanted to have any children. He was married five years, and no children had come of that marriage.

Rachel put those thoughts aside. Brian had never given her any reason to doubt his sincerity. Maybe it was because of their recent misunderstanding, but she was feeling a bit anxious. When her phone rang, and she recognized Brian's number, she took a deep breath before answering.

"Hey there," he said. "How did it go?"

"The home test was right. We're having a baby. You're going to be a father."

There was silence on the other end.

Rachel waited for what seemed like minutes but was only seconds. "Brian? Is something wrong? Are you upset about this?"

"No, babe. I'm not upset. I wanted to believe it was true, and I know you said those home tests are almost always accurate, but I guess I was preparing myself in case the test was wrong."

"Would you have been disappointed?"

"Yeah. And if you weren't pregnant, I wasn't sure how you'd react. I didn't want you to be hurt. But if the results hadn't gone the way we wanted, I would have still been right by your side to support you."

Tears formed in Rachel's eyes. "You mean that, don't you?"

"Yes, I do. And I'm happy about the outcome. Just a little overwhelmed at first."

"You do realize I didn't plan this. I mean, that night... I knew there was an outside chance, but—"

"Rachel, stop. We've been there before. There were two of us. You aren't solely responsible."

"I know, but—"

"No buts. We're in this together, remember?"

"Okay."

"I guess we should tell our families first."

"Yeah. Want to go together to visit your mother?"

"Yes. Hopefully, we can catch her on a good day. What about your family?"

"It would be ideal to tell them in person, but I have no interest in driving to Austin this weekend. Cecilia, my stepmother, invited me for Christmas, but I'd rather not wait until then. Guess we can talk about it tonight."

"Works for me."

"I'm at the mall right now. Need to do some shopping. Why don't you come to the house around six? I'll make dinner."

"Okay. See you then."

Rachel put the phone in her purse, tossed the remainder of the smoothie in a trash can, and walked to the nearest department store.

***

It was only by chance he had seen Rachel Jackson at the medical complex. He shouldn't even have been there, and wouldn't have been if he hadn't been required to see a psychiatrist. The idea was ludicrous. He didn't need a shrink. If he told half the things he'd done or a fraction of the thoughts in his head, he'd be locked up in a mental facility faster than he could blink an eye.

At first, he was surprised to see Rachel there, knowing she had her practice in Driscoll Lake. But then again, doctors are also patients.

She stepped into the elevator as it stopped on the second floor, and his first instinct was to bolt. It took a few seconds for him to calm down. There was no reason to panic. She didn't know him. Doubted she would remember their brief encounter. Chances were slim she had noticed his presence at any of the events she had attended the past few months.

Still, he kept his head down to avoid eye contact. He was grateful other people were on the elevator. Rachel probably didn't even notice his presence.

When they reached the first floor, he waited for others to exit, then he made his way into the lobby. Curious, he walked over to a directory sign to see what types of physicians were on the second floor. Not that he cared, but curiosity got the better of him. Could the good doctor be harboring secrets?

After a quick glance at the list of clinics, he couldn't be sure of the reason for her visit. Not that it mattered. When he exited the building and started toward the parking lot,

Rachel was still sitting in her Corvette. By the time he reached his car, she was driving away. On impulse, he decided to follow her.

Arriving at the mall, he followed her to the food court, careful to keep his distance. After she ordered her drink and sat down at a table, he went to another vendor and purchased a soft drink. Careful to sit behind her, he chose a place close enough that he could overhear any conversation she might have.

A moment of panic swept over him, and he reached into his shirt pocket for a cigarette before putting it back. He hated anti-smoking laws. There was a time when it was acceptable to smoke indoors in designated areas. Unless he went outside, he would need some other way to calm his nerves. Deep breaths. He could do this.

What if Rachel was meeting Nichols here? Brian would recognize him. Maybe it was best he leave, although he didn't want to make too hasty of an exit and draw attention to himself.

It wasn't long before Rachel's phone rang. As luck would have it, he didn't have any trouble hearing her side of the conversation. She was obviously talking to Nichols. The information she shared was interesting.

He waited for her to end the call and watched as she walked to a nearby store. He knew what had to happen now. Rachel would die first. The satisfaction of seeing Brian grieve over his lover and his unborn child sent a rush of adrenaline through his system. Then, his last task would be to ensure Brian also died.

Revenge was sweet.

Chapter 34

Greg Sikes glanced across the table to where Matt Bradford sat drumming his fingers while waiting for the others to join them. Matt's actions echoed Greg's frustration. He should have been able to solve this case a long time ago. Maybe he would have had it not been for Richard Abbott's dogmatic insistence that Brian Nichols was the culprit. He couldn't blame Abbott. He went along with the theory even though his gut feeling told him otherwise.

But he had been trained to rely on evidence and motives, not inner suspicions. Just like he'd been taught not to allow his personal feelings to affect an investigation. Abbott was running on emotions, allowing the history between his son and Nichols to overtake sound judgment. Greg looked up to see Stan Gardner, Carlos Gonzales, and Richard Abbott. Everyone exchanged greetings as each man took a seat, then grew silent as they waited for the mayor's arrival.

They didn't have to wait long until Andrew Reeves entered the room and sat down at the head of the table. "Gentlemen. Sorry, I've been out of town for a few days, but I understand there has been a new development."

Greg exchanged looks with Abbott and nodded for him to speak.

"Last Friday night there was a fire at a residence in Brewster. Because of the similarities with the Driscoll Lake fires, I contacted Agent Sikes. We have every reason to believe it is the same perpetrator."

Mayor Reeves cleared his throat. "I see. Anything new on a suspect?"

Greg shook his head. "Negative. However, we did rule out someone. There isn't any connection to Brian Nichols with either the resident or the house. He also had an alibi for the time of the fire. We have eliminated him as a suspect in the other fires."

"So, there is no one else?"

"Not at this time. However, I have concluded that Carlos was right. Nichols is the target. I believe the arsonist is out to extract revenge on him and this person won't stop until he has reached his goal." Greg went on to explain the reasons for his theory and provide everyone with updates on the evidence.

"You're telling me all we have is inconclusive DNA evidence and the presence of a white Honda or similar car in the area of several fires. However, no one bothered to get a license plate number. And Nichols has no idea of anyone who would want to frame him." Andrew Reeves looked around the room as he spoke, but Greg knew the statement was directed at him.

"Afraid so. There is something that could work, but some of you might think it's a bit unconventional."

Matt nodded. "Go ahead. Tell us your idea."

"In the early nineties, there was a series of arsons in Seattle. The perpetrator set over one-hundred fires during a six-month period. A potential witness helped lead authorities to the arsonist through forensic hypnosis."

Andrew Reeves looked stunned. "Hypnosis?"

"Yes. The witness was able to describe the suspect as well as remembering a partial license plate number. Because of her, authorities released a composite drawing through the media which led to the suspect's capture and arrest."

"I'm familiar with the technique," Carlos said. "We used it on occasion when I was in San Diego."

"You think someone who spotted the car may be able to help?"

"That's exactly what I'm saying Mayor."

"Do we have anyone who might be willing to help?"

"Vic Stewart lives across the street from the Tippet home. He was the first to report seeing a white car in the area before the fire. Rachel Jackson's office manager reported seeing a suspicious car a couple of days before the fire at the clinic. Maybe Jim Davenport, although we don't know for sure if the car he saw has any connection. The neighbor in Brewster might be willing. However, it's a risk because some judges won't allow the prosecution to use evidence obtained under hypnosis."

"Do what you have to do, but let's save the hypnosis as a last resort." Mayor Reeves stood up, a sign he had adjourned the meeting.

***

When Rachel entered her office on Wednesday morning, she was surprised to see Wendy in the breakroom surrounded by boxes of Christmas decorations.

"I hope you don't mind," she said. "I always decorated for Dr. Jacobs. With Thanksgiving behind us, I figured this was a good time to start."

Rachel smiled. "I don't mind. Time to get into the Christmas spirit. Lord knows with everything that's happened in this town of late, lots of people could use some cheering up."

"You don't seem to need help in regards to that. In fact, you're almost glowing this morning."

It was hard not to say anything about the baby, but she and Brian hadn't talked to his mother yet. They planned to visit her in the evening and hoped she would be lucid enough to understand. Last night, she and Brian had called her father and stepmother. Rachel's thoughts drifted to the phone call.

They were surprised, but after the shock wore off, Cecelia immediately began making plans for a baby shower. She was elated at the prospect of not one, but two, grandchildren to spoil. Rachel didn't doubt Cecelia would treat this child no different from her biological grandchildren.

"First Nicole and now you. And maybe your brother and Melissa won't wait too long after their marriage to start a family. I hope the two of you will come for Christmas."

Rachel wanted to say yes, but she glanced at Brian. He seemed hesitant somehow, so she merely said. "We'll have to see how things go here. You know I have my practice and Brian also runs a business. I assume everyone will gather at Abuela's house on Christmas day."

"Of course. Family tradition," Cecelia said.

"Please think about coming," Ron Jackson said through the speakerphone. "We'd love to have you both visit."

"I'll let you know something soon." She hung up the phone and turned to Brian.

"Who's Abuela?" he asked.

"Cecelia's mother. She's Hispanic, so I've always called her by the Spanish name for grandmother. You would love her. She accepted me as one of her own when I went to live with Dad."

"I'm not sure about visiting."

"Brian, why are you hesitant about meeting my family?"

"Maybe they won't think I'm good enough for you. After all, your father is one of the most prominent surgeons in Austin."

"Have I ever told you the story about my father? He grew up in a low-income family and had to work his way through college and into medical school."

"And you once said you thought the reason he and your mother couldn't make their marriage work was because of the difference in their backgrounds."

"That's true, but I had a long talk with Dad when I visited a few weeks ago. He blamed himself for their failed marriage. I think if you got to know him, and talk with him, you'd realize the two of you have a lot in common."

"I'll think about going. It would be nice to get away from here for a few days."

Rachel looked up at the sound of Wendy's voice. "Penny for your thoughts."

"Sorry. You were saying?"

"You seem very happy."

"Let's say that even with everything that's happened, I have a lot to be grateful for, and I'm not going to let recent events get me down."

"Doesn't it bother you that an arsonist is probably targeting you and Brian?"

"I'm concerned, but I won't live my life in fear. Neither will Brian. Besides, I have every confidence Agent Sikes will catch the perp soon."

"They asked me about the possibility of undergoing hypnosis. I told him I was willing."

Rachel couldn't help but feel anger over Sikes initially thinking Brian might be the guilty party. Then again, she'd expressed doubt, which nearly destroyed their relationship. Shaking aside her thoughts, she went to the exam room to see her first patient of the day.

The morning was busy, and it was almost noon when Rachel's cell phone rang. The caller ID indicated it was Hamilton Realty. She pressed the answer button. "Hello?"

"Rachel, this is Debbie McDade. I have some news for you about the investment firm in Florida."

"Great. I didn't expect to hear from you so soon."

"I got lucky. My friend was quite familiar with the name. Turns out the owners live right here in Driscoll Lake."

***

Rachel ended the call, grabbed her purse and car keys, and hurried to Wendy's office. "What time is my first appointment this afternoon?"

Wendy looked at the computer screen. "Not until one-thirty. Why? Do I need to fit someone in?"

"No. I have to run an errand, and I may be cutting it close. I'll see you then." She rushed to her car, drove toward the downtown area, and turned onto Main street. Parking her car in a nearby lot, she got out and marched toward the building that housed the Parker and Davis law firm. Taking a deep breath to calm herself, she opened the door and went inside.

"May I help you?" the receptionist asked.

"I need to see Alan Davis right away. Is he in?"

"He is. Do you have an appointment?"

Rachel held up her hand. "I don't, but tell him Rachel Jackson is here."

"Okay, but—"

"Just tell him my name. He'll see me."

The woman picked up the phone and pressed a number. "Mr. Davis, Rachel Jackson is here to see you. Okay, I will." She turned back to Rachel. "He said to go right in."

"Thank you." Rachel's heels clicked on the parquet floor as she made her way to Alan's office. She reached for the handle just as he opened the door.

"Rachel, this is a surprise. To what do I owe the pleasure of this visit? Please, have a seat."

"I won't be here that long." Rachel walked to the center of the room and stood with her arms crossed. She glanced around, taking notice of the framed law degree hanging above Alan's desk. "I see it didn't take you long to move into Miles' office."

"Why not? I'm the senior attorney around here now."

"You're the *only* attorney. Word around town is that you're not getting much business these days. But that's not surprising. When Miles left, integrity walked out the door with him. Truth and honesty count for a lot with people in Driscoll Lake."

"What are you talking about?"

"Why did you do it? Partner up with Curtis Lawrence?"

"I don't know what you're talking about."

"Don't play dumb with me. I know all about that fake investment firm. I have to admit the name threw me at first. C. R. Investments. Wasn't hard to believe the "c" stood for Curtis, but the "r" threw me until I saw your diploma just now. Richard Alan Davis."

Alan rubbed the back of his neck and looked away.

"If the two of you wanted my property that bad, why didn't you just make an offer? Why be so secretive about the entire thing?"

"Because he didn't think you would sell to a Lawrence."

"He's right about that, but it's not because he's a Lawrence. I wouldn't sell anything to Curtis because of the way he treated his son. Kyle was a good man. Granted, he made mistakes, but his life must have been hell growing up in that house."

"Getting the property was important to him."

"Why are you involved?"

Alan lowered his voice. "Because Curtis Lawrence is my father."

Rachel's head jerked up. "*You're* Curtis's son?"

"Yes. My mother was his secretary years ago. They had an affair. When she found out she was pregnant, Curtis wanted things kept quiet. You can imagine he didn't want his image tarnished. Mother left here and went to live with her folks in Florida. She later married a man named Raymond Davis, and he legally adopted me. I didn't know about my biological father until I was in college."

"Yet you formed a partnership with him."

"His idea. Said he wanted to make things up to me. He's the one who encouraged Miles Parker to bring me in as a partner in his law firm."

"And you moved to Driscoll Lake and went along with his schemes to get his hands on Cameron property."

"He claimed the factory site was rightfully his."

"Yeah, I've heard about some long-standing feud between our ancestors. Curtis couldn't let it go. He wanted to marry my mother. When that didn't work, he tried to match Kyle and me before we were old enough to date.

Wait a minute—that's why you've shown interest in me. In Curtis's mind, Kyle failed, so he used you to get to me."

"No, I—"

"Don't try to deny it. You were the one responsible for hiring Heather Stevens, and when Miles found out she was spreading rumors last year, he fired her. You couldn't very well hire her back, so you put her up to trying to seduce Brian to keep us apart."

"It wasn't like that."

"You're lying. You wanted Brian out of the picture. I honestly believe you'd stop at nothing to get what you want."

"It was all Curtis's idea. Rachel, believe me, I do care for you."

"Liar! You didn't see Brian behind my office the night of the fire, did you? It was all to make me think he wanted to hurt me. You're more devious than Curtis."

"Okay, so I lied. I never saw Brian that night."

"Then you admit to lying. What else haven't you told me? Who did you see?"

"No one."

"Then if you didn't see anyone... Were you even there? Or did you also lie about that?"

"I was there. I just didn't see anyone."

"Then why? No, you wouldn't." Rachel clasped her hand over her mouth. "I've got to get out of here." She turned and fled the building. When she reached her car, she called Brian's phone.

"Hey babe. What's up?"

"Where are you?"

"At Rosa's eating lunch. Why?"

"Meet me at Matt's office in five minutes. It's important."

Chapter 35

Rachel paced the floor of the interrogation room, waiting for Brian to join her. Matt had suggested they meet in there since it afforded them more space than any of the offices. The small, windowless room contained a table, four chairs, and smelled like stale coffee. Rachel wasn't claustrophobic, but the tiny space was confining, making her wish she had waited outside.

Chalk it up to a state of mind. Even though she had heard the words come from Alan, she found it hard to believe he was Curtis Lawrence's son.

Her thoughts drifted toward Christine. Wonder how she would feel, knowing she has a brother-in-law. She had been through enough without having to deal with anything else.

When Brian stepped into the room, Rachel met his gaze. He rushed toward her and drew her into his arms. "What's wrong, babe?"

"You're not going to believe it. I always knew he was a jerk, but I never thought he would be this underhanded."

"Who?"

"Alan Davis. I went to see him at his office."

"You went to Alan's? Why?"

"Because I found out he's the one who tried to buy the factory site."

"Alan is involved with C. R. Investments?"

"Yes, and there's more to it than that. But let's wait for Matt and Agent Sikes. I don't want to have to repeat everything."

"Agent Sikes? Then I gather you know something related to the fires."

"Yes." Rachel drew away from him and threw her hands in the air. "I told Matt this was important. You'd think they would realize that and hurry up."

"Calm down honey. Getting upset isn't good for you or the baby. Come sit down." Brian took her hand and led her to the conference table as Matt and Agent Sikes walked into the room.

"Matt tells me you may have some information related to the arsons," Agent Sikes said as he took a seat.

"Yes, I think so." Rachel took a deep breath and began to tell about the events of her morning. She left nothing out, including the fact that Alan was Curtis Lawrence's son.

When she finished, everyone was silent for a few minutes. Matt rubbed the bridge of his nose. Brian frowned and crossed his arms. Agent Sikes narrowed his eyes and then looked at the notes he had jotted down.

Matt was the first person to break the silence. "Rachel, you can't be serious. The fact that Alan is a liar and went about things a bit underhanded doesn't make him an arsonist."

"But it all fits. Alan lied about seeing Brian at my office that night. The judge wanted the factory site for years. After I sold the place to Brian, he needed him out of the way, so he got Alan to help. Need I remind you that's where the first fire was? I think they hoped to ruin him financially so they could get their hands on the property."

"That's a pretty strong accusation."

"What about the second fire? That house also belonged to Brian."

"What about the others? Why would Alan burn his father's house?Rachel, I think I speak for everyone in this room when I say we want the guilty person behind bars, but what you've told us today isn't enough for us to charge Alan with the crimes. "

Sikes took this opportunity to speak. "Matt is right. What you've told us is circumstantial at best."

"You're just going to let Alan walk? All you had before was circumstantial evidence when you were convinced Brian was guilty."

Sikes sighed and rubbed his forehead. "You're right. I was wrong, and that's why we need to make sure before questioning anyone."

Brian reached for Rachel's hand. "Relax, honey. I've never cared for Alan Davis, and I agree the way he went about things was sneaky. But if they arrest the wrong man, we're no better off. The arsonist will still be free to carry out his plans."

"We appreciate you coming forward with this. Rest assured we will follow-up. Just give my men and me a little more time to investigate. If we feel it's warranted, we'll bring Davis in for questioning."

Rachel took and deep breath and exhaled slowly. "Thank you Agent Sikes. Guess that's all I can hope for."

***

Brian walked Rachel to her car. "You okay?"

"I will be. Still, I find all this hard to believe. I keep wondering when Curtis Lawrence will cease to be the bane of my existence." Rachel shook her head. "Makes me feel even more sorrowful for Kyle. He couldn't have had much of a life growing up as Curtis's son."

"Yeah, well, neither one of us did well in the father department. At least I had a loving and supportive mother. Kyle didn't even have that."

Rachel took both his hands in hers. "Honey, I'm sorry. I know your father made your life miserable."

"Hey, it's okay. I'm getting over it."

"Are we still on to visit your mom tonight? I can't wait to tell her the news."

"Yes. We should get there no later than six-thirty. Mom goes to bed early."

"I see my last patient at four-thirty, so I should be finished around five." Rachel glanced at her watch. "Speaking of patients, I need to get back to the clinic. Otherwise, I'll be behind schedule all afternoon."

"I'll knock off early. We can meet at my place around six and head over there. Grab some dinner afterward."

"Sounds good."

"Why don't you stay at my house tonight? That way you won't have to drive back to the lake."

Rachel reached up and placed a quick kiss on his lips. "Sounds even better. See you at six."

***

It was almost midnight when he finished his shift at Riverbend. What is it with Christmas these days? It wasn't even December, and already people were holding Christmas parties and holiday functions.

He hadn't expected to work late, but when his boss asked, he could hardly refuse. Since the night of that fundraiser, he had been under a microscope. If it hadn't been for that fancy lawyer's wife... He smirked, thinking

322

about the revenge he had planned. Her day was coming soon. But tonight, he had another job to do.

Wonder how Brian Nichols will react to his mother's death?

He left Brewster and drove the short distance to Willow Lake. A few days earlier, he had scoped out Woodbine Nursing Home and learned which room belonged to Dorothy Nichols. Fortunately for him, her room was located on the back side of the building. She'd had that nasty fall a few weeks earlier and most of the time still relied on a wheelchair to move about. Even if she did wake up to the smell of smoke or the sound of a fire alarm, it wouldn't be easy for her to get out of the room before it was too late.

Others would likely die also, but that's how it had to be. To kill one person, he would need to sacrifice others. He parked his car a couple of blocks away. Looking around to make sure no one was watching, he got out of the car and began walking toward the nursing home. His pulse quickened with excitement as he neared the building, and he reached to light a cigarette.

This time, he wouldn't be able to stay and watch the aftermath. He would just have to watch it on the local newscast.

***

Brian hunkered further beneath the covers and tried to ignore the intermittent noise coming from the direction of the bedside table. He put his arm around Rachel, drawing her closer to him.

"Brian?"

"Hmmm?"

"Your phone is ringing."

"Okay." He rolled over and reached for the phone. "Hello?"

"This is Matt."

Brian frowned and looked at his watch. "What the—Why are you calling at this hour?"

"There was a fire at the nursing home. It started outside your mother's room."

"What? Is she hurt?"

"She's okay but is asking for you."

"I'll be right there." He jumped out of bed and started throwing on his clothes.

"What's wrong?" Rachel asked.

"That lunatic struck again. Stated a fire outside Mom's room. No one was hurt, but I'm going over there."

"I'm coming with you."

***

Brian wasn't surprised that his mother was confused after the fire. Only a few hours earlier, she was lucid and talked as if nothing was wrong. She had been excited to learn of Rachel's pregnancy.

"It's about time I had grandchildren," she had said.

Now she didn't seem to recognize Brian or Rachel. She didn't call either of them by name, nor did she mention the baby.

"How come I can't stay in my room? I like it there."

Not wanting to alarm her, Brian said. "There was a fire near your room."

"Did my things burn?"

"No Mom. Everything is okay."

"How soon can I go back?"

"In a few days. It's late, so why don't you try to get some sleep? Will you be okay for a while? I need to talk to someone."

"I'll stay with her," Rachel said.

"Thanks," he whispered. "I'm going to look for Matt and Agent Sikes."

"Once she's asleep, I'll join you."

Brian found Matt and Sikes near a back entrance, talking with three men. Two of them wore jackets with ATF printed on the back. The third man wore scrubs.

"Hey, man," Matt said as Brian approached. "How is your mother?"

"Confused, but I expected it."

Greg Sikes dismissed the man in scrubs and spoke briefly to the two investigators before turning to Brian. "If it hadn't been for the quick actions of a nurse, we probably would have had a tragic situation on our hands. He had gone outside for a smoke break and happened to notice the flames. He also saw a man running from the scene. Unfortunately, it was too dark for him to get a good description."

"He didn't go after him?"

Sikes shook his head. "Figured it was more important to sound the fire alarm and assist with the evacuation of patients, if necessary."

Brian sighed and hit his fist on the door frame. "Damn. Then you're no closer to learning the identity of the suspect than you were days ago."

"Unfortunately, no. We'll gather evidence and look for DNA. As with the other fires, the suspect dropped a cigarette butt on the ground, but he is always careful not to leave fingerprints. Nichols, are you sure you don't have any idea of who it might be?"

"Wish I did. I can take it if someone comes after me, but when it begins to affect people I love, it's another matter.

First Rachel, now my mother. If I could get my hands on this guy…"

"Leave that up to us. I understand how you feel. I've been there when someone tried to hurt Stephanie. Rachel and your mom are going to need you." Matt's cell phone rang, and he turned away to take the call.

A couple of minutes later, Matt walked back to Brian and Sikes. "That was one of my officers. Got a call from a resident on Bishop Street who saw a man running along the side of the road. The suspect got into a white Honda and drove away."

"Sounds like our man."

"Yes, and this time the resident was able to get a partial license plate number. Texas plates beginning with SQZ, and it contains the number seven. We'll contact the DMV to search their database. At least now we have something more to go on."

***

He had arrived home long after midnight but still awakened before dawn. He had a restless night—tossing, turning, unable to sleep. Part of it was due to the frustration of not being able to watch the fire. The other was when that stupid nurse decided to walk outside.

If he had taken more time to scope out the place, he would have known there was a dedicated smoking area close to Dorothy Nichols' room. He'd noted shrubbery nearby where he could have hidden. Instead, he panicked and ran away. Fearful the nurse had followed him, he didn't slow his pace until he reached the car. Another mistake. If anyone saw and could identify him, everything he had planned would be in vain.

He climbed out of bed and threw on an old shirt and jeans. The nicotine craving was intense this morning, and his stepmother didn't allow him to smoke inside the house.

For that matter, she didn't even want him around, but his father convinced her everyone needed a second chance. Had it not been for his father's intervention, his stepmother wouldn't allow him to live there.

He tiptoed down the stairs, hoping to slip outside without anyone knowing. The last thing he needed this morning was to face his father, or even worse, his stepmother.

But when he got to the bottom of the stairs, a light was already on in the kitchen. His father was talking to someone on the phone, so he stopped to listen.

"At least there was a witness this time. Even without a positive ID, that's more than you've had before. I think that fact alone means the suspect is getting careless."

His ears perked up at that statement and moved to where he could listen more closely without anyone seeing him.

"A partial license plate number? That's good. I'd say this guy's days are numbered."

Only quick thinking kept him from emitting an audible gasp. He didn't want his father to know he had been listening, so he turned and went back upstairs. The cigarette would have to wait, although now he needed it more than ever.

It would take a lot more than nicotine to calm his nerves. Authorities were closing in on him. He went back to his room to plan his next course of action and waited until his father and stepmother left the house.

Once he was sure they had gone, he slipped into their bedroom and removed the handgun from his father's nightstand. Carrying a firearm was a violation of his parole, but he didn't care. If someone caught him, he would at least have the satisfaction of knowing he had destroyed Brian Nichols.

Chapter 36

He wasn't following Rachel. At least, that wasn't his intent, although she was a beautiful woman. Not that she would pay him any attention. The one time he had seen her up close, she had been rude.

At any rate, she belonged to Brian. He always got the girl. Tiffany, Angie, Rachel. However, when the opportunity to eavesdrop presented itself, he took advantage of the situation. He needed all the information he could get to finish his task at hand.

There was a time when he almost idolized Brian. Wanted to be like him. In high school, Brian had been the "bad boy" that girls gravitated toward. Maybe it was the would-be rock star image. Not to mention his good looks and devil-may-care attitude.

He began to run around with Brian and some of the other boys from Driscoll Lake. The old abandoned house on the outskirts of town was the perfect place to hide out and smoke, drink beer, and party.

He had no delusions of being anything other than an outsider. And it wasn't because he didn't live in Driscoll Lake. He didn't fit in with any crowd. Not with the athletes like Matt Bradford. Definitely not with Kyle

Lawrence and the other rich kids. Not even with rebels like Brian.

But still, he kept pretending and showing up for their parties. One night he had gone to the old house, hoping to have the place to himself. He had worked up enough courage to ask Tiffany McDade to a high school dance. When he arrived, he could hear Brian's voice inside. And he wasn't alone—he was with Tiffany, of all people. It was apparent they didn't want anyone else around.

He managed to slip away without being noticed. That was the night when he realized he would never be like Brian. And he began to hate him. He stopped hanging around as often. When he accidentally set the old house on fire, no one was the wiser. He chuckled to himself. No one had suspected him, and several people thought Brian was to blame.

Later, after he started doing drugs and got caught, Brian took a chance on giving him a job. Brian was married to Angie then. The only reason he took the job was that she managed the office, and he could see her when he picked up his paycheck each week.

Not that she ever noticed him. Once again, Brian got the girl. But the pay wasn't enough to support his habit, and he started stealing from job sites. When Brian found out, he was left without a job.

Brian should have understood. If he had kept his job, he would have never had to rob that convenience store in Brewster. He'd gotten careless that night. Didn't use caution when exiting the store. Of all people to see him, it had to be Brian whose testimony helped send him to prison.

He spent five years planning his revenge. After the factory fire last year, he was the one who planted a seed of doubt in his father's mind.

A burst of laughter from the next booth brought him back to the present. Rachel and Stephanie might be laughing now, but their happiness wouldn't last. Not if his plans were successful.

It had to be fate that had them choosing a café in Brewster. A place where he happened to frequent. Luck had put them in the booth behind him. Even with the lunch crowd, he was able to overhear bits of their conversation.

His pulse quickened with excitement when Rachel told Stephanie her plans for that evening. "Brian's band is playing at Pinnacle again. I'm going. Why don't you ask Matt about the two of you joining us?"

"I'm not sure Matt can make it. They have some leads on the arsonist, and he may work late. I'll ask him."

Stephanie's words confirmed what he already knew. Time was short.

***

Greg Sikes looked up from his desk to see Richard Abbott standing in the doorway. "What brings you here so late on a Friday evening? If you're looking for Chief Bradford, he's already left for the day. Detective Gonzales convinced him to take the evening off. I think he was taking his wife to that new club in Brewster."

"Actually, I came by to talk to you."

Greg motioned him in. "What's on your mind?"

Abbott sat down in front of the desk. "We got off to a bad start. I resented you being brought in for the investigation. I wanted Nichols to be guilty because I blamed him for sending my son to prison."

Greg nodded. "Matt told me about it."

"Yeah, well, I was wrong. Clay is my only son. I realized early on he had problems, but when you're a parent, you want to give your children the benefit of the doubt. But there's no question my son was guilty of robbing that convenience store. I let my feelings cloud my judgment, and I feel it impeded this investigation."

"Not entirely your fault. At first, it seemed plausible Brian could be the culprit. With the first two fires, anyone could have made a case that he needed the insurance money. Then the others had some connection to him."

"I hear you have a new lead."

"We do. Hoping to get a match on a partial license plate. A witness stated the car he saw was a white Honda Accord with Texas plates beginning with SQZ and the number seven."

Abbott's face turned ashen. His voice barely a whisper. "I know who the arsonist is."

***

Matt took a sip of beer, hoping the alcohol would help loosen the tension he felt. After the long and trying week at work, he had looked forward to a relaxing evening.

As usual, Brian was in his element behind the drums. With everything he had been through lately, he deserved a break. Both Stephanie and Rachel seemed to be having a good time.

Matt smiled, and Stephanie reached to take his hand. She leaned toward him and whispered in his ear. "Are you okay? You seem restless tonight."

"I'm fine. Just trying to relax."

It wasn't exactly a lie. He *was* trying to unwind. But since he and Stephanie arrived at the club, he'd been uneasy. Something told him he needed to be alert.

Observant. He almost ordered something non-alcoholic, not wanting anything to hinder his ability to focus. He could handle a couple of beers, but he couldn't shake the feeling that something was going to happen. Maybe that was the reason he decided to bring his handgun, even though he was off duty.

When he felt his cell phone vibrate, he pulled it from his pocket and recognized Greg Sikes' number. Mumbling something to Stephanie, he excused himself and went outside to take the call.

"What's going on, Sikes?"

"We have an identity on the arsonist. We think he's going to make a move tonight at the club."

Matt listened as Sikes relayed the information. "You're kidding me? He's the arsonist?

"Wish I was. He didn't show up for work tonight, and he's not at home. We think he's going to try something at the club. Are you carrying?"

"Yeah."

"Good. Stay on the lookout. Keep this quiet, we don't want panic, but you might want to alert club security. We're on our way there, and I've notified Brewster police. I'll keep in touch."

Matt hung up the phone and walked back inside. He took a quick look at the restaurant area before approaching the hostess to ask for the manager. "I'm Matt Bradford, Driscoll Lake Police Chief. It's important I talk to your manager immediately."

If the hostess was surprised at his request, she didn't let on. After speaking into the phone, she turned back to Matt.

"The manager will be here in a couple of minutes."

"Matt. Is something wrong?"

Matt turned at the sound of Vince Green's voice. "Glad you're here, Vince. I may need your help," Matt said as the club's manager approached them.

"Chief Bradford, I'm Aaron Chambers, the manager here. I understand you needed to see me."

Matt extended his hand. "Yes. Is there a place we can talk privately? This is FBI Agent Vince Green. I'd like him to join us."

"Of course. Let's go to my office."

***

Clay crouched behind the wooden fence surrounding the dumpster and waited while the police car made its way slowly down the alley. There was no way to know whether they were looking for him. It could have been a cop on routine patrol. At any rate, they wouldn't find his car. He wasn't stupid enough to park close to his intended target. Instead, he had hidden it in the crowded parking lot of a nearby shopping center.

But when the patrol car stopped beside the dumpster, he held his breath. The cop must have had the window lowered because Clay could hear his words.

"Negative. No sign of the car and no one is in the alley… Ten-four… I'll check that location and return here."

When the cruiser pulled out of the alley, Clay rose from his hiding place. There wouldn't be enough time to start a fire. He had to do something else. Looking in both directions to make sure no one was watching, he walked between two buildings until he reached the front door of Pinnacle.

Taking a deep breath, he patted the gun hidden inside his jacket, walked into the club, and approached the hostess.

"Do you have reservations, sir?" she asked.

"No. Just in the area and thought I'd drop in to hear the band."

She shook her head. "Sorry, there aren't any tables available. Unless you'd like to sit in the bar. The view isn't the best, but at least you'll be able to hear the music."

He glanced toward the stage. Brian sat behind the drums, singing lead on a song. Clay followed Brian's gaze and saw Rachel seated at a nearby table. Stephanie Bradford was with her, but there was no sign of Matt. It didn't matter. What he had in mind wouldn't take long. No one would have time to react once the damage was done.

He turned back to the hostess. "The bar is fine."

She smiled at him. "Go right in."

Clay walked up to the bar and took the only empty seat. He turned the stool to look around the room. There weren't a lot of places where he could slip away unnoticed. He needed to be close enough to the stage and Rachel's table, but far enough away from anyone so that he wouldn't get caught.

After a few minutes, he saw it. There was an emergency exit sign not far from the stage. It was near a darkened alcove. Perfect. When the shots rang out, people would panic, and he could slip out the door in the midst of the chaos.

"What can I get you?" The bartender's voice jarred him from his thoughts.

"Nothing. I just came to hear the music."

"Look, pal. Either you want a drink or get away from the bar. Other paying customers would like your seat."

"I don't plan on being here that long."

"And I don't care."

"Fine. Give me a beer." *And you'll pay for being rude to me.*

***

Matt ended the call and placed his cell phone back in his pocket. "That was Sikes," he said to Vince Green and the club manager. Brewster police found Clay's car in a parking lot a block away."

Aaron Chambers looked at Matt. "You think he's coming here?"

"If he hasn't already arrived. Police are discreetly watching the back alley. They want to draw him out, not frighten him away. Sikes believes Clay knows we're on to him. He's out for revenge and getting desperate."

"How can I help?" Aaron asked.

"We need to keep an eye on things inside."

"I have a couple of off-duty officers who help with security. Give me a description of the suspect, and I'll let them know."

Matt held up his cell phone. "Abbott texted me a recent photo."

"I'll get out there." Vince turned to leave the room, glanced up at the security camera monitors, and stopped. "He's here. Sitting at the bar."

Matt followed Vince's gaze. "I doubt he's here to listen to the music."

As Matt spoke, Clay moved off the bar stool and started walking toward the opposite side of the room.

"He has something planned," Vince said.

"Is there a back door?"

"Yes, an emergency exit."

"We'd better get out there."

Matt and Vince walked out of the manager's office.

"There's a shortcut," Aaron said, pointing toward a hallway. "It will take you to the back exit. I'll notify security."

"Thanks." Matt turned to Vince. "You go that way. I'll circle back toward the bar, and we can come at him from both sides."

Vince nodded as he walked away.

Stephanie met Matt in the doorway of the club. "There you are."

"Where is Rachel?"

"Still at our table."

The music stopped, and the band's leader announced they were taking a short break. Matt glanced at the stage and saw Brian making his way toward Rachel. He turned back to Stephanie. "I want you to go to the car and wait for me there."

"What's going on?"

"No time to explain. Just—" Matt's words were cut short by a loud popping sound, and people in the club began to scream.

**

Brian was surprised that neither Matt nor Stephanie were at the table. He looked at Rachel and raised his eyebrows in question as he stepped off the stage. She shrugged and motioned for him to sit down.

A sudden movement to his right caught his eye, and he looked in that direction. He saw the muzzle flash and heard the sound of gunfire and people screaming. Brian lunged for Rachel and pushed her to the floor, covering her body with his.

It was over in seconds. Brian stayed on the floor until he heard a voice say, "I've got him."

Someone began barking orders. "Ladies and gentlemen, we've had an emergency. Everything is under control, but we ask that you leave the club quickly and orderly. There is no need to panic."

People had begun to leave when Brian and Rachel stood up. "Are you okay? Did I hurt you?"

"I'm fine."

"Thank God. I could have lost you." Brian pulled her into his arms. "Are you sure you don't need to go to the hospital? Get checked out? What about the baby?"

"Brian, I'm okay."

A Brewster police officer led a handcuffed man away while Vince Green stood nearby with Greg Sikes. Brian did a double take when he recognized the suspect as Clay Abbott.

Matt walked over to stand beside them.

"Was anyone hurt? Where is Stephanie?" Rachel asked as she looked around.

"Stephanie is fine. She's outside. Fortunately, Vince was able to grab the gun before Clay could hurt anyone."

"What was Clay doing here? And why was he shooting into the crowd?"

"He was looking for you."

"Me? Why?"

"You helped send him to prison. We also have strong evidence to show he is the arsonist."

"So that's why Sikes is here?"

"Yeah. He called me right before this happened to say he believed Clay was going to try something tonight. We think Clay knew we suspected him, and he was desperate. We didn't know he had a gun."

Sikes walked up to Brian and extended his hand. "I know we got off to a bad start, and I was wrong about you. I'm confident we've got the right man."

"I never would have guessed Clay was responsible for the fires. All this because I testified against him?"

"I believe it goes deeper than that. Clay is a very disturbed individual. He was out to get revenge. That's why the locations of the fires were connected to you in some way."

Brian shook his head. "Unbelievable."

"It's over now," Matt said. "Why don't you and Rachel go home? We'll take care of things here."

Brian looked at Rachel. "You ready?"

"Yes."

"Good. First I'm taking you to get checked out."

"I told you I'm okay, but if it will make you feel better..."

"It will." Brian looked back at Sikes. "Never thought I would say this, but thanks."

Epilogue

Three weeks later.

Brian glanced toward the passenger seat where Rachel was sleeping. She needed the rest. When she first asked him about spending Christmas with her family in Austin, he had been a little apprehensive. But making the trip was the right decision.

His mind drifted to the events of the last few months. Clay Abbott confessed to starting the fires. It was revenge. In Clay's mind, Brian was the enemy. Curtis Lawrence was the judge who sentenced him to prison, hence the reason for torching his house. Clay even admitted to setting fire to the old house where they hung out as teenagers, although he did maintain that one was accidental. Even with leniency due to his confession, he still faced a lengthy prison sentence.

Richard Abbott was a broken man. It had been hard for him to learn his son was a serial arsonist. "I've spent years investigating fires," he had said. "Never thought my son would be responsible for so much destruction."

Abbott's subsequent apology had taken Brian by surprise. "I wanted to blame you for all Clay's problems. I knew Clay had issues—even when he was a teenager. You didn't influence him to do drugs or steal to support his habit. If anything, he could have pulled you down with him. I'm sorry for everything."

Brian turned at the sound of Rachel's voice. "Penny for your thoughts."

"Just thinking about Clay. I still find it hard to believe. Never guessed he hated me so much."

"It's hard to say what makes some people act they way they do. I'm glad he's back in prison. He needs some psychiatric counseling."

"Guess you're right."

"I'm curious as to why there were almost nine months between the fire at the factory and the one in Woodland Hills."

"Clay set the first fire shortly after his release. Afterward, he went to live with his mother in Houston. He returned to Brewster just before the second fire."

"Guess that explains it."

Brian slowed the 'Vette as he neared their exit. The heavy Austin traffic made him appreciate the laid-back feeling of Driscoll Lake.

"You look good behind the wheel of this car. Too bad it won't be practical in a few months. There's no way I'm transporting our child in something like this."

"Back to an SUV, huh?"

"Yeah. But you know something? I'm no longer afraid to look over my shoulder. Guess I've buried those ghosts of Phillip."

"I've buried a few of my own."

"Your father?"

Brian nodded. "I've talked with Dan Bradford several times over the past few weeks. Although I thought I'd exorcised those demons a long time ago, he helped me realize I was still holding on to some things."

"I can't begin to imagine what growing up was like for you."

"Dad didn't make it easy. I realize now his constant criticism of me affected the way I acted toward others. Especially those I'm closest to. That's the reason I overreacted when I thought Matt was accusing me of things. And why I acted the way I did when you questioned me."

"I never meant to hurt you."

"I know. And I'm sorry for walking out on you. But all that's behind us now. I refuse to allow my father's memory to dictate my life. Although he would probably turn over in his grave if he knew about us."

"Why?"

"He always told me I wasn't good enough for someone like you. I remember once when he picked me up after band practice. You were walking with some friends and Dad saw me looking at you. He told me you were a Cameron and beyond my league."

Rachel reached to squeeze his hand. "Is that the reason you were hesitant about our relationship at first?"

"Yeah. And about meeting your family."

"I guess now you're ready."

"Unless your father shows up to the door with a shotgun aimed at me for getting you pregnant."

Rachel laughed. "He wouldn't do that. Although he will be glad to know we're getting married."

"Think so?"

"I know so. Besides, as I said before, the two of you have a lot in common." Rachel motioned with her hand. "Turn right at the stop sign. The house is the second on the right."

A couple of minutes later, Brian pulled into the driveway. When he and Rachel got out of the car, he took her hand, bent down, and kissed her. "I love you."

"I love you, too. Ready for this?"

"Yeah. Let's do it. Together."

Author's Note

When I began writing book one of the Driscoll Lake Series, I thought it would be a stand-alone novel. However, there are times when certain characters speak to writers, necessitating a change of plans. Such was the case with my character, Brian Nichols.

In *Unseen Motives*, I planned for Brian to be one of the bad guys. A juvenile delinquent who never quite changed his ways, despite appearing to be a model citizen. Beneath his suave exterior was a cold-hearted, deceitful, and manipulative person who held a long-term secret.

But after writing only two or three paragraphs of Brian's first scene, he said, "That's not me. I'm not an evil person." He was so adamant I created two characters—one who held the secret, the other one deceitful. If you don't already know how I worked out the details, you can find the answers by reading *Unseen Motives*.

Even after I let Brian off the hook, he continued to speak to me, imploring me to tell his story. That's how *Unknown Reasons* came about. And as I continued to introduce minor characters, I realized they too had stories to tell. Look for Christine Lawrence and Vince Green to take center stage in book three, *Unclear Purposes*, in the fall of 2018.

If you enjoyed reading *this book*, please consider leaving a comment on Amazon or Goodreads. Thanks.

Until next time,
Joan

Other Works

Driscoll Lake Series

Unseen Motives

Unknown Reasons

Unclear Purposes (Coming Fall 2018)

Novellas

The Stranger

Anthologies

Unshod

Macabre Sanctuary

Bright Lights and Candle Glow

Quantum Wanderlust

Acknowledgements

I'm grateful to many people who supported me during the process of writing and publishing this novel as well as those who support me every day through friendship and love.

Sandi, Brett, Tj, Ken, Patti, Sandy, Annette, and Laura... my Monday night writer's group for their feedback and support.

Adrian... for beta reading the raw, rough first draft and providing feedback and encouragement.

Adam of Writer's Detective... for answering my questions about criminal investigations.

To all my family and friends... for their understanding and putting up with an often-temperamental writer.

Staci... for your support and friendship.

The staff of AIW press... for publishing this book.

And most of all to John...for being the best and most understanding husband I could ask for.

About The Author

Joan Hall likes to create character-driven fiction with strong, determined female leads and male characters that are sometimes a bit mysterious. Her favorite genre is mystery and suspense—often with a touch of romance.

When she's not writing, Joan likes to take nature walks, explore old cemeteries, and visit America's National Parks and historical sites. She and her husband live in Texas with their two cats, Tucker and Little Bit.

You can connect with Joan at http://joanhall.net or on the following social media sties: